BESIDE THE TURQUOISE SEA

EMMA BURSTALL

First published in Great Britain in 2025 by Boldwood Books Ltd.

Cover Design by Head Design Ltd.

Cover Images: Shutterstock and iStock

A CIP catalogue record for this book is available from the British Library.

Paperback ISBN 978-1-83561-547-8

Large Print ISBN 978-1-83561-548-5

Hardback ISBN 978-1-83561-546-1

Ebook ISBN 978-1-83561-549-2

Kindle ISBN 978-1-83561-550-8

Audio CD ISBN 978-1-83561-541-6

MP3 CD ISBN 978-1-83561-542-3

Digital audio download ISBN 978-1-83561-543-0

This book is printed on certified sustainable paper. Boldwood Books is dedicated to putting sustainability at the heart of our business. For more information please visit https://www.boldwoodbooks.com/about-us/sustainability/

Boldwood Books Ltd, 23 Bowerdean Street, London, SW6 3TN

www.boldwoodbooks.com

To Kate O'Connor, my dear, true friend for more years than I care to remember. Thank you.

PROLOGUE

Way up in the White Mountains of southern Crete, dotted with peaks, ravines and deep gorges, a funny-looking, higgledy-piggledy stone cottage seemed to spring from the rugged landscape as if it had grown there.

The rough, rocky terrain on which it perched soon gave way to a sudden, plunging hillside. At the very bottom lay miles of craggy coastline and beyond that, the sparkling Libyan Sea.

As it was night-time and pitch-black, there was no one admiring the view right now, though. The shutters of the cottage were shut tight and inside an elderly woman sat at a coarse wooden table in the centre of her kitchen, thinking about someone she'd never met.

In front of her was an open laptop and in her right hand she held a small, brown woollen pouch. This she gently squeezed, feeling with her fingertips for the objects inside: a miniature vial of olive oil, some dried laurel leaves and a silver pendant with a double-headed Minoan axe – her lucky talisman.

Katerina Papadakis, for that was the elderly housekeeper's name, nodded slightly, as if in satisfaction, and continued staring into the distance, a small smile playing on her lips. The only light came from an overhead ceiling lamp, which emitted a dim glow.

From the sparse surroundings, you'd think Katerina was as poor as a church mouse, but you'd be wrong. In truth, she was a wealthy woman, thanks to her former employer, who'd bequeathed her a grand villa a little way down the mountain.

Instead of living there herself, however, Katerina preferred to rent the villa out, but only to certain, special people; she wouldn't take just anyone. Secretly, she was convinced Villa Ariadne chose its occupants, not the other way round, but she tended to keep this to herself.

Her own kitchen, unlike the villa's lavish one, consisted of just a sink, a rickety-looking gas cooker and stone worktops. There was no sign of a washing machine, dishwasher or even a fridge. It was as if the Industrial Revolution had yet to arrive in this remote corner of the island.

Wooden shelves of various sizes were laden with pans, mugs, glasses, jars and tins, all neatly labelled in a faded Greek script. The flagstones on the floor had become uneven and flaky with age.

Yet the cottage wasn't ugly or depressing. Far from it. Little vases of wild flowers and pots of herbs were neatly arranged on windowsills and surfaces. Meanwhile, one wall was dominated by an eye-catching painting of three beautiful, smiling Minoan women.

The women, in richly coloured clothes and jewels, had intricately coiled black hair. They were set against a vivid blue background and the whole work was surrounded by a smart, white wooden frame. It was such a happy picture, you couldn't help but smile, too.

After a time, Katerina rose with a sigh from her chair and poured herself a glass of water from a jug by the sink. Then she padded in well-worn slippers down the dark corridor to the little bedroom at the very back and felt for the lamp switch.

Once the room was lit, you could see there was just enough space for a small double bed, which had been neatly made with white sheets and pillowcases, and embroidered, red scatter cushions.

A multicoloured woollen throw was sitting folded at the other end, ready for chilly nights.

Both floor and ceiling were covered in panels of dark wood, while the stone walls had been left bare. In pride of place above the bed hung a painting of two bright blue peacocks against a backdrop of green, gold and pink. Similar to the picture in the kitchen, it was also a riot of colour, like a celebration of life itself.

Katerina glanced at it and her eyes lit up. It had been given to her by a local artist, named Marina, who'd painted it many years ago when she was little more than a child.

Her work had changed and developed since then and become more abstract. The newer stuff was worth more on the open market, but Katerina wouldn't swap this painting for all the tea in China; it had become as much a part of her as the cottage's roof, beams and foundations.

After placing her slippers beside the bed, she climbed under the sheets, pulled them up to her shoulders and lay back with her eyes closed.

It had been a long day, it was very late and she was tired, but her mind was still busy.

She was already planning the arrival of the Englishwoman she'd never met, plus her husband and friends; she couldn't help it. The stranger hadn't confirmed her booking yet or paid the deposit, but Katerina had made sure not to charge too much and was certain she soon would. She could feel it in her bones.

Thankfully, since the summer season had ended in October,

she'd had plenty of time to spruce up the villa ready for the arrival of the new guests. She'd had both the swimming pool and plunge pool drained and swabbed, the rugs, blinds and curtains cleaned and she'd bought brand-new bed linen and crockery.

The bedrooms had been redecorated and the bathrooms, too. The exterior woodwork also needed repainting, but this would have to wait till the weather improved.

Come May, she could guarantee the place would be ship-shape and gleaming from top to bottom. Her visitors deserved the best, and she took great pride in making sure that's what they got, right down to the little welcoming touches, such as putting fresh flowers in the bedrooms and leaving out a selection of *kalitsounia*, her traditional homemade pastries.

Once the guests were happily ensconced, Katerina's work would be largely done. Her job was to set the scene, so to speak, and engage the actors. The rest was up to them.

What would Edie – Mrs Lovell – be like? Katerina suspected she'd be well-mannered, attractive and intelligent – but with a secret sadness, a longing.

As for her friends, there was a story there, too. The elderly woman could sense it from afar.

She took a deep breath and said a little prayer, as she always did, thanking God for a good day and asking Him to guide and comfort the lonely, sick and suffering.

The world was full of folk, she thought sadly, with a hole in their soul so deep, they believed it could never be filled. If only Villa Ariadne had space for them all!

1

Today, Edie's sandwich was mature cheddar topped with sliced tomato in brown granary. Nothing wrong with that. But she'd been in such a rush to get out of the house this morning, she'd forgotten to add mayo and the bread was dry and hard to swallow. She should keep a jar of the stuff in the staffroom fridge for emergencies.

Chewing disconsolately, she glanced out of the wide, rectangular window and all she could see was grey: the sky above, the concrete forecourt below, even the grassy area beyond the school railings seemed to merge with everything else into an indistinct gloom.

And it was spitting with rain. Of course it was. It had been like this for most of January and February. Barely a sliver of sunshine and not a single sprinkling of snow all winter to liven things up.

'Grim, eh?'

She glanced round and exchanged smiles with Tom, who taught Geography. He couldn't have been more than twenty-five or -six and had only been here since September, but seemed amazingly confident – in a good way.

He plonked his Tupperware container on one of the round, white, melamine tables in the centre of the room and started to pull out a chair, which squeaked on the vinyl floor.

'It's terrible; it never stops raining,' Edie agreed from her position on the pale blue sofa.

She always settled here, with her sandwich on her lap, rather than at a table; she'd sat or stood behind a desk all morning and it was a relief to be able to stretch out her legs and lounge back for a bit.

Tom removed the lid from his Tupperware box, fished out a wooden fork and shovelled in a mouthful of green pesto pasta. Edie didn't want to move from where she was but wondered if it would be rude not to join him.

She needn't have worried, though. The staffroom door swung open and Miss Bamford hurried in, clutching a pile of books.

'Hi, Tom!' she said, flashing him a dazzling grin. Edie smiled inwardly. He was a good-looking chap, for sure, and charming with it; she'd bet all the young female teachers had their eye on him. Some of the older ones too, probably.

Miss Bamford – Martha – plonked her books on his table. 'Mind if I join you?'

Tom's face lit up. 'Of course – be my guest.'

Martha sashayed over to the tall white fridge on the far side of the room and fetched her lunch, wrapped in tinfoil, and a can of Diet Coke.

Tom went back to his food, but Edie thought he couldn't have failed to notice his colleague's pretty features and neat figure in a tight-fitting, cinnamon-coloured polo neck, flattering black trousers and black heels. She'd seen the two of them chatting animatedly a few times in the corridor between classes; there was clearly an attraction.

She felt quite wistful, remembering the electricity between

her and Ralph when they first got together. It had been such an exciting time, full of fun and promise.

Twenty-six years on, their eldest child had left home and the younger one was away at university. They seemed to have packed all the light in their suitcases and taken it with them.

Placing her half-eaten sandwich back in the box, she laid it to one side and picked up her phone to make a call. Several more staff came through the door; the room was filling up fast. She'd have to be quick.

'Hi, Hannah, can you speak?' she said, keeping her voice low, so as not to annoy anyone.

'Sure,' came the reply. 'I'm having lunch at my desk.'

Edie could picture her friend in trackie bottoms and a baggy sweatshirt, chomping into a salad. She always ate salads. She was forever trying to lose weight, but sabotaged every diet by snacking on peanuts and biscuits in between.

She was probably spilling bits of lettuce and smearing olive oil on the keyboard. She was awfully messy, but as she worked from home, there was no one to call her up on it.

'Have you thought any more about that holiday I suggested?' Edie went on. 'The weather's so shit, it's getting me down. I need something to look forward to.'

'I have actually. What about Crete? I've never been and it's supposed to be lovely. May half-term should be perfect weather, too. Warm but not too hot.'

'Ooh!' Edie's mind instantly filled with images of sandy beaches, bright white buildings and sparkling azure waters. 'Ralph and I had our honeymoon there. We loved it, but for some reason we've never been back.'

'I'm slightly up to my neck with work at the moment,' Hannah mumbled. She was quite hard to understand when her mouth was full. 'Can you look into villas and I'll research flights and hire cars?'

'Sure,' said Edie. 'Any preference as to which part of the island we stay on?'

There was a crunch, followed by chomping noises. Celery? Raw carrot?

Edie waited patiently while her friend finished chewing.

'Anywhere's fine by me,' Hannah said eventually. 'Let's not stay too far from the airport, though. Mac hates having a massive long drive straight after getting off the plane.'

'Agreed. I'll do a bit of googling and report back.'

They said goodbye and Edie forced herself to finish her dry sandwich, or she'd be hungry later. After that, she popped a dark red grape in her mouth and nearly swallowed it whole when someone tapped her firmly on the shoulder, making her start.

Jessica, the History teacher, was standing right behind her. Edie quickly chewed the grape a couple of times before gulping it down.

'Oh! Hi!' she said, managing a smile, though her eyes were watering.

'How was your morning?' Jessica asked, seeming not to notice Edie's face had turned red, too.

'Fine, thanks. My Year Nines were a bit rowdy, but I've got my lovely A-level English group to look forward to this afternoon. How about you?'

Jessica switched her black leather bag from one shoulder to another. She was tall and slim with a long, pale face that was interesting rather than pretty, and small, clever, bright blue eyes.

She had a passion for ancient history and though it was rarely taught in state schools nowadays, she'd managed to persuade the head teacher to include it as an option.

'My GCSE lot are finally getting to grips with Echo and Narcissus. They seem quite enthralled. One pupil said if Narcissus was alive today, he'd be obsessed with selfies. I love it when the penny drops and they realise it's not just a dusty old story; it still has relevance.'

Edie smiled again. 'Great they've made that link.'

Jessica was wearing a maroon-coloured dress, tied at the waist with the buttons done up to her neck. Her straight, mid-brown hair was in a ponytail, with hairpins on either side to anchor any stray strands.

It was well known pupils found her intimidating; even some of the staff were a bit scared of her. Not Edie, though, who found her intriguing.

Jessica was in her late forties, single and with no children, but she didn't seem remotely sad or lonely. Highly intelligent, she had numerous interests as well as ancient history, including classical music, poetry, crochet, travel, marathon running and, perhaps surprisingly, crime novels.

She took no nonsense from anyone and had a reputation for being strict, while Edie was the one people turned to in a crisis. Even the other teachers would come and cry on her shoulder if they'd had a row with the boyfriend or husband or a dressing-down from the head. Edie didn't ask for it; it just seemed to happen that way.

Jessica's exam results were the best in the school and gossipy staff claimed this was only because the children were terrified of her. But as Edie would point out, those brave enough to pick her subject at A level seemed to end up hero-worshipping her, so she must have something special.

The phone flashed on the seat and Edie's train of thought flitted from Jessica, Echo and Narcissus and ancient Rome, to Greece.

'I've just been speaking to a friend,' she said. 'We're thinking of going to Crete in May half-term. Have you been?'

Jessica shifted from one foot to another and nodded.

'A very long time ago, when I was in my twenties. I remember visiting Knossos, centre of the old Minoan civilisation. I went to some beautiful beaches, too, but I can't recall which ones.'

'I need to find us a nice villa. I'm sure there are loads. I just hope we haven't left it too late.'

'Oh, you'll find something,' Jessica replied distractedly, checking her watch. 'Goodness! Time's ticking. I'd better hurry up and have lunch.'

Walking briskly over to one of the high tables in front of the window, she pulled out a stool, settled down and reached for the sandwiches in her bag. She rarely joined Edie on the sofa unless they'd made a prior arrangement, or Edie specifically invited her.

After finishing her grapes, Edie wiped the crumbs off her lap and took a sip of water. She'd have liked a strong coffee but needed a pee and also had a bundle of worksheets to print off before the next lesson.

One of her former pupils, a young woman with dark curly hair and big brown eyes, was coming through the door as she was leaving.

'Hello, Amina. How are you?' she asked, pausing. She was always pleased to see her.

'Good, thanks, Mrs Lovell.'

Amina had arrived at the school six years earlier speaking barely any English and traumatised by the war in Syria, from which she and her family had fled.

Edie had been her form tutor for that first year and had taken her under her wing. Amina was smart and keen to learn as well as polite, funny and personable.

Impressed by her attitude, Edie had given her extra language lessons in her own time and lent her books to read. Amina could soon keep up in class and before long, she'd even started to overtake many of her peers.

She went on to achieve first-class exam grades. Disappointingly, though, she hadn't got into the university she most wanted to attend.

Encouraged by Edie and her other teachers, she'd decided to take a year out and reapply. In the meantime, she'd come back to school for two terms on a paid, part-time basis to assist the IT department.

Edie was super proud of Amina but also knew she was vulnerable. She felt quite maternal towards her and sometimes had to stop herself clucking round her like a mother hen.

'Can I ask you something?' Amina said suddenly, moving to one side to let another teacher enter the room.

Edie raised her eyebrows. 'Of course. Anything.'

Amina explained she was having trouble filling in one of the many university forms, some of which had changed in the past year. She had to do it all by herself as neither of her parents spoke much English.

Edie offered to stay behind after school the next day to go over things with her.

'They're absolute pigs, those forms. As you know, I had to help my kids do theirs. I should find it easier third time round.' She made a face. 'Famous last words, perhaps.'

Amina laughed.

'Thanks so much. I really appreciate it.'

The afternoon went quickly and Edie had a spring in her step when she left the school building, clutching a canvas bag stuffed with Year Seven essays to be marked.

It was dark outside but at least it had stopped raining. Her black VW was in the staff car park at the back of the school and she waited for another car to leave before pulling out.

It was only a twenty-minute drive through the winding Surrey lanes to her village outside Guildford, and she found herself reflecting on how much longer her commute might have been if she and Ralph had stayed in London.

They'd decided to move when Maisie was six and Ollie four, wanting them to have more space and freedom. The children loved the area when they were young but had complained as teenagers, because everything was so spread out.

As soon as they were old enough to drive, however, their parents had helped buy each of them a second-hand car and the moaning had stopped.

Overall, Edie thought, she and Ralph had made the right call. It was a relief not to have to deal with London traffic, road cameras and 20mph speed zones.

Here, they could hear birds tweeting and were surrounded by gorgeous countryside. She sometimes hankered after West End shops, theatres and restaurants, but not the crowds.

Cobbler's Cottage was in a row of cosy-looking, detached Victorian homes set back from the lane and facing a common. The double-fronted, red-brick property had a smallish front garden surrounded by a white picket fence and filled with neatly trimmed shrubs.

There were white-painted plantation shutters on all the windows and in summer, pink roses rambled over the triangular-shaped porch canopy. Beneath it, the blue-black front door, with its heavy iron, horseshoe-shaped knocker, seemed to beckon to you.

'Come in!' it seemed to say. 'You'll be sure of a warm welcome here!'

Edie pulled into a special bay, cut into the grass verge just across from her gate, and turned off the ignition.

The hall light was on but the rest of the house was in darkness. She guessed Ralph was still in his garden office out back. As she walked up the front path she could hear Dilly, their Border Terrier, yapping wildly on the other side of the door.

'Shh, Dilly! Be quiet. It's only me,' Edie whisper-shouted while she fiddled with the key in the lock. You had to use a special knack, or it wouldn't turn properly.

The yaps morphed into ear-piercing squeals and Edie hoped she wouldn't find a puddle on the floor. When she opened the door at last, Dilly hurtled out, running rings round her heels before jumping up and scratching her calves with sharp little claws.

'Ouch!' Edie plonked the heavy bag of school books on the ground and bent down to pat the dog's head and stroke her soft, pointy ears. 'I must remember to make an appointment with the groomer.'

Dilly rolled on her back to expose her round, pink tummy.

'Soppy dog,' Edie cooed, giving her a tickle. 'Now, out of my way. I need to get in the house.'

Once inside, she abandoned her big bag at the foot of the stairs and strolled down the narrow hallway. She could hear the dog's nails tap-tapping on the wooden floor as it trotted after her.

Flicking on the overhead spots in the kitchen, Edie blinked several times in the bright light. It wasn't long before her eyes adjusted, and she made a beeline for the kettle.

'A nice cup of tea is what we need, isn't it, Dilly?' she said, glancing at the dog at her feet while turning on the tap.

With some satisfaction, she reached for her favourite blue-and-white-striped mug, neatly placed in one of the sage green, Shaker-style cupboards.

The kitchen never ceased to give pleasure; they'd saved up for ages and it had only been finished eighteen months ago. Everything in it had been carefully chosen, from the antique brushed brass taps and handles to the polished concrete floor.

After popping a bag of Yorkshire Gold into the mug and filling it up with boiling water, she turned to the oak-topped island in the middle of the room.

It was virtually crumb-free, but she gave it a quick wipe anyway, and it was only now she noticed a note poking out from beneath the rough, blue ceramic fruit bowl sitting on top, which she loved. It had been made for her by a potter friend.

The handwriting was Ralph's. Glancing out of the glass doors into the garden, she realised his office was in darkness. He was out then. Surprising. He normally worked till about 7 p.m.

Afterwards, they'd have supper together, then she'd do her marking while he, well... He usually sloped back to his office and read or listened to music. Or he'd watch TV in the sitting room with the door shut, so as not to disturb her.

She went back to the note and read it quickly.

Hi hon, hope today was OK. Gone to golf lesson. I'll have a bite in the pub with Peter after. Might be late! Don't wait up xx

Peter was his best local mate. A bit of a boozer, so they'd no doubt hang about till closing time. Had Ralph told her he was taking golf lessons? She didn't think so. But why would he? Pilates with the girls was more her thing.

A nasty niggle in her stomach made her pause. When did they stop telling each other stuff? After the children came along? It couldn't have been that long ago; she and Ralph were a team back then.

True, he'd never been a big talker and she'd sometimes

wished he'd open up about his feelings more. But it hadn't seemed to matter much when they first met because they were so much in love and lust that in her eyes, he could do no wrong.

Later, once they had kids, they were just so busy getting by, she barely thought about it, and they were certainly good at divvying up the tasks so family life ran smoothly.

Maybe the cracks began to show once the kids became more independent, Edie mused. He'd set up his own, one-man publishing business and started working from home about eight years ago, when Maisie was fifteen. That was when they'd installed the garden office, aka his man cave.

It soon became his favourite place in the world and he often went in there just to chill. This used not to bother her; after all, she was usually busy with work and the children anyway.

But now Maisie had moved out and Ollie was at university, the house felt empty. Edie hadn't realised quite how big a presence they'd both been, Ollie, in particular.

She used to like nothing more than having a full table, and his mates would drop by a lot. She'd whip up huge bowls of pasta for them all, or a giant chilli con carne, and listen in on their chat.

It was Ralph who'd driven Ollie to university for his first term and Edie had wept bitterly when she'd said goodbye; she couldn't help it.

'I'll be back soon, Mum,' Ollie had said, giving her a big hug and kissing her on the cheek before pulling away.

'I know.'

Edie had wiped her eyes and managed a smile. She didn't want to make him feel sad or guilty; it wouldn't be fair.

'Just think – no more smelly sports kit or filthy rugby boots to trip over,' he'd added, with a laugh. 'You and Dad can do whatever you want. Why don't you book a weekend away? You've always said you want to explore the Lake District. Why don't you go there?'

'Good idea,' she'd replied, acting keen. But in truth, she couldn't muster any real enthusiasm. It would probably rain every day and the prospect of being holed up with Ralph in some typically shabby UK hotel or guest house was, frankly, unappealing. What on earth would they talk about?

Ralph must have missed their son, too. They used to go fishing at the weekend and watch footy on TV. He and Edie had never talked about their new situation. Perhaps they both found the subject too painful.

Dilly was scratching on the bifold door so Edie let her out into the garden. It was just after 6 p.m., too early for supper. Picking up her mug of tea, handbag and an open packet of shortbread biscuits, she strolled over to the squashy cream armchair in the corner and sat down, kicking off her shoes and curling up her legs underneath.

'Right,' she said to herself, placing her mug on the floor and reaching for the phone in her bag. 'Time for some research.'

Soon, she was lost in features and travel blogs about Crete, its history, food and culture, as well as the best areas to visit. She remembered she and Ralph had been to the north side of the island on their honeymoon, so this time she focused on the south.

Nowhere seemed too far from either of the two international airports, but she couldn't decide which towns or villages to home in on.

Idly, she typed, 'luxurious peaceful villa to rent in southern Crete, near sea, own swimming pool'.

Expecting the search engine to throw up a raft of links to suitable rental companies, to her surprise, the very first name that came up was that of a single establishment – Villa Ariadne.

Curiously, the description contained the exact same keywords she'd used. It even claimed it was perfect for two couples, though it could sleep up to five people.

She clicked on the website link and was taken straight to the home page. The pale blue font looked old-fashioned and the photographs were grainy, leaving her to suspect the site hadn't been updated for some time. However, the outside of the house looked very appealing, with a grand yet welcoming façade and an avenue of olive trees leading up to it. And the blurb, written by the housekeeper, was really rather charming.

Katerina Papadakis welcomes you to the magic of Villa Ariadne and Porto Liakáda. No roads, no cars, no mopeds. You will arrive here by ferry from Chora Sfakion, fifteen minutes away, and immediately feel as if you have left behind the stresses of the modern world.

Villa Ariadne is a historic jewel. Built by the Venetians, sections date back to the fifteenth century. While retaining many traditional features, however, it has been lovingly updated to create a modern, luxurious yet laid-back and uniquely calming home.

Everywhere you look, there is some piece of art, pottery or sculpture to delight tired eyes and soothe weary souls and senses. Everywhere you go, you will be able to lose yourself in nature, whether in the mountains, by the coast, in the azure Libyan Sea, or just at home in the villa's gardens, filled with aromatic flowers and trees.

The villa is set high up in the White Mountains overlooking Porto Liakáda, where discos and clubs don't exist, just a few quiet bars and restaurants by the beautiful bay. Night life is you, your conversation, your next drink, as you gaze up at the night sky and feel yourself start to reconnect with what really matters in life...

Edie thought it could have been written just for her; it was uncanny. It was almost as if someone or something out there knew she was feeling sad and wanted to reconnect with her husband, but didn't know how.

Quickly scrolling through the photo gallery, she found herself impressed with everything the villa had to offer: the large, airy bedrooms, some with sea views; the modern bathrooms and kitchen; the spacious dining room; interesting artwork; and most of all, the pool and lush green garden, filled with brightly coloured flowers.

Tucked away in a private stone courtyard, there was even a square-shaped plunge pool, decorated with beautiful blue and white mosaics. Edie could already picture herself with her nose in a book, cooling off in the crystal-clear water.

On the third and final website page, there was a lot of information on things to do and see around Porto Liakáda. There were no reviews of Villa Ariadne, however, and she couldn't see anything about the price.

The only way of finding out was to email Mrs Papadakis. Edie suspected the house would be taken already and even it was free on the dates she asked for, it would probably be far too expensive. Still, nothing ventured, nothing gained...

'*Dear Mrs Papadakis,*' she typed, before going on to explain what she wanted and asking how much it would cost.

She was about to sign off when something made her hesitate.

'*My husband and I had a dreamy honeymoon in Crete many years ago,*' she quickly typed, '*but we haven't been back since. Now our children are all grown up, I'd love to try to recreate some of those happy memories and maybe even recapture some romance!*

'I look forward to hearing from you.

'All very best, Edie Lovell.'

Swiftly, she reread what she'd written and wondered if she should delete the final paragraph. Perhaps it sounded too personal and odd. After all, most couples seeking a romantic holiday wouldn't invite their friends, too. Mrs Papadakis had no idea Edie wanted Hannah and Mac as a buffer, in case the silence between her and Ralph became deafening, the atmosphere between them unbearably chilly.

There again, it was unlikely the villa would be available anyway, so why waste time fretting about what the woman might or might not think?

She pressed send and waited to hear the satisfying *whoosh* as the email went on its way. It was done.

Her tummy fluttered. Crete, the birthplace of Zeus, king of the gods, and also El Greco, the Renaissance painter. The centre of Europe's first advanced civilisation and home of the fearsome half man, half bull, the Minotaur.

A place of rocks, mountains, deep gorges, pebbly beaches and secret coves with soft, golden sand. In other words, a land of contrasts.

It could be exactly what she needed.

2

She was lying in bed with her eyes closed when Ralph got home around midnight. After finishing her marking, she'd run a bath and soaked in lavender-scented water for a while, hoping it would make her sleepy.

Instead, to her annoyance, she'd remained wide awake, listening for the key in the lock.

Now she could hear Ralph as clear as day, talking nonsense to the dog in the kitchen in the silly sing-song voice he reserved specially for her.

'Hey, bubba... Who's a good little doggie, then...?'

He was obviously tipsy and she hoped he'd remember to put Dilly out in the garden for one last pee, then bring her back in and lock the door properly afterwards.

She heard his heavy steps coming upstairs and when he pushed open the bedroom door, the glare of the landing light made her flinch. Lumbering in, he caught his leg on the edge of the bed on his way to the bathroom.

'Fuck me, that hurt!'

She had to suppress a giggle.

Soon, the bathroom lit up, too, and the bedroom, no longer soothing and peaceful, felt like the inside of an airport terminal. Ralph relieved himself loudly, sighed, then washed his hands and buzzed away with the electric toothbrush for what seemed like an age.

There was no way she could have slept through that, though he seemed surprised when she sat up and said hello.

'I didn't realise you were awake. Sorry. How was your day?' he muttered, beginning to undress.

'Fine, thanks. You?'

'Yeah, same.'

She was about to ask about the golf but before she knew it, he'd chucked his clothes on the floor, climbed into bed and turned his back on her. Within minutes, his breathing became slow and ponderous.

Edie, of course, was more awake than ever now and rolled from one side to another and back again, trying to find a comfortable position. She wanted to tell Ralph about the Crete idea and the villa, but he was fast asleep and snoring. All right for some.

The bed felt too hot then too cold and her neck hurt, even when she plumped the pillow and rearranged it under her head. Her mind was soon preoccupied with problems which, by day, would scarcely trouble her, but now seemed insurmountable.

After about half an hour and unable to bear it any longer, she climbed out of bed and reached for her dressing gown, hanging on a peg on the back of the door. Ralph didn't even stir as she left the room and padded back downstairs, forgetting to avoid the third step, which gave a loud creak.

Dilly was in her basket and squinted at Edie when she walked into the kitchen, but soon shut her eyes again as if to say: 'What sort of time do you call this?'

'Shh!' Edie said involuntarily, as if the dog were causing a disturbance, not the other way round.

She made herself a mug of tea before tiptoeing into what used to be Ralph's study, a small room just off the kitchen, later appropriated by Maisie and Ollie. Then she switched on the battered task lamp and woke up the family computer.

There were already quite a few new emails in her inbox, which she'd only checked a couple of hours ago. Most could wait till tomorrow, but one in particular caught her attention.

It was from Katerina Papadakis, the housekeeper who took bookings for Villa Ariadne. Edie quickly read to the bottom and breathed in sharply.

To her amazement and delight, the villa was not only free on the dates she wanted, it was also far less pricey than she'd feared.

'Please can you advise me as soon as possible if you would like to make the booking and forward the deposit, using the details below,' Mrs Papadakis wrote. *'I hope you and your husband and friends will reap the benefits from all that Villa Ariadne has to offer. It is a most unusual and very special place, like nowhere you have ever been before.'*

The wording was slightly odd, Edie thought, seeming to suggest they'd be in for something more than simple relaxation. What did the housekeeper mean? She decided to put it down to language differences and was tempted to say yes straight away, but reminded herself she'd better check with the others first.

'Dear Mrs Papadakis,

'Thank you for replying so quickly,' she wrote back. *'I'll speak to my husband and friends first thing tomorrow and get back to you by the end of the day.'*

This way, she hoped the housekeeper would be persuaded to give her a chance and keep the booking on hold, at least for a short while, before passing it on to someone else.

After closing her inbox, Edie browsed the Web for a bit,

looking for swimsuits and holiday wear. It was the wrong time of year, though, and nothing much caught her fancy. She soon grew bored. Best wait till nearer the time.

She resolved not to forward the villa's rather old-fashioned website link to Hannah or Ralph, in case it put them off. She'd rather talk to them first and explain why she thought it was so perfect. She could be persuasive when she wanted.

Back in bed, Ralph was flat out on his back, making strange little moaning sounds. She gave him a gentle nudge and he rolled onto his tummy and went quiet.

As Edie's breathing slowed and she finally began to drift off, she found herself thinking about Mrs Papadakis, trying to picture how she looked and sounded, and wondering what she'd made of Edie's first message.

For some reason, Edie became convinced the housekeeper was thinking about her, too, that there was some sort of synchronism. She imagined she could see Mrs Papadakis sitting by herself on a wooden chair, gazing into the distance, reaching out and trying to make a connection.

Edie shook her head and told herself not to be silly. No doubt Katerina would be tucked up and dreaming by now. After all, Edie, Ralph and their friends meant nothing to her. They were just a bunch of potential clients. She'd have pushed the whole lot of them right to the back of her mind.

* * *

At lunchtime in the staffroom the following day, Edie received the news she'd been hoping for.

'Villa Ariadne sounds ideal,' she heard Hannah say on the phone. 'I can't believe the price! It's much cheaper than I thought.

I checked with Mac and he gave it the thumbs up, too. Let's go for it.'

'Great!'

Edie mentally punched the air. Having set her heart on Villa Ariadne, she'd been afraid either Hannah's husband, Mac, or Ralph might veto the idea. Mac could be tricky at times.

He, Ralph and Hannah had met at university and when Edie started dating Ralph a couple of years later, they'd all become firm friends.

She thought back to their first ever holiday together, when they'd hired a barge to cruise up and down the Norfolk Broads. They must have been about twenty-three or -four and just starting out on their careers.

The barge was small, dark and cramped and it had rained most days but no one cared. Ralph and Edie, who'd met about six months before, were head over heels in love, while Mac and Hannah were already well-established and talking about saving up to buy a place together.

Edie could remember drinking cheap red wine below deck, while thunder crashed and lightning flashed around them and their sides hurt from laughing so much.

Back then, she'd thought Mac and Hannah the ideal couple, who balanced each other perfectly. He was funny, smart and creative, a dreamer with big ideas, while Hannah was the level-headed one who kept his feet on the ground.

She'd sometimes tease Mac for being impractical; for instance, when he'd suggested they buy a run-down lighthouse and convert it into a home. He'd seen it advertised for sale in a local newspaper he'd picked up when he'd gone to buy milk and bread.

'You must be mad,' Hannah had said with a laugh, when he'd returned to the barge. 'I'm not living in the middle of nowhere.

You'd definitely underestimate how much it would cost and we'd run out of money and it'd never get finished – and imagine all those stairs!'

'It wouldn't be great if you had children,' Edie had agreed. 'You'd spend all your time rushing them to A and E!'

Mac had groaned. 'We could have it for a few years and really enjoy it.' He'd looked to Ralph for backup. 'It'd be fantastic for parties. We could always sell up if kids came along. Come on, you've got to enjoy the present; who wants to be sensible all the time? We're only young once.'

There was something immensely appealing about his enthusiasm and Edie had no doubt if anyone could make a go of converting a lighthouse, it was him. He had great vision and was amazing with his hands. He'd make the place stunning.

But she could see Hannah's point of view, too.

'I wouldn't fancy it myself,' Edie had said. 'I bet lighthouses are damp and a bit smelly.'

When Mac sighed, Ralph had affectionately ruffled his friend's thick, dark hair.

'Looks like you're on a loser here, mate. Maybe buy a boat instead.'

'You can have parties on that,' Hannah had added, somewhat sarcastically, pointing to the rain slashing down outside the porthole window. 'See how much fun we're having! You don't need to be in a lighthouse to experience nature in all its glory!'

Almost thirty years on from that holiday the four were still great friends, particularly Edie and Hannah, who happened to share the same birthday. They were godmothers to each other's children, too.

Edie knew Mac and Hannah's marriage wasn't easy. As the years had gone by, Hannah had increasingly complained about her husband's moodiness, which Edie put down mostly to work stress. Mac was a landscape gardener and was either on a high or a low, depending on how well his business was going. Rarely anything in between.

Another bone of contention was Hannah's sociability. She loved nothing more than a big party or gathering, while Mac had become more introverted, preferring the company of one or two others or just his own. Hannah grumbled he was boring, while he accused her of being out all the time.

They also struggled with money, which undoubtedly put more strain on the relationship. His job was either feast or famine, more often the latter, or so it seemed to Edie.

Hannah's online recruitment job was commission-based and she often worked incredibly long hours. She earned quite a lot, but had a tendency to live beyond her means.

When things were going well, she'd splash out on herself and the kids. But then when she went through a lean patch, she'd realise there was scarcely enough in the bank to pay their big bills and even bigger mortgage.

Despite all this, she and Mac appeared to jog along well enough and Edie was fond of them both. Recently, though, she'd noticed more bickering between them and Hannah seemed to have lost some of her bounce. She hoped Mac had nothing to do with it.

As soon as she'd rung off, she started an email to Mrs Papadakis.

She'd already discussed the villa in bed with Ralph this morning. He'd been so hung-over he'd have said yes to anything.

'Dear Mrs Papadakis,' she wrote. *'I'm delighted to say my husband, friends and I would love to take Villa Ariadne for the week of Saturday 24 May to Saturday 31 May. I hope it's still available? I'll transfer the deposit as soon as I hear back from you.*

'We look forward very much to meeting you and spending time on your beautiful island.

'Thanks and very best wishes...'

'Hello, you!'

Edie swung round, blurry-eyed, propping herself up on an elbow on the back of the sofa. She realised she'd been miles away, staring into space.

'I was thinking about Crete,' she told Jessica, apologetically. 'I may have found us a villa to rent.'

'Well done.'

Jessica was standing very straight, with a pile of exercise books clutched to her chest. She was smiling but something about her seemed different; Edie couldn't put her finger on it.

'Nearly the weekend, thank goodness,' Edie said brightly. It was Friday and the mood in the staffroom and round the school was always cheerier. 'What are you up to? Got any nice plans?'

Jessica would normally reel off a list of arrangements: a visit to some or other historical site, a running challenge, a tennis match or theatre trip, for instance. Whatever she'd organised always sounded interesting. Edie sometimes felt a teeny bit envious.

Her weekends were mostly taken up with marking, housework, catching up on admin and watching TV with Ralph, possibly with a takeaway thrown in. She'd occasionally suggest inviting friends for supper or offer to book theatre tickets, but he was never that keen. He always said he had work to catch up on.

It seemed Jessica did most of her activities alone – she rarely mentioned friends. Feeling a little sorry for her and also seeing her as a potential companion, Edie had once asked her along to a film they'd discussed. Jessica reciprocated soon after with an invitation to a blues event.

Both evenings had gone well and Edie had suggested arranging another night out soon.

Jessica had never followed her up on the idea, however, and not wanting to be pushy, Edie had decided to park it. Perhaps her colleague preferred her own company. She was certainly very independent.

Edie was slightly in awe of Jessica, actually. She herself would never go to a film, play or concert alone; she'd be far too self-conscious. Silly really. She probably missed out.

She was mulling this over while she waited patiently for a response from Jessica but for once, she seemed lost for words.

'Are you OK?' Edie asked, looking more closely at her friend and noticing her downcast eyes and the slight quiver in her lip.

'Actually, no.'

Jessica's face reddened and her features sort of scrunched together, as if she were fighting back tears.

'What's happened?' Edie asked in alarm, patting the empty space on her right. 'Come here. Tell me what's wrong.'

Jessica hurried round to the other side of the sofa and sat down. It was a shock to see her so vulnerable, her thin knees, encased in opaque black tights, pulled together as if for comfort, and she was staring blankly at the pile of books on her lap.

'It's my dog – Ernest,' she began, with a catch in her voice.

Edie frowned. She knew Jessica was very fond of her pet, a dachshund. She mentioned him quite often.

'His heart's been bad for a while but he was doing OK on medication,' Jessica continued. 'But last night when I got back from work, he was coughing and gasping for breath. He seemed really distressed.

'I rushed him to the vet and they kept him in for tests. The vet rang just now; I just spoke to her. She said his heart's giving up and there's nothing more they can do.' She swallowed, wincing as if it hurt.

'They've dosed him up with sedatives and painkillers but he's not happy. They said the kindest thing would be to put him down.'

'Oh, Jessica, I'm so sorry.' Edie wrapped an arm round her friend's shoulders and squeezed.

It was too much for Jessica, who let out a sob, attracting the attention of a group of nearby staff, who were sitting round a table eating lunch.

Most looked away quickly but Janine Murray, the gossipy Art teacher, caught Edie's eye and raised her brows in question. Edie quickly glanced in the other direction, pretending not to notice.

Jessica's hands shot up to cover her face.

'He's been such a dear friend to me these past twelve years,' she said falteringly. 'I couldn't have asked for more. I'm going to the vet's after work today to say goodbye.'

Tears pricked in Edie's eyes, too. She could only begin to imagine how Jessica must feel, and she didn't even have a husband or partner to support and comfort her.

'I'll come with you,' Edie blurted, before hesitating. 'If you'd like me to, that is.'

There was a pause, while Jessica weighed up the offer.

'That's very kind of you,' she replied at last, 'but no. You've got enough on your plate. I'll be fine. I knew something like this was going to happen sooner or later. I'll miss him, that's all.'

'It's no trouble, honestly,' Edie persisted. 'I can drive you there. I'll wait outside if you prefer.'

She wouldn't have wanted to be on her own if Dilly had to be put down; she'd be an absolute mess. But Jessica's mind was made up.

'No. I'm a big girl. I can cope,' she said, before inhaling sharply and straightening her back.

'I want him to have a calm, peaceful death; it's the least I can do. Hopefully he'll just drift off to sleep on my lap.'

Clearing her throat, she pushed back a strand of loose hair and secured it tightly with a clip. Seeming more composed now, she rose, still clutching her pile of books, and Edie did the same.

'Thank you for your kindness,' Jessica said.

She was back to her old, polite, slightly formal self.

'I hope it goes OK later, or as well as you could hope for,' Edie replied. 'Let me know if you change your mind about the lift.'

It wasn't long before the bell rang and Edie didn't see Jessica again until the end of the day. Children were spilling out of her ground-floor classroom, jostling with each other in the corridor and chattering excitedly. It was Friday, after all.

'Er, excuse me,' Jessica said in a loud, commanding voice, appearing at the door just as Edie approached. 'Lower the volume, please, and walk, don't run. We don't want any accidents.'

Edie's lesson had finished promptly and she'd been on her way to the car park with her coat in one arm, her heavy canvas tote bag, packed with exercise books, in another.

She paused, waiting for the last pupils to leave, before asking Jessica how she was feeling.

'All right, thanks. I think I've got my head round it now. He's a dog, after all, and he's had a very good life. One mustn't be silly and sentimental.'

Edie was surprised. As far as she was concerned, it was totally natural to be sentimental about the death of a much-loved pet. Still, she admired her friend's stoicism.

'You're right,' she said, doubtfully. 'That's a very sensible attitude. I'd be blubbing all over the place if Dilly died. I don't know what I'd do without Ralph—'

The comment just slipped out and Edie inhaled sharply, wanting to kick herself. If only she could take it back! The last thing she wanted was to make things worse by drawing attention to the fact Jessica didn't have a partner. But she needn't have worried.

'Oh, I've never needed a man to hold my hand,' Jessica replied airily. 'In my experience, most of them aren't up to much.'

Edie was momentarily stung on Ralph's behalf, but quickly recovered. After all, it's not as if she hadn't been aware Jessica was somewhat anti-male. Indeed, she'd sometimes wondered if her friend had had a bad experience or if she were gay, but there'd never been any evidence.

She drew herself up with a nod.

'I agree. Women are much stronger than men,' she said, touching Jessica lightly on the arm. 'Good luck. I'll be thinking of you.'

3

Ralph was in the kitchen pouring himself a glass of white wine when Edie arrived home. There was another, empty glass waiting for her on the island, along with a bowl of crisps and some green olives.

'Want some?' he asked, waving the wine bottle in her direction.

She nodded. 'Please.'

After handing her a drink, he pecked her lightly on the cheek before pulling out a stool from under the bench and sitting down. She did the same, kicking off her shoes and placing her stockinged feet on the foot bar.

Moments like this with Ralph were unusual. He didn't normally leave the office till later, and she felt an unfamiliar glow of pleasure. She took a sip of wine, savouring the mellow, fruity taste, before breathing in deeply with her eyes closed, allowing herself to bask in the warmth that was slowly spreading through her body.

'Good day?' he asked.

Her eyes flickered open again and she was surprised to find

him gazing at her intensely. It was slightly unnerving.

'What?' she asked, squirming on the stool. 'Do I need to blow my nose?'

He laughed. 'No! I was just thinking you look very attractive tonight. Am I allowed to say that?'

Now it was her turn to smile. 'Of course, but you never normally comment on my appearance.'

'Don't I?' He seemed surprised. 'Sorry. But you do – look very attractive, I mean.'

'I can't think why.'

Her hand shot up to smooth her dark, wiry curls, now flecked with silver and cut into a chin-length bob. Taming her hair was a never-ending battle; it had a tendency to spring forth in all directions, like Medusa's snakes.

Ralph leaned over and gently took her hand away, holding it lightly in his palm and stroking the back with his thumb. His hand felt big and warm and, for some reason, she wanted to cry.

'Hey, what's up?' he asked, noticing her expression.

'It's just...' she began, before stopping. He didn't move.

'Just what?'

The weather outside was cold but inside felt warm and cosy. Edie broke away from him to take off her navy-blue cardigan and put it carefully in her lap, playing for time.

Mustering courage, she raised her head once more and looked him in the eye.

'Are we all right?' she blurted. 'You and me?'

His body tensed and his sandy-coloured eyebrows shot up.

'I think so.' He laughed nervously. 'Aren't we? Why? What's brought this on?'

She was tired and wished she hadn't embarked on the conversation; she'd been ruminating on the way home but hadn't planned to put her thoughts into words. Now, it was too late to stop.

'It's just, we don't seem to do anything together any more,' she said, before swallowing. 'I mean, this is lovely, us having a glass of wine together. Most of the time we seem to lead parallel lives.'

Her eyes felt dry and stingy, and rubbing them only made things worse.

'We're always working and if not, we're so tired we can hardly speak. I thought things would change when the children left, but they haven't. We see less of each other now than we did before—'

'That's not true,' Ralph responded. 'We watched *Family Guy* together the other night.' He laughed again, trying to make light of it.

'That's not talking, it's co-existing.'

She took another swig of her drink and put the glass down, running a finger idly round the rim. Her head had started to buzz; the wine must be strong.

'Is this about – you know?'

As Ralph spoke, Edie noticed his expression change and his features distorted into a frown.

'I thought we'd moved on from that,' he went on. 'Why are you bringing it up again?'

That 'it' was such a small word, yet with such deep resonance.

'I'm not,' she insisted. 'This has got nothing to do with it.'

She meant it. At least, she thought she did. Maybe she was kidding herself.

Her mind flashed back to about this time ten years ago and his one-night stand. He'd been to a works do in central London and had booked a hotel room in advance, knowing he'd struggle to catch the last train home.

She'd only found out about the fling because he'd acted so strange and guilty afterwards. Her suspicions raised, she'd confronted him a few days later and he'd confessed immediately; he'd always been the world's worst liar.

In his own words, it had been 'a moment of madness'. The opportunity arose and temptation, coupled with copious amounts of alcohol, had got the better of him.

Plus, he and Edie had been going through a tricky patch; she was up to her neck in work, preparing for an Ofsted inspection, and the kids were being extra demanding. He'd been feeling unloved and unappreciated and, well, this other woman had happened to cross his path...

He'd wept bitter tears and begged Edie to give him another chance. Shaken to her very core, she'd initially asked him to leave, not at all convinced she could get through the pain and hurt and come out the other side.

But while he'd been staying at a hotel, she'd realised she missed him terribly, and it had dawned on her how much there was to lose. Besides, she still loved him, and in the end, she'd chosen to forgive. At the time it had felt like the least-worst option.

After that, they'd seemed to pick up where they left off but beneath the surface, something had changed. Edie supposed it was a matter of trust and these days, she was more watchful and insecure.

Certainly, the anguish had lessened over time, but you don't forget these things completely; it was as if a small but significant part of him had slipped from her grasp and she'd been searching for it ever since.

Recently, though, she'd begun to despair of ever finding it again. In the depths of her gloom, she'd even thought of leaving him, or having an affair herself. Perhaps that would bring back some spark into her life and make Ralph sit up.

But her heart wasn't in it and the thought of being on her own terrified her. She wasn't as strong and independent as Jessica. Edie was like an Antarctic penguin; she needed warmth and closeness.

Ralph brought her crashing back to the present. 'OK, let's go out then,' he said suddenly.

For a moment she forgot what they'd been talking about and stared at him blankly.

'What do you want to do?' he went on. 'Go to the pub? Have a meal? See a film?'

'I've no idea what's on,' she replied, forcing herself to refocus.

She knew most films started around eight and the nearest cinema was several miles away. She checked her watch: 6.45 p.m.

'Anyway, it's too late now.'

'What about a meal then?'

'The restaurants will be booked up. We need to arrange things like that in advance.'

He sighed. 'The pub?'

She shook her head and he sat back and crossed his arms defensively.

'Why don't you suggest something then?'

The good mood he'd been in earlier had well and truly evaporated, and it was all her fault. Now she felt guilty, too.

'No, let's not bother,' she replied. She wouldn't force him and besides, she'd gone off the idea, too. 'We're both knackered. I'll do a quick pasta. We've got mushrooms and parmesan and I think there's enough for a salad. I'll do some marking later if I've got the energy. I've got masses to get through.'

His shoulders relaxed in evident relief, but her chest felt as heavy as a dark stone beneath the grey-blue sea. She gave herself a mental shake. What did she expect after twenty-five years together? Champagne and red roses? To be whisked upstairs in his arms and smothered in kisses? Marriage was no fairy tale. At least they were still together – just, unlike some of their friends.

Ralph took a handful of crisps and looked at her apprehensively. Perhaps he didn't believe she wasn't seeking to dredge up his past infidelity; maybe he thought she wanted to punish him further.

Whatever the truth, she decided to drop it.

'I'm hungry, how about you?'

She took a crisp herself and popped it in her mouth, before licking the salt off her fingers one by one.

'D'you want to lay the table? The pasta won't take long.'

They ate supper side by side at the round oak table overlooking the garden. It was the biggest they could locate at the time and seemed far too large now for just the two of them.

Since the children left, she'd found herself huddling ever closer to him while they ate. Sometimes, she'd accidentally bump against his arm with her elbow and feel the need to apologise.

If it annoyed him, he never let on. Perhaps deep down he found the closeness comforting, too.

He had a habit of feeding Dilly little titbits from his plate, which had turned her into an awful nuisance.

'Get down!' Edie said sharply when the dog jumped up, scratching her thighs with her sharp claws.

Dilly only obliged when Ralph whistled to her to come to his side, holding out a juicy piece of penne.

'You really shouldn't do that,' Edie said with a sniff, as she had done countless times before, to no effect.

'I can't help it.' Ralph ruffled the dog's head affectionately. 'She always looks so hopeful.'

The conversation felt stilted at first, which was no doubt Edie's fault for getting heavy earlier on. She was determined not to resort to talking about the children for once, though.

Instead, she told him Hannah and Mac had given the OK to Villa Ariadne and she'd sent an email to secure the booking.

'It does sound really lovely and it'll be nice to explore the island. I don't remember much about it from our honeymoon, do you?'

'Didn't we spend most of it in bed?'

Glancing his way, she noticed a slight smile on his lips as he raised a forkful of food to his mouth.

They had, indeed, made love so often on that trip they'd worn themselves out. Towards the end, he'd even begged for a night off, saying he needed time to recover.

In truth, she was quite surprised he remembered how passionate they'd been back then. He didn't seem particularly interested in sex these days and her libido had plummeted, too.

Sex happened once a week, max, and often less than that. To her, it felt they were both doing it more out of duty than genuine desire.

'We'll be able to see the sea from our bedroom, just like last time,' she commented, keen to keep the romantic theme bubbling.

'I hope Mac and Hannah don't squabble,' Ralph replied. 'I can't stand listening to their rows.'

Edie shivered, as if she'd walked into a cold shower. Ralph certainly knew how to spoil the moment.

Laying down her fork, she stared out of the window at the blackened garden. She'd done quite a bit of work out there last spring and summer, planting new shrubs and adding colour to the borders. But you wouldn't know it now.

'I think those two have got worse, don't you?' she said, turning back to her half-eaten food with little enthusiasm. 'I'm a bit worried about them, to be honest. Mac's always snapping at Hannah and putting her down. I don't think he appreciates her.

'It's her income that keeps that family afloat but you'd never know it from the way he behaves. He doesn't earn enough to feed them, let alone pay the mortgage.'

Ralph finished his mouthful and laid down his fork as well. 'That's a bit strong.'

He ran a hand through his longish, straight hair. It used to be honey blond but had faded to a sort of pale, brownish grey.

'She can be pretty sharp with him, too, I've noticed. She's more restrained in company, but I bet she gives as good as she gets when no one's looking.'

Edie snorted. 'Rubbish. Hannah hates conflict. She wouldn't say boo to a goose.'

'I wouldn't be so sure.' Ralph raised an eyebrow. 'You don't get to her position without being tough.'

The mobile rang in Edie's bag and she fished it out to check the number.

'Unknown caller,' she said, replacing the phone. 'I'll deal with it later.'

Remembering how she'd made a mental note to check on Jessica later, she decided now to recount the story of Ernest, the sick dog.

'Jessica was heading straight to the vet's after school to have him put down, poor thing. She was so upset. I offered to go with her but she refused. I hope she's OK.'

'Didn't she have anyone else to go with?' Ralph asked.

'No.'

'Is she single, then?'

'Yes.'

Edie realised she hadn't talked to him much about Jessica, even though the two women had been out together a couple of times. Perhaps she'd thought he wouldn't be interested.

'She's an amazing person,' she said now. 'You'd like her. She's very intelligent and she's got loads of interests, including running. She does marathons and triathlons and things.'

'Impressive.'

Edie had had an inkling this would draw him in, and she was right. He ran, too, but only round the local woods and parks; he'd never entered a race, though he'd recently talked about attempting a half-marathon.

When she'd first set eyes on him, she'd thought he must be an athlete because he was so slim and tanned, with ripped muscles showing through his tight white T-shirt.

Later, he explained he'd been working in New Zealand all summer, cutting logs for a family friend's forestry business. He'd had bulging biceps but they were nothing, he'd insisted, compared with those of the local men he worked with, who were built like tanks.

Edie wasn't the only one who'd found him irresistible and she'd had to fight off several rivals to win his affections. His six-pack had long since gone, but he was still in pretty good shape.

'How old is Jessica?' he asked now, picking up his glass and sipping his wine.

'About my age, maybe a little younger. Late forties?'

He nodded, putting the glass down. 'Has she ever been married?'

'No. I'm not sure why. I guess the right person never came along. She's attractive – tall and slim, with long brown hair and these amazing blue eyes. She can seem a bit intimidating at first but once you get to know her, she's really interesting to talk to.

'I get the impression she's happy being on her own. She's always busy. I've never picked up on any regrets about not having a partner or children.'

'Good for her.' Ralph wiped his mouth with a blue napkin.

'Maybe I should have a chat with her about marathon training. Sounds like she'd be good person to ask.'

'I'm sure she'd be delighted.'

Edie glanced at his food, which was three-quarters gone.

'Finished?'

He nodded.

'There's fruit and ice cream for pudding, if you fancy.'

After gathering their plates, she walked over to the dishwasher.

'I might ask Jessica here sometime, actually. For lunch, maybe. I do feel sorry for her. She adored that dog.'

While Ralph chopped up a banana, which he ate with vanilla ice cream, Edie loaded the dishwasher and put on the kettle. She was convinced her husband would make some excuse and disappear into his office again the moment he'd finished, but he suggested watching TV with her instead.

'Later,' she replied, shaking her head. She needed to decompress. 'I'd better call Jessica. I don't want to leave it too late in case she goes to sleep.'

'Fair enough.'

Ralph slunk off to the sitting room, while she took a mug of tea upstairs and sat on their bed, sinking back against a pile of soft pillows and cushions.

The buff-coloured walls and carpet, the thick, earthy-coloured curtains and the fluffy cream throw had a soothing effect on her. She must try to relax more. Picking holes in her marriage wasn't the right way to bring them closer. She resolved not to raise the thorny issue of their relationship again.

Her mind drifted back to Katerina's strange email: *'I hope you and your husband and friends will reap the benefits from all that Villa Ariadne has to offer. It is a most unusual and very special place...'*

She'd just have to hope the villa – and indeed, the holiday in general – would live up to her expectations and help her and her husband remember why they got together in the first place. If a week in glorious Crete didn't do the trick, nothing would.

* * *

'It was a good death, the best, really, under the circumstances. He died in my arms; I sort of stroked him off to sleep. It was all over quickly and he wasn't in any pain. Everyone was so kind. They let me sit with him for as long as I wanted. All the staff were in tears, too, even the vet. Ernest would have been chuffed; he loved being the centre of attention.'

Just listening to Jessica's description of her pet's demise made Edie's eyes fill up. She could hear the heartache in her friend's voice, though Jessica was trying really hard to be brave.

'Do you want me to pop over?' Edie offered. 'I can – it's no problem. I'm not doing anything tonight. I've got some delicious hot chocolate in the cupboard. I bought it in France and it's so good, much better than anything I've found here. I could bring it with me? Unless you'd prefer wine?'

She hated to think of Jessica being all by herself. Even lone wolves needed company sometimes.

'No, thank you.'

Jessica's voice wobbled and Edie wished she could give her a big hug.

'I need to hide away tonight and lick my wounds. I'll be better tomorrow, honestly. I bounce back pretty quickly; luckily, I'm fairly resilient. I really appreciate your concern, though.'

'OK, if you're sure,' Edie replied doubtfully. 'How about lunch here tomorrow – or Sunday if you prefer? Ralph said he'd be interested to meet you. He's thinking about signing up for a half-marathon. He'd appreciate some tips.'

The offer proved irresistible. Jessica loved dispensing advice. Many of the school staff found this habit of hers infuriating, especially as she usually knew more than anyone else and was almost always right.

Edie, though, couldn't see the problem. She liked being able to tap Jessica's brains and was constantly impressed by her knowledge of almost any subject you cared to mention. It was like being friends with an encyclopaedia.

'Sunday would be great, thanks,' Jessica said, after a short pause. 'I look forward to it.'

Edie's spirits lifted. 'Fab, see you around midday.'

Her mind immediately flitted to what to cook and whether to invite anyone else to join them. Mac and Hannah, perhaps? They hadn't been over for a while and it would be fun to discuss the holiday.

She hurried downstairs to run the idea past Ralph, who was surprisingly receptive.

'Let's have a big joint of beef. I'll get it tomorrow from the village butcher. His meat's always better than the supermarket stuff.'

Happily, Hannah and Mac weren't busy and as soon as Edie came off the phone, she returned to the kitchen and pulled out her favourite cookery books.

There was a recipe for roasted vegetables with olive oil, garlic and crushed coriander, which always went down well, and she'd do sticky toffee pudding for afters. Pure comfort food for wintry days.

After lunch, they could do a circular walk round the common and through the woods – the snowdrops were still out – then home for cups of tea and cake. She'd make a lemon drizzle. Hannah was particularly partial to it.

A damp cloud appeared from nowhere and seemed to settle

just above her head. What if Jessica didn't like Hannah or Mac and vice versa? The couple weren't exactly academic; in fact Mac sometimes joked the only book he ever read these days was *The Gardeners' Almanac*.

Edie liked a bit of gardening talk, but Jessica might find it dull. And Hannah knew nothing about ancient history; she'd done Accounts and Marketing at university and probably hadn't even heard of Socrates or Plato.

There again, Jessica had only just lost her beloved pet and would no doubt be feeling fragile. It might be a relief not to have to deep-dive into some intellectual discussion or other. She could just sit back, relax and let the chit-chat wash over her.

Whatever the outcome, why was Edie even fussing? She was only trying to be nice. Jessica wasn't exactly a close mate and Hannah and Mac were such dear old friends, Edie could throw anyone into the mix and they'd do their best to get on with him or her.

4

When the snowdrops faded at last and yellow, cream and orange daffodils started to pop up in gardens and along roadsides, Edie began to sense that the holiday wasn't so far away now at all.

As it turned out, she needn't have worried about the lunch with Jessica. It had been a big success, so much so, in fact, that Jessica had been invited on the Crete holiday, too.

She and Hannah had got on extremely well, and when Jessica had left, it was Hannah who'd suggested asking her along.

'I mean, she obviously loves Crete and wants to go again,' Hannah had said. 'She's good company and we'd get lots of history lessons. She said she's free that week and I read somewhere the villa can sleep up to five. I guess if she comes it would cost us all a bit less. What do you think?'

She'd scanned the others' faces for clues.

There had been a pause while everyone pondered the question. Edie had been taken aback, because it was so unexpected, and she'd initially felt slightly offended. Wasn't her and Ralph's company enough? And maybe an extra person would ruin the vibe.

But she'd quickly berated herself for being childish and mean. Jessica was on her own, had told them she'd nothing arranged for May half-term and had just lost her beloved pet. She'd said she badly wanted to go to Crete again and it would help Hannah and Mac if they didn't have to pay quite as much for the villa. It would help them all, in fact.

It wasn't as if Edie didn't like Jessica, either. She thoroughly enjoyed her company. And Jessica was so independent, she'd probably push off on her own quite a bit. What's more, if Edie and Ralph wanted time alone, they could say so. They didn't have to do things together all the time.

Ralph didn't have a problem with the idea, but Mac hadn't seemed all that keen.

'She'd change the atmosphere,' he'd said, slightly sullenly.

Sensing he and Hannah were about to have a row, Edie had pretended to misunderstand.

'So, we're all in agreement then,' she'd said, fake-innocently. 'Excellent. I'll invite Jessica and let you know what she says.'

At school the next day, Jessica had seemed delighted with the proposal, and so it had all been settled.

With big exams coming up soon, Edie didn't mention the impending trip to her GCSE or A-level students, knowing the poor things would be mired in revision throughout half-term.

However, the day before she left, she did tell her ex-pupil, Amina, who was still helping out in the IT department.

'I hope you have a wonderful time, Mrs Lovell,' she said, watching Edie stuffing books and items of clothing from the staffroom locker into a big carrier bag.

The school bell had just rung and they could already hear pupils pouring out of classrooms and thundering down the corridor, excited to be having a week off.

'Thanks, Amina. I hope you have a nice break, too,' Edie said. 'What are you up to?'

Amina looked down at her feet. She was wearing a white hijab over loose black trousers, black shoes and a purple tunic top.

'I need to look after my little brothers while my mum's at work.'

Edie felt a rush of sympathy. Amina had so many responsibilities for a girl her age, but never complained.

'Let's hope it's good weather and you can take them to the park,' Edie replied brightly. She knew the brothers were about eight and ten.

Amina nodded. 'They're a bit too old for the swings but they like playing football.'

'Or what about Frensham Ponds?'

'What's that?'

'It's a wildlife sanctuary and there are two ponds, surrounded by lovely woods. You're allowed to swim in the big pond. It's quite safe and the water's tested regularly. There's a sort of beach – and a café where you can get ice creams and things. You could catch a bus. The boys would love it.'

Amina's eyes lit up. 'That sounds great. Thanks. I'll take a look at it.'

Edie was pleased. She knew the family was hard up and Amina and her brothers didn't have many treats. This could be a fun activity for them all and it wouldn't cost much more than their bus fares.

As she slung her bag over her shoulder and headed down the corridor towards the stairs, she found herself thinking how different Amina's life was from Maisie's.

There was Maisie, earning a handsome salary and working hard but having the time of her life with her boyfriend and pals in central London, while Amina struggled to fit her job around helping her parents and caring for her younger siblings. And all because of an accident of birth.

It wasn't fair, but then nor was life itself. At least Edie could be a listening ear for Amina and give her a little of her time. It wasn't much, but it had to be better than nothing.

Jessica was just coming out of her classroom on the ground floor when Edie passed. She was wearing a smart tan trench coat, belted at the waist, with her black handbag slung over one shoulder and a heavy-looking brown holdall over the other.

'Are you packed?' Edie asked with a grin. She was already dreaming of boarding the plane tomorrow morning and arriving in Crete to bright blue skies.

'Almost.'

Jessica turned to check she hadn't left anything behind before switching off the lights and closing the heavy wooden door. Then they walked, side by side, towards the car park.

'Are you sure you don't mind picking me up?' Jessica asked, her black court shoes clip-clopping on the tarmac. 'It's a bit of a detour.'

'It's fine,' Edie assured her. 'The taxi driver knows already; he's got your address. We should be with you by six thirty, but don't worry if we're a few minutes late. Ralph usually forgets something and has to run back.'

In actual fact, it was normally Edie who forgot something, like her sunglasses, phone charger or book, but she didn't say so.

They stopped by Jessica's car – a newish-looking, electric blue Mini – and she fished the keys out of her bag.

'How are the others getting to the airport?' she asked.

'I think one of the children is taking them. It's useful when your kids can drive. Unfortunately, mine are both otherwise engaged.' Edie raised her eyebrows. 'Typical.'

'I hear that all the time from people with children,' Jessica replied with a sniff. 'It's all take and no give. I can't think why anyone has them. Most of them are spoiled brats.'

Edie was so taken aback, for a moment she couldn't speak.

'Oh! I wouldn't go that far,' she said at last, pulling herself together. 'They're not all bad. Maisie even brings me a cup of tea occasionally when she's around.'

'You're one of the lucky ones, then.'

Jessica opened the car door and plonked her bags on the passenger seat. 'From what I see, given half a chance, most of them would have the coats off their parents' backs.'

Edie found herself blinking rapidly, thinking she must have misheard. Surely Jessica didn't disapprove of Edie's choice – or anyone's choice, for that matter – to have children. That couldn't be what she meant.

She was a teacher, after all. You had to like young people in their job. It was just one of those silly, throwaway comments folk make when they're overwrought.

'I've got such a lot to do,' Jessica said, as if to confirm Edie's hunch. 'I'd better get home. See you at crack of dawn tomorrow.'

She climbed into the car and drove off with a quick wave, leaving Edie standing in the darkened car park, staring after her.

* * *

After Edie had dropped Dilly at the dog sitter's, she popped upstairs to check on Ralph. He was lying on their bed watching TV, his open suitcase beside him. It was full but on closer inspection, he'd packed only one pair of shorts and forgotten his swimming trunks.

'I can wash the shorts if they get dirty,' he insisted, when Edie queried him. 'We're only going for a week and it's not as if

Crete's the back of beyond. There'll be a washing machine at the villa.'

Ignoring him, she dug out two more pairs of shorts and two pairs of trunks before fetching her own case from the top of the cupboard.

She'd never found packing easy and dithered over which summer dresses to take. She had several, some short, others below the knee or ankle-length.

Then there was the tricky issue of cardigans and sweaters. One warm layer mightn't be enough and besides, she'd like to have a choice, but sweaters were so bulky.

In the end, she opted for a grey sweatshirt, which she'd wear on the plane, and a dressier cream cardigan, plus a pale blue, woollen wrap, which had accompanied her on almost every trip.

When Ralph wasn't watching, she slipped in some new sexy black lacy knickers with a matching bra, all wrapped in pale pink, scented tissue paper.

There was a posh lingerie shop in the neighbouring village, which she'd popped into one weekend. She'd never been there before and the wide choice of styles and colours had been a revelation.

For one wild moment she'd almost opted for scarlet, but decided it might be a step too far. If the black was a success, she could always go back for another set. Perhaps she'd end up buying the whole colour spectrum. Even if it did cost her a month's wages, it might be worth it.

Ollie called while she and Ralph were having supper and wished them a great trip. He was driving a group of friends to a house party in the countryside. They were waiting till the traffic died down before setting off.

'Drive carefully,' Edie said. She always worried, even though her son was pretty sensible behind the wheel. 'And don't drink too much.'

'I won't,' he replied, with a sigh.

They both knew he was lying but for some reason, it made her feel better.

Neither she nor Ralph slept particularly well that night and they were ready and waiting for the taxi when it arrived five minutes early at 6.15 a.m.

Edie felt a tickle of excitement after locking the front door and climbing in beside Ralph.

'Got your passport, phone and wallet?' she asked and he patted his jacket pockets.

'Yes.'

She opened the bag on her lap to check for her own things and was relieved to find everything there. No turning round and running back this time.

Jessica was waiting on the pavement when the taxi pulled up, with one small suitcase and an even smaller rucksack.

'How on earth did you manage to get everything into that bag?' Edie asked, shuffling closer to Ralph to make room on the back seat. 'Mine's twice the size.'

'I don't know. I guess I'll be wearing the same things every day. Why? Have you packed your ball gown? I didn't think we'd be going anywhere grand.'

Edie laughed. 'No ball gown, I promise. But I can never choose, so I end up throwing loads of things in. I've probably got far too much.'

Ralph made a disapproving noise. 'Did you remember the kitchen sink?' Edie laughed again. It was the first time he'd spoken for a while; she'd assumed he was still half asleep.

Hannah and Mac were already in the queue when they

arrived at the airport. They were easy to spot, as Hannah was wearing a bright pink fluffy cardigan.

They were in their own worlds, not speaking, but Hannah's face lit up when she saw Edie, and Mac leaned over the barrier to shake Ralph's hand before pecking Edie, then Jessica, on the cheek.

As soon as they'd checked in, they made their way to a café and the women bagged a table while Ralph and Mac went to buy food and drinks.

Edie, who'd been feeling weary, perked up after coffee and a croissant and noticed a book sticking out of Jessica's open rucksack.

'What have you brought to read?' she asked.

'*Zorba the Greek*.' Jessica pulled out the book and showed it to her. 'I can't believe I've never read it. I saw the nineteen sixties film, starring Alan Bates and Anthony Quinn, but never got round to the novel. It's such a classic.'

'I haven't read it either,' Edie admitted, turning the book over to scan the blurb on the back. 'You'll have to let me know what you make of it.'

'I haven't even heard of it. What's it about?' Hannah said. Edie hadn't realised she was listening.

'In a nutshell, it's about two men with completely different world views,' Jessica explained. 'One is bookish and serious; the other, Zorba, believes in living every day as if it were his last.

'It was first published in 1946 and it's set in Crete. The writing is supposed to be colourful and beautiful. It's quite controversial, though. Some people think it's highly misogynistic.'

Hannah's eyes widened. 'Ooh! Can I get some book recommendations from you sometime? I don't read enough – I spend far too much time on my phone. I could do with a list of must-reads-before-you-die, if you see what I mean.'

'Sure. I'll have a think.'

Edie stared into her empty coffee cup, feeling slightly put out. After all, she was the English teacher but Hannah never asked *her* for book suggestions, despite how much she read. She quickly dismissed the thought, though. Hannah wouldn't have meant to offend.

The place was very busy and a group of people pushed past, knocking Edie's arm, which sent Jessica's book flying to the ground.

'Sorry,' said a young woman in a baseball cap, bending down to pick it up.

'No problem,' said Edie, then, 'Oh dear!' A corner of the book was bent and there was dirt on the cover, which she tried to brush off with her hand.

The woman apologised again and Jessica responded with such a fierce stare, Edie found herself blabbing like a fool; she couldn't help herself.

'It's OK... no problem... no harm done... We can easily get another one...'

'Gate twenty-one,' Ralph announced suddenly, squinting at the board a little way off. 'Let's go.'

Edie felt her shoulders relax and she exhaled, swiftly passing the book back to Jessica before rising. By the time she looked again, the woman with the baseball cap had gone.

They hadn't managed to get seats all together on the plane. Hannah and Mac were at the back and Edie and Ralph in the middle while Jessica was on her own up front.

'Will you be all right?' Edie asked, concerned Jessica might feel left out, but she needn't have worried.

'I'm looking forward to getting stuck into my book,' she replied. 'I just hope I don't have a screaming baby next to me.'

It was surprisingly enjoyable sitting beside Ralph, looking out of the window at the fluffy clouds below and feeling her cares drift away. For once, Ralph couldn't take himself off to his office or get stuck in front of the TV. Edie put a tentative hand on his thigh and rested her cheek against his shoulder, breathing in his warm, clean scent of soap, fabric conditioner and skin. He didn't push her away.

'I'm so glad we're doing this,' she said, giving his leg a small squeeze.

'Me too.'

'I hope the villa's nice.'

'I'm sure it will be.'

'D'you think it'll be OK, having Jessica with us? We haven't made a mistake, have we?'

Ralph shuffled in his seat, making her raise her head.

'It's a bit late to be asking that now,' he said, turning to look at her.

Her brow wrinkled and he gave a reassuring smile.

'Don't worry. She'll be fine. She can take as many photos of dusty ruins as she wants while we laze on the beach and eat nice food and have long siestas. She's used to being on her own. I doubt she'll bother us at all.'

5

They went in one big taxi from the airport to the ferry terminal, then caught a boat to Porto Liakáda, a journey of about twenty minutes. The sun was shining brightly and the turquoise sea looked so tempting, Edie could hardly wait to jump in.

Feeling the heat, they all stripped off their top layers. Edie was concerned her pale, winter skin might burn, and she'd buried her sun cream in a sponge bag at the bottom of her suitcase. Luckily Jessica had a small tube to hand.

'It's factor thirty,' she said, passing the tube across. 'Use as much as you want. I've got plenty more.'

After applying some cream to her own face and arms, Jessica turned away from the others and gazed out at the rocky, mountainous coastline, dotted with spiky low ground bushes.

While Hannah and Edie chatted, she remained silent and self-contained, looking neat and business-like in skinny black jeans, clean white trainers and a pale grey T-shirt, with her slender hands resting, one on top of the other, in her lap.

Before long, they rounded a bend and Porto Liakáda came into view. Edie gasped in delight. The small, semi-circular harbour was surrounded by sparkling, whitewashed buildings with bright blue shutters, which seemed to cling to the rocky, reddish-brown mountains behind.

Painted wooden boats bobbed merrily by the shore and the water was so clear, you could see the rocks at the bottom.

'It's even prettier than the photos,' Edie said to Ralph, who was beside her. They'd both risen to their feet to enjoy the view and she tucked a hand under his arm. 'It looks completely unspoiled.'

'It's gorgeous,' Hannah murmured, standing up, too, and moving away from Mac, who remained sitting on the wooden bench. 'It's like a painting. It hardly looks real!'

As the boat pulled into the jetty and the first passengers began to disembark, Edie scanned the faces of folk waiting by the quayside. Some were clearly tourists like them, with backpacks and suitcases, while others, unloading crates of water, wine, vegetables, fruit and kitchen supplies, must have been locals.

Mrs Papadakis had promised to meet them there when they arrived but there were no likely candidates who might have been her. Perhaps she'd forgotten.

'What does she look like?' Ralph asked, as Edie led the way down the gangplank onto the cobbled street, wheeling her suitcase behind her.

'No idea. I don't even know how old she is,' she admitted. 'I probably should have asked for a photo.'

All of a sudden, she heard her name being called – 'Mrs Lovell?' – and a tiny woman in a blue and white headscarf pushed her way through the small crowd towards them.

Dressed in a white, short-sleeved blouse tucked into smart navy trousers, the woman was considerably older than Edie had imagined, with a skinny neck and arms and tanned, wrinkled skin. But as she drew near, Edie noticed her straight back, raised chin and intelligent black eyes.

'I am Mrs Papadakis,' she said, stopping in front of Edie and looking at her steadily with an extended hand. 'But you can call me Katerina. Welcome to Porto Liakáda.'

Her voice was clear, strong and heavily accented and her handshake was surprisingly firm. 'I hope you will be very happy here.'

Edie introduced the others, then, at Katerina's suggestion, they started on the mile-long, uphill walk to the villa. Edie had been warned about this in an email, and her friends were prepared.

The main street overlooking the harbour was bustling with visitors going in and out of shops selling clothes, jewellery and beach items, or sitting in bars and restaurants at tables right by the water.

With no cars or angry motorists to worry about, Edie felt her stress levels subsiding. The air smelled clean and fresh and you could wander freely in any direction for as long as you liked.

When they'd almost reached the end of the street, Katerina stopped.

'Here's the mini-mart where you'll probably want to buy your groceries. You'll find basic things like milk, tea, coffee, sugar and white and red wine at the villa.

'I've also made supper for tonight – just cold meat, rice and salad, you understand, and Greek yoghurt with fruit for afters. I thought you mightn't want to go out again this evening. But you'll have to buy what you need for the rest of the week another time.'

'Thanks so much,' Edie said. 'We weren't expecting you to provide supper.'

Peering inside the shop, she could see the shelves were well stocked with tins, jars and packets of assorted shapes and sizes. In one corner was a giant-sized rotisserie with delicious-looking golden chickens roasting on the spit, while outside two stands were stacked with fresh fruit and vegetables: white and green asparagus, cucumbers, juicy red tomatoes, big heads of garlic, peas and beans, peppers, radishes, courgettes, fennel and aubergines, plus apricots, loganberries, lemons, peaches, strawberries and mounds of pistachios.

Her mouth watered and she found herself looking forward to eating big salads drizzled with local olive oil good enough to dip your bread into, and even your finger.

Katerina was about to get going again when she and Edie heard a screech behind them.

'Look out!'

Edie spun round to see Hannah and the others pointing, wild-eyed, to a spot by her feet.

Glancing down, she was startled to see a very small, dark child in nothing but a nappy squatting in front of her, trying its best to pick up a pebble from the ground.

One more step and she'd have fallen over, or worse, on top of the infant.

Her heart fluttered, then started banging against her ribs.

'Naughty boy!' came a strange, strangled voice. 'Put that down!'

A blonde woman with a red face was hurrying out of the shop. She barged past Hannah and Jessica, who were standing side by side, and raced in Edie's direction.

Just in time, Edie noticed the child succeed in picking up the pebble between finger and thumb and raising it to his mouth. Quick as a flash, she bent over and snatched it from his pudgy little fingers, causing him to wail in high-pitched fury.

'Sorry, sweetie,' Edie said, at once relieved and also stricken with guilt. She squatted down to comfort the child.

'There there... sorry, darling... it's all right...'

She would have picked him up but his mother got there first.

'Bad boy, naughty Nikos,' the woman repeated over and over again, scooping the sobbing toddler into her fleshy arms and squidging his grimy wet cheeks in a hand.

Amid much jiggling and scolding, she kissed him hotly on the lips, forehead and nose.

'Mamma's told you not to eat stones. You might've choked.'

After a while, the woman glanced up and caught Edie's eye. Feeling rather as if she were being ticked off herself, Edie quickly popped the offending pebble into a pocket, noticing its hard, sharp edges and thinking it could have done some serious damage.

While all this was going on, a fair-sized crowd had gathered round.

Katerina starting shooing them away as if they were geese, in a rather confusing mixture of Greek and English.

'Everything is all right, there's no need to gawp,' she said fiercely, flapping her arms like imaginary sticks. '*Elá!* Will you please give us some space.'

Reluctantly, the crowd began to disperse, but not until Edie heard some busybody Englishwoman mutter, 'Irresponsible mother!' to which her friend replied, 'Poor child. Did you see its dirty hands and knees?'

When at last the toddler stopped crying, Katerina gave a satisfied nod.

'Good afternoon, Mrs Vasillis,' she said to the blonde woman, as if the drama of the last five minutes or so had never taken place. 'I was just pointing out your shop to my new guests. They're spending a week at Villa Ariadne.'

The blonde woman, who seemed somewhat recovered, blew a straggle of hair off her face and smiled apologetically. She was really rather pretty when she wasn't shouting, with a round face, dimples in her cheeks, a small squashy nose and sparkly grey eyes.

'I'm so sorry,' she said, still clutching the little boy while looking at each of the visitors in turn. 'He's that quick, one minute he was there, the next he'd vanished into thin air.

'One of the others usually looks out for him when I'm serving, but they've done a disappearing act on me, too.'

'The others', as it turned out, were her three older children, a boy and two girls.

Although Katerina gave the woman no encouragement, she seemed intent on filling everyone in on her life story.

She was called April, grew up in Leeds, had met her husband, Georgios, on holiday in Crete and they now had four kids, two large Bernese dogs and two cats. And they all lived in a flat above the supermarket.

She missed Boots, the chemist, Marks and Sparks and cheese and onion crisps, but not the English weather. She loved Georgios to bits and still fancied him rotten, but he was useless in the shop or at helping with the kids, unless given strict orders.

'Goodness!' Edie said when April had finished her account. 'I'm not surprised you lose a child from time to time. I found it hard enough keeping tabs on my two – and I had my parents and a childminder to help!'

Katerina gave her what she took to be a disapproving look.

'I-I mean, I never *really* lost them,' Edie stammered. 'They were just misplaced. They always turned up in the end, thank goodness. We never had to call the police. Well, just the once...'

Realising she was only digging herself in deeper, she quickly clamped her mouth shut.

'Oi! Meaty!'

Another screech from April made them all jump, including

Nikos, whose bottom lip trembled and his eyes started to refill with tears.

Before Edie knew it, the child had been thrust into her arms while April hurried towards an older boy on the other side of the street, who was kicking an empty Coke can into the harbour wall.

This boy was about nine or ten, Edie guessed. Dark-haired and skinny, he was dressed in jeans shorts, a khaki T-shirt, which was rather tight and small, and grubby white trainers.

Looking over his shoulder at April thundering towards him, he gave the can one last almighty kick. It pinged against the wall before bouncing off and coming to a clattering halt in front of a surprised-looking elderly gentleman in a Panama hat. He'd been sitting at a café table sipping coffee and generally minding his own business.

April rapidly changed course, veering in the elderly gentleman's direction and bending down to retrieve the can by his feet.

'I'm so sorry,' she said, stuffing the offending article into the pocket of her flowery apron. 'My son's lost his manners.'

The man didn't seem put out and merely shrugged, before returning to his coffee. Meanwhile April lunged at Meaty, grabbing the neck of his T-shirt and dragging him, kicking and squirming, towards the shop.

'My eldest,' she said, depositing the boy in the middle of the group and looking down on him disdainfully, rather as if he were a disobedient puppy she didn't know what to do with.

'His name's Demetrios but we call him Meaty for short.'

Nikos, who was still being held by Edie, yelped and struggled to get down. She put him carefully on the ground and he toddled towards his big brother, wrapping himself round his skinny legs as if his life depended on it.

Meaty tried to pick the toddler up but he was too heavy, so he crouched down and gave him a cuddle instead.

'Ah! They adore each other,' April said affectionately, momentarily forgetting her anger. 'Nikos copies everything he does. He wants to *be* him.'

Her expression hardened again and her eyes clouded over as she stooped to Meaty's height, jamming her face right up close.

'And that's why you have to set a good example,' she barked. 'Now, get inside and take your little brother with you. You can mind him till supper – and don't you dare let him out of your sight for one second.'

Meaty clearly knew the fight was over and Edie and the others watched him take Nikos by the hand and lead him back into the shop.

'We must proceed,' Katerina said strictly after a moment or two. 'We have a long way to climb.'

After saying their goodbyes, the group turned left up a steep flight of stone steps between two buildings. Edie and Hannah struggled with their wheelie suitcases and their husbands had to help them, but Jessica, who was super fit, bounded up some of them two at a time.

She didn't manage to overtake Katerina, however, who was sprightlier than a woman half her age. There wasn't an inch of fat on her; she must have been all muscle.

'Almost there!' she cried, turning round at the top, hands on hips, and smiling, with some amusement, at the slowcoaches lagging behind.

'Thank God,' Edie muttered to no one in particular, her thighs and calves screaming. 'My legs feel like jelly.'

There then began a long, slow ascent up a gravelly donkey track lined with gnarled bushes, rocks and scrub.

Assorted trees dotted the landscape – pine, lemon, orange and fig – along with swathes of brightly coloured wild flowers that seemed to flourish miraculously despite the dry conditions.

The air was filled with the scent of wild thyme and sage and herds of goats, with bells round their necks, perched precariously on rocks, munching lazily on blades of grass while they watched the strangers from afar.

Occasionally, they'd break into a chorus of mournful, wavering bleats that seemed to echo round the mountain like a lament.

Before long, the group came to a tumbledown stone cottage with a rusty, vine-covered pergola outside, providing some shade. A clean white sheet and two matching pillowcases had been hung on a nearby olive tree to dry.

The brown-painted wooden shutters were open but there was no one to be seen. In fact, the only sign of life was a flock of hens in a chicken-wire pen at the side of the cottage, pecking at the dusty soil round their rickety henhouse.

'That's where my neighbour, Eleni Manousaki, lives,' Katerina explained, pausing for a moment to allow the others to rest. She didn't appear remotely tired herself.

Jessica scrutinised the cottage, rather as if it were an ancient relic. It certainly *looked* like one, Edie thought, as if it hadn't seen a lick of paint, a new gutter or replacement roof tiles for years.

'Do you live in Villa Ariadne – when there are no visitors, I mean?' Jessica asked.

Katerina shook her head. 'Oh no. It's far too grand for me. I have a little cottage further up the mountain.'

'Do the owners ever visit?'

Katerina took a deep breath before answering. 'No. They are far away. I look after it for them and try to manage it in the way they would wish.'

Her reply piqued Edie's interest and she would have liked to ask more, but the old woman seemed keen to move on.

'We still have some way to go,' she said, beckoning the group to follow. 'I told you it was quite a hike.'

The donkey track curved left then right before reaching a particularly steep incline. Everyone went quiet when they spotted it, except Edie.

'Jesus!' she said, despairing. 'Not another bloody precipice!'

Ralph, beside her, tutted. 'I think someone needs to up their cardio fitness,' he commented, with an annoying little smirk. 'You're out of breath.'

'Rubbish,' Edie retorted. 'There's nothing wrong with my cardio. Anyway, you can't talk. You're puffing like a steam train.' She wrinkled her nose. 'And dripping in sweat.'

She was so hot and cross, the spat could easily have escalated. Luckily, though, they'd almost reached the top of the steep bit. Just ahead, they could see where the gravelly path petered out to become a rough sandy track, lined with gnarled old olive trees. And, to Edie's joy, at the very end was a set of tall, shiny, black iron gates.

Behind them, an imposing building made of the same grey-beige stone as Eleni Manousaki's cottage seemed to rise majestically from the land. In the centre was a rectangular tower so tall it appeared to be reaching up to touch the sky.

'Wow!' said Hannah, and Mac whistled.

Edie, having quite forgotten her irritation, hopped up and down on the spot like a child and Ralph smiled, amused.

'Looks like you've chosen well.'

'I hope so. Fingers crossed it's nice inside.'

Now the finish was in sight, the group's pace quickened. In preparation for their arrival, Katerina pulled an enormous bunch of keys from the brown leather messenger bag she wore, cross-body style, and clutched them in her fist.

Half running, half walking, she started to pull away from the others, who were hampered by their suitcases. The closer she got to the villa, the smaller she seemed in comparison. She reminded Edie of a worker ant, marching determinedly towards its colony.

Finally, on reaching the metal gates, Katerina stopped, put one of the keys in the big black lock and turned. The gates looked very heavy and Edie thought she might need some help opening them.

Before she had a chance to offer, however, Katerina swivelled round, bent almost double and used all the strength in her shoulders, back, legs and bum to force the gates apart.

'This way,' she said when the rest caught up, as if there'd been nothing to it. 'Mind your feet. The ground's a bit uneven in places.'

Once inside, they felt as if they'd entered a different world. The villa was surrounded by a wall, partially obscured by trees and greenery, which was so high, no one could possibly see over the top.

There was a wide, curved gravel courtyard and in the centre stood a set of stone steps. These led to an archway and at the end, a large, solid-looking wooden front door.

You could tell the place had been lovingly renovated. There were no cracks or gaps in the stonework or weeds poking through broken window frames. The sky-blue shutters looked freshly painted and on either side of the steps were giant terracotta pots, bursting with interesting-shaped palms and colourful blooms.

Edie's eye was particularly taken with two large statues of dogs, set on giant plinths at the top of the stairs. Tall and thin with pricked ears, wedge-shaped heads and curled tails, they seemed to be guarding the entrance. They had such noble, gentle faces, however, it was doubtful they'd deter anyone.

'They're Cretan hounds,' Katerina said, noticing Edie's interest. 'They're one of the oldest hunting breeds in Europe, possibly the oldest.'

'They don't look very scary.'

'No, they're very polite and mild-mannered. They make wonderful pets. You wouldn't want to be a cat or rabbit, though. They love chasing small animals and can run extremely fast.'

Jessica, who was nearby, came and joined them.

'When was the villa built?' she wanted to know.

'Sections date back to 1462,' said Katerina. 'It was built by the Venetians but has been greatly modified since.'

'Did the current owners make many modifications themselves, or was it all done before they bought the place?'

Katerina frowned as if for some reason the question annoyed her.

'The renovations have taken place over very many years,' she said. 'You will see what miracles have been achieved when you step inside.'

After crossing the threshold, Edie gazed in wonder round the open entrance hall with its high ceilings, smooth, whitewashed walls and creamy marble floor tiles. They were so clean, she imagined she could see her reflection in them.

A number of curved archways led off the hall into smaller rooms, one with comfy-looking red velvet armchairs and a TV, another with a desk, bookshelves, more chairs and an antique wooden table with a fancy chessboard on top.

The place, though light and airy, didn't feel clinical or impersonal. Quite the opposite. It seemed as though every painting, object and piece of furniture had been carefully selected by someone with immense taste and style.

In the very centre of the hall was a polished dark wood table on which sat an unusual, chunky, greenish-grey ceramic vase with a round bottom and narrow neck. There was something very pleasing about the irregular shape and uneven texture, and the piece could only have been made by hand.

Another, bigger archway at the end of the hall led into a dining room with a cream-coloured marble table, flecked with black. It was so large, it could easily seat at least twelve people.

From here, Katerina showed them into the kitchen at the back of the villa, which was a spacious, square-shaped room painted yellow and white, with French doors overlooking the garden.

It seemed to have everything they needed, including a brand-new dishwasher and a giant, American-style fridge-freezer. There was even a heavenly scent of citrus in the air, thanks to the lusty-looking lemon tree growing just outside the open window.

Beyond the kitchen lay a shady patio, complete with a rectangular wooden table and chairs. It was here, Edie decided, that they'd eat most of their meals.

Next, she followed a small pathway through a trellised archway, covered in climbing roses and a trailing vine. The others followed a little way behind.

Soon, she reached the main pool area, looking out over the mountains, town and sea. Five wooden sun loungers, with thick yellow cushions, beckoned invitingly from an area to the left, shaded by leafy foliage.

On the other side of the pool was a walled courtyard, largely hidden behind lush trees. On investigation, Edie was intrigued to find this housed a square-shaped plunge pool, decorated with beautiful blue and white mosaic tiles.

At the far end, water trickled out of the open mouth of a fierce-looking, bearded man's face, which was made of white stone, stained green in places by algae.

'I wonder who that's supposed to be?' Hannah said, pointing at the fountain.

'Poseidon, I expect,' Jessica replied, coming alongside. She stuck her hands in her jeans pockets and tilted her head, studying him from afar. 'He was God of the sea, earthquakes, horses and storms.'

Hannah put her hands in her own pockets and stared at Jessica, wide-eyed.

'Is there *anything* you don't know?' She seemed genuinely amazed.

Jessica gave a small smile. 'Oh yes. Lots.'

Edie pursed her lips. She was beginning to find the hero worship a tiny bit bugging.

'This'd be a great place for nude sunbathing,' she commented, changing the subject.

'And skinny-dipping,' Hannah replied with a wink.

Mac must have overheard because he came up behind his wife, wrapped his arms round her waist and rested his chin on her shoulder. Ralph was on the other side of the pool, deep in conversation with Katerina about something.

'Did I hear you say skinny-dip?' Mac asked with a grin. 'Can I watch?'

'You must be joking!' Hannah said sharply, shaking him off.

He wasn't to be deterred that easily, though.

'Aww! Why not?' The whiny childish voice he used was probably supposed to be funny. 'I'll hide behind a tree. You can't stop me.'

But Hannah wasn't amused and remained silent, scowling at him.

'I'd be careful if I were you,' Jessica piped up all of a sudden.

Mac's focus shifted and his eyes narrowed. 'Why's that?'

'You know what happened to the hunter, Actaeon?'

He shook his head. 'No, but I'm sure you're going to tell me.'

'When he saw the goddess Artemis bathing naked, she was so

angry she turned him into a deer and he was torn to pieces by his own hounds.'

'That's terrible!' Edie said, with a nervous laugh. 'A bit over the top of her, don't you think?'

Mac ignored the comment and remained fixed on Jessica, who held his gaze.

'It's different if it's your wife,' he said slowly and deliberately. 'I've seen it all before, remember.'

Jessica didn't flinch. 'I think you'll find the law disagrees with you. A woman's body is her own, whether or not she's married. Spying on your wife without her consent is still voyeurism.'

Mac's mouth twisted and his eyes darkened. Edie's pulse started racing. The mood had taken an unpleasant turn and she stared hard at Ralph, who was still talking to Katerina, willing him to sense something was wrong and come to her rescue.

She was about to call him when Mac gave a loud, unexpected laugh. There was no humour in it, but the tension lifted. Katerina must have heard and started making her way towards them.

'Follow me! I'll quickly show you the rest of the villa, then I'll leave you to settle in. You must be tired after your journey.'

Edie took a deep breath and waited for Ralph before trailing after the housekeeper. He must have picked up on his wife's anxiety because he caught her eye and mouthed, 'You OK?'

Nodding, she mouthed 'Yes' back. She'd have to wait till they were alone to tell him what had happened.

She was thankful the upstairs didn't disappoint. At least one thing was going right. All the bedrooms were simply but tastefully decorated with linen blinds in shades of orange, red and blue, original paintings and wooden floors scattered with rustic, woven rugs.

Two of the rooms had balconies and stunning views, while

the third was slightly smaller, though still a double with an en suite, and it looked out over the back garden.

'I'll take this one,' Jessica said, plonking her backpack on the bed.

'Are you sure?' Edie asked, relieved. If she were the only single person in the group, she'd have done the same, but she wasn't certain about Jessica.

While the others unpacked, Edie and Ralph went back downstairs with Katerina, who handed over a spare set of keys.

'Don't forget your supper's in the fridge,' she said.

'We won't,' Edie promised. 'Thank you.'

'You might like a cup of tea and one of my *kalitsounia* pastries,' the old woman went on. 'They're made with thyme honey from our local mountain bees. It's very good for you, you know. It protects the heart and kidneys and it's an antiseptic, too.'

'How amazing!' said Ralph, who had a sweet tooth. 'I can't wait to try it.'

They were standing just inside the front door now and Katerina appeared to be on the point of leaving. Without any warning, however, she suddenly stopped and looked up intently at Ralph then Edie, pausing on their features, taking her time with each of them, as if seeking something out.

Edie scratched her arm uneasily.

'You are a good couple,' Katerina said at last, still gazing at them.

Edie felt as if she were being examined under a microscope.

'Please, look after what you have. It's very precious.'

It was such an odd comment, Edie's mouth dropped open and she was lost for words. Ralph, though, remained composed.

'Thank you for your advice,' he said slowly, in a voice Edie knew well. It was his professional, polite-but-firm, 'I mean business' tone – the one he used for tricky clients making unreasonable demands or refusing to pay up. 'I think we both value our marriage. We know perfectly well how lucky we are,' he went on. 'Now, if you'll excuse us, we'd like to settle in.'

If Katerina was offended by the brush-off, she didn't show it.

'Of course!' she said, clapping her hands. 'How rude of me! I mustn't detain you any longer.'

With that, she pulled her ready-folded, blue and white scarf out of her bag and knotted it beneath her chin before opening the door and stepping outside.

'You are going to have a very big adventure,' she added, turning briefly to give them both a strange, close-lipped smile that seemed to whisper of hidden truths and secrets never to be told.

6

'I've got a bad feeling about all this. I wish we hadn't come.'

A tear trickled down Edie's cheek and Ralph went into the bathroom to fetch some tissues.

She was sitting on the end of their bed. The shutters were wide open and the turquoise Libyan Sea seemed to be winking at them mischievously in the distance.

'It's such a gorgeous place,' she went on, wiping her eyes and sniffing. 'It's hard to imagine *not* having a wonderful time. But Hannah and Mac are horribly snappy and I get the feeling Mac already hates Jessica and vice versa.

'It was a stupid idea to invite her. In fact, we shouldn't have invited any of them; we should have gone somewhere on our own. I can't think why we didn't.'

Ralph sat down beside her and put an arm round her shoulders.

'Don't beat yourself up, Edie,' he said gently, giving her a rare, reassuring squeeze. 'Inviting Jessica was Hannah's idea, remember? She was the one who suggested it.'

Edie sniffed again. 'I know but—'

'Look,' he interrupted. 'It's done now so let's make the best of it. It's a stunning place, as you say, and *we* can still enjoy ourselves. If Hannah, Mac and Jessica are at each other's throats, let's leave them to it. We can push off on our own and they can bicker and row as much as they like. At least we're miles from the nearest house so no one will hear them.'

Edie giggled; she couldn't help it. He sounded like the old Ralph, the one with a sense of humour.

'You couldn't make it up, could you?' she said. 'That comment Jessica made about voyeurism was *weird*. I think she's got it in for Mac and he knows it. It feels like we're on the brink of war.'

Ralph inhaled deeply. 'Maybe it's a good thing if she calls him to account. It might make him reflect on his behaviour. Personally, I don't think there's anything sinister going on between him and Hannah, but they're certainly not love's young dream. Not like us,' he added, giving Edie another squeeze.

She glanced up to see if he was being sarcastic, but his expression seemed genuine. Straightening up, she turned to peck him on the cheek. It was a bit scratchy as he hadn't shaved, but she didn't mind.

'And what about Katerina?' she asked suddenly, with a jolt. 'What on earth was she on about?' Edie had been so busy filling Ralph in on Mac's tense exchange with Jessica, she'd put the housekeeper's odd comments before she left to one side.

'Oh, she's just a funny old lady,' Ralph replied dismissively. 'A bit fey. She probably spends too much time up the mountain on her own.'

Edie gave a big sigh and he swivelled round, pressing her face between his palms.

'Don't worry,' he said, gazing steadily into her eyes.

He hadn't done that in a long time and his breath seemed to

fill her with warmth and newfound strength. She scarcely dared move, in case his mood suddenly changed.

'Thank you,' she said, when he finally lowered his hands. 'I feel a lot better now. Let's have a swim, then I'll investigate supper.'

The sun was just beginning to set when they entered the garden in their bathing suits and flip-flops and made their way to the pool area, through the trellis arch, covered in vine leaves and climbing roses.

The air was still balmy and they stood for quite a while with their elbows resting on the stone balustrade, watching the sky and sea turn through a kaleidoscope of colours, from greenish-blue to orangey pink, streaked with lilac and indigo.

Now and again a goat further down the mountain would bleat out a solo. Soon, the others would join in, accompanying their piteous cries with a jangling of bells.

Meanwhile, the cicadas struck up sporadic choruses of clicking and chirping. It was nature's cantata, specially composed, Ralph and Edie decided, for the two of them.

Just before the sun dipped below the horizon, when the sky was now crimson red, Ralph nudged Edie in the ribs.

'Come on, let's swim.'

Reluctantly, she turned her back on the magnificent spectacle unfolding before her very eyes, and watched her husband dive into the darkening water with a loud splash, before resurfacing.

'It's the perfect temperature,' he called. His wet hair was slicked back and the droplets of water in his eyes made them gleam bright.

Bracing herself, she stood on the edge of the pool, pinched her nose between finger and thumb, closed her eyes – and jumped.

The cold water whooshed into her sage green swimsuit and

up her body, instantly making her blood rush and her heart pound with exhilaration.

She went down far enough to touch the bottom with her tiptoes before pushing herself off and resurfacing with a pop, like a cork and the bubbles from a champagne bottle.

'Wow! Bracing!' She smiled at Ralph with water streaming down her face.

'Fancy a race?' he asked, starting to swim towards the shallow end. 'I don't know why I'm asking. You always win!'

'Ready, Steady, Go!' she shouted, and soon they were crashing through the water using their best front crawl, as if their lives depended on finishing first.

For a few strokes, she was aware of Ralph alongside her, but she soon started to pull ahead.

Just before reaching the end, she stretched out an arm as far as she could, preparing herself for victory. But before she could touch the edge, Ralph swerved sideways, bumping into her, and they ended up in a tangle of arms and legs.

'Cheater!' Edie screamed, coming up and gasping for air. 'You did that on purpose!'

'Sorry,' he replied, panting and grinning at the same time. 'I didn't want you to get all cocky.'

By now the sun had completely disappeared and long shadows were creating strange, other-worldly shapes round the garden. A sound of clinking, coming from somewhere near the house, alerted them to the fact they weren't alone.

'Shall we get out?' Ralph asked, and Edie nodded.

'We'd better find out what the others are up to.'

Wrapped in towels, they padded back to the villa just as Jessica was leaving the kitchen with a pile of plates. The patio table was already half laid with placemats, napkins, glasses and cutlery.

'Oh gosh!' Edie stopped to hug her towel round her while a puddle of water collected at her feet. 'You shouldn't have to do that on your own. I'll get some clothes on quickly and come and help.'

'No worries!' Jessica smiled. She'd changed out of her black jeans and sweatshirt into a pair of skimpy white shorts and a pale blue, sleeveless top.

Edie had never seen her friend's bare legs before and they were long, thin and pale but strong-looking.

'What time shall we eat?' Jessica asked, putting down the pile of plates and checking the fitness watch with a pink strap she always wore. 'It's eight thirty now. Shall we say nine o'clock?'

'Goodness!' Edie replied. 'Is it really that late? It was only seven the last time I looked.'

'We're on holiday,' Ralph commented. 'Time's more elastic. It's nice not to be tied to a routine.'

Edie loosened her towel and rubbed her hair dry with one end.

'Agreed. Still, I don't know about you, but I'm hungry. I'll tell the others to come down for nine. Don't do anything more, Jessica. It won't take me long to get changed.'

She felt a little apprehensive about knocking on Mac and Hannah's door, in case they were asleep or having a row. It was Mac who opened up and when Edie peeped inside, she saw Hannah looking perfectly relaxed, sitting on the bed and combing her damp hair.

She must have showered and was fresh-faced and make-up-free. She'd changed, too, into a white cotton dress with short sleeves.

'Is it chilly outside? Will I need a jumper?' she asked, when Edie told her about supper.

'Not really. I'm cold now because I've had a swim. Maybe bring an extra layer just in case.'

It was impossible not to feel content, sitting round the wooden patio table, surrounded by lemon and olive trees, with plates of delicious-looking food in front of them.

Jessica had found three white pillar candles in giant glass hurricane jars and had placed one in the centre of the table and the others on a nearby wall.

As soon as she lit them, the garden was transformed into a sort of fairy land and everyone's face glowed mysteriously in the flickering flames.

Katerina had prepared a big bowl of Greek salad, with tangy feta cheese; crunchy cucumber; sweet, vine-ripe tomatoes; earthy green bell peppers; strong, salty kalamata olives; fresh oregano and red onion.

In addition, there was a dish of cold pulled pork flavoured with honey and fresh herbs, including sage, rosemary, thyme and coriander. They ate this with rice flavoured with onion, garlic, lemon juice, parsley and fresh dill, washed down with a chilled local white wine, also kindly left in the fridge for them by Katerina.

'My! This is so good! I didn't realise I was quite so ravenous.'

After popping a forkful of the cold meat into her mouth, Edie reached out while she was still chewing and spooned some more onto her plate. Only then did she push the dish towards Mac, who'd been eyeing it greedily.

They talked a bit about plans for tomorrow and Edie said she'd like to stroll into town in the morning to have a browse.

'Typical!' Ralph said with a laugh. 'You just can't keep away from shops, can you? I swear they've got some sort of magnetic power over you. I think I'll stay here and chill, if you don't mind. I'm looking forward to doing absolutely nothing.'

'I'm not going clothes shopping, if that's what you're thinking,' Edie replied tetchily. 'We'll need some supplies from that mini-market, unless we decide to eat out tomorrow. Also, I want to get the lie of the land. I noticed there are ferries to quite a few different places, including the Samaria Gorge and Gavdos. That's the southernmost island in Greece. It might be worth a visit. I'll try and get a timetable.'

'I'll come too,' Jessica said, before lowering her eyes. 'That's if you don't mind.'

'Of course not.' Edie glanced at Hannah. 'Fancy making it a threesome?'

Ralph put down his knife and fork and stretched his arms above his head. 'Ah!' he said, finishing his stretch and bringing his arms down with a theatrical sigh. 'Music to my ears. The women go food shopping while the men relax. Just how things ought to be.'

Edie and Hannah knew he was kidding and merely raised their eyebrows. Jessica, though, rose to the bait.

'I hope that was a joke,' she said sharply.

Ralph quickly backtracked, raising his hands, palms forward. 'It was, I promise. A bad one. Sorry.'

'Well, it wasn't very funny.'

Her sour face seemed to amuse Mac, who gave a loud laugh.

'God, you women are so easy to wind up.'

There was a pause while Jessica weighed up her response. Sensing danger, Edie cast round desperately for some form of distraction.

'Who do we think will win in the local election?' she said fake-chirpily, breaking her own rule about not mentioning politics at the dinner table. It was the first thing that had come into her head.

'The Tories again, unfortunately,' Ralph said quickly. 'Labour's making a bit of a mess of things nationally. I reckon it'll be a landslide.'

'Agreed.' It was Mac, who'd already forgotten about Jessica. Edie's plan had worked. 'God help us. They're a bunch of hypocrites.'

Jessica raised her glass of wine and stared at the contents thoughtfully. 'The Tories are supposed to be the party of low tax, but taxes skyrocketed the last time they were in power. Then Labour whacked them up even more. No wonder the country's in chaos.'

'We need more investment, not less,' Mac replied, quick as a flash. 'The NHS, schools, social care, they're all fucked.'

Jessica shook her head. 'That's because we can't cope with the numbers. We're desperately overcrowded and getting more so by the day, but no one seems to be able to do anything about it. As a single person with no children, I resent having to pay more and more for services I barely use.'

Mac's eyes glittered dangerously and even Edie felt a shiver of dislike. Jessica seemed smug and self-satisfied, sitting there in these beautiful surroundings, with a delicious plate of food in front of her and no one to think about but herself.

Edie's other single friend, Marianne, who also had no kids, was the complete opposite. She had numerous godchildren and even paid for ballet classes for one of them, because the parents were hard up. She also had a voluntary job, mentoring troubled teenagers, and often sang the praises of the NHS. Edie had rarely met anyone more community-minded.

'It's the kids who are in schools now who'll be paying for your pension,' Mac snapped. 'And funding your healthcare needs when you get old.'

Jessica sniffed. 'I'm not saying education's not important. Of course it is. I work in it, for heaven's sake. But having children is a choice. No one forces you to have more than you can afford. Why should I have to pay through the roof for other people's irresponsible decisions? And for your information, I have private healthcare. I barely use the NHS.'

Mac's face puffed up and he turned so red, he looked as if he might explode. The first supper of the trip was supposed to be a relaxing affair, but it was turning into a battle zone and Edie could feel the blood pounding in her temples.

Hannah, who'd been quiet up to now, made a half-hearted attempt to defuse the situation.

'I do see your point,' she said evenly to Jessica. 'But most people can't afford private healthcare. Surely everyone should have access to good doctors and hospitals, regardless of income or the number of children they have? But equally, of course, you can't have people abusing the system. It's not fair on everyone else.'

Jessica was about to respond when Edie abruptly rose from her seat.

'Enough politics!' she said in a loud, stern voice, which surprised even her. 'I'm on holiday. I haven't come here to listen to you lot arguing.'

'Quite right!' Ralph raised his glass. 'Hear, hear!'

Edie shot him a small smile; she was grateful for the support.

Mac looked daggers at Jessica on the opposite side of the table, but she ignored him, smiling graciously at Edie, Hannah and Ralph instead.

'I totally agree,' Jessica said, rising like Edie and raising her glass, too. 'This is the most perfect place. I think we should give a toast to Edie, who was so clever to find it for us!'

'Here's to Edie,' they all said, even Mac, though he looked as if he'd eaten a lemon from one of the nearby trees.

All of a sudden, a gust of wind blew out the candle in the centre of the table, plunging them into semi-blackness.

Edie squealed, 'Help!' and instinctively went to Ralph's side, while Mac howled like a werewolf: 'Ow ow oww!'

'Shut up!' Hannah hissed.

It was Jessica who marched over to the wall to fetch a box of long matches before swiftly relighting the candle.

'There!' she said, her pale face glowing once more while her bright blue eyes had turned a strange shade of purple. 'No cause for panic. Now, you all stay there and chat. I'll fetch the pudding.'

* * *

Hope flight was OK. How's the villa? And the weird woman you invited too?! Have fun! Your favourite daughter xx

Edie was pleased to see Maisie's message when she and Ralph returned to their bedroom, but she wasn't quite sure how to respond.

'What shall I say?' she asked her husband, who was standing naked at the washbasin, cleaning his teeth. She'd been watching him through the open bathroom door.

'I can't really tell her the truth, can I? *"The villa's great but Mac and Jessica want to kill each other"*.'

Ralph took the toothbrush out of his mouth and turned, giving her an eyeful.

'I'd leave out the last bit,' he replied, scratching his side unselfconsciously. 'No need to involve her.'

Edie nodded, but she wasn't really listening. It was a long time since she'd looked – really looked – at her husband in the nude. At home, it seemed they were always rushing to get somewhere, barking orders at each other and making arrangements on the hoof.

Either that or they were too tired even to notice whether or not they were naked before diving into bed.

Now, though, they were in no hurry to go anywhere or do anything and Edie liked what she saw.

She was about to send a quick message to say everything was fine when the phone rang. Maisie had always been impatient; she clearly couldn't wait.

'I still think it's weird, inviting a random person with you on holiday,' she said, not even bothering to say hello. 'What if you realise after a few days you don't like her? What if she *smells*?'

Edie switched her mobile from one ear to the other and smiled. She could always rely on Maisie to lower the tone.

'She doesn't smell,' she replied. 'I see her almost every day at work, remember? I wouldn't have agreed to her coming if she was whiffy.'

'You might find she does terrible farts. She wouldn't do them at school but maybe she stores them all up and lets them out when she's on holiday.'

'She's not the kind of person to fart in public. She's far too proper.'

'She sounds really boring,' Maisie replied with a sniff. 'I hope I don't ever have to meet her.'

There was a loud bang in the background and the sound of a sweary male voice.

'What's happened?' Edie asked, alarmed.

'It's only Sam,' came the nonchalant reply. 'He's cooking

supper – spaghetti Bolognese. He's just dropped the saucepan and there's boiling water all over the floor.'

'Oh dear. It's very late to be doing supper. Do you need to give him a hand?'

'Nah. He has to learn.'

'Learn what?'

'How not to drop saucepans, of course.'

'Oh, I see.'

Ralph replaced his toothbrush in the holder and rinsed his mouth with water before padding over to the bed and lying on top of the cool white sheet beside Edie.

It was terribly distracting, but as Maisie rarely answered calls or rang herself, Edie didn't want to hurry her along; she might not hear from her again for a week.

Maisie was just over a year into her first job on a graduate banking scheme, and was working and playing hard. She shared a flat in Hackney with three former university friends but seemed to spend more time in Sam's one-bed apartment in trendy Kentish Town, bought for him by Daddy.

'I hope you've stocked up on nice bikinis?' she asked her mother next.

'Not really. I think my bikini days are almost over, I'm afraid.'

'Nonsense,' Maisie retorted. 'You've got a great figure, Mum. None of my friends can believe you're in your fifties. They all think you look much younger.'

Edie laughed. 'Well, that's nice. Don't disillusion them!'

Maisie decided to switch subjects.

'How's Ollie?' she wanted to know. 'I haven't heard from him for ages. He never replies to my texts.'

'Nor mine.' Edie sipped from her glass of water, which had been sitting on the bedside table. 'I did manage to speak to him briefly before we left, but he was in a rush as usual. He sounds fine. I'm not sure how much work he's doing, though.'

'No one does any work in their first year,' Maisie said confidently. 'I didn't do much till the third year and I still got a 2:1.'

Edie shuddered. 'Don't tell him that, whatever you do.'

When they finally hung up, she replaced her glass, put her phone face down in her beside drawer and firmly closed it. As Ralph was engrossed in his book, she decided she wouldn't disturb him yet and allowed her mind to wander freely.

Soon, she found herself reflecting on Hannah's delighted reaction to the news Jessica would be coming to Crete, too.

'I know Mac thinks she'll change the atmosphere, but maybe that's a good thing,' Hannah had said to Edie on the phone after work. 'He can say what he likes with you and Ralph because he's so comfortable with you. He might behave better when she's around.'

Hannah had laughed, as if it were a joke, but Edie's mind had clouded over.

'Are you all right, Hannah?' she'd asked seriously. 'You and Mac, I mean?'

Hannah had caught her breath and there was a pause before she'd replied. 'Yes,' she'd said at last, breathing out. 'Why do you ask?'

'I just wanted to make sure, that's all.'

'You know what he's like – Mr Grumpy. But we're not about to get divorced, if that's what you're implying.' She'd laughed again.

'Good. You would tell me, though, wouldn't you, if you were in any trouble?'

'Yes.'

'Promise?'

'I promise.'

But still, Edie didn't entirely believe her.

An uneasy feeling in her stomach made her wriggle restlessly and she applied some lavender-scented hand cream before turning to switch out her light. Ralph was still totally absorbed in reading and didn't notice.

Lying there with her eyes closed, Edie thought, not for the first time, that it was strange the way Jessica had pressed her on Hannah and Mac's relationship sometime after the holiday invitation.

Jessica had been about to eat her lunch at her usual table in the staffroom when Edie had beckoned her to come and join her on the sofa.

'You wouldn't put Hannah and Mac together, would you?' Jessica had commented, opening up her brown bread sandwiches, neatly wrapped in tinfoil. 'They're such different people. She's so laid-back whereas he seems, well, he seems *angry*.'

Edie had nodded. 'I know what you mean. He hasn't always been like that. He was funny, a real character when we first met. I'm not sure what's happened.

'It's interesting you've raised it, though. I'm a bit worried about Hannah, to be honest. She was fine at that Sunday lunch you came to, in good spirits, but I sometimes think she seems quite down. I don't like the way Mac picks on her—'

Jessica had fixed her small, clever, bright blue eyes on Edie, making her stop in her tracks.

'Do you think he's a bully?'

Edie swallowed. 'I... I don't know.'

Jessica's eyes had narrowed. 'My father was a bully. I can't stand them. Mac had better watch himself in Crete.'

At the time, Edie hadn't paid much attention to Jessica's words. Her mind had been too focused on finishing lunch and leaving plenty of time to think about what she needed for her afternoon lessons.

Now, though, as she lay on the cool bed, feeling the tension in her body drift away, she recalled again the sense of relief she'd experienced sometime later.

Hannah's relationship with Mac had been at the back of her mind more than she'd realised and Jessica's blunt question had brought these concerns to the fore.

If Mac did bully Hannah in secret, she'd mused, Jessica would sniff him out, for sure. She was sharp as a tack and fierce as hell when she wanted to be, as she'd already demonstrated.

Edie just hoped her ferocity wouldn't spiral out of control and spoil the holiday for everyone. She was someone you'd definitely want in your platoon, but woe betide you if you got on her wrong side.

Edie was so far away, she jumped when Ralph snapped his book shut and plonked it on the floor beside him. His skin was still slightly pink after his shower and he smelled delicious.

'Mm! Herbs!' Edie said, sniffing his shoulder. 'It's the body wash. The shampoo and soap smell the same. Have you noticed?'

'Um, yes.'

She nudged him playfully in the ribs. 'Liar! I expect it's made locally. The washing stuff, I mean,' she added, lying on her side and snuggling right up close.

Now, she could run a fingertip across his chest, down to his tummy button, round his abdomen and up again, drawing little circles and figures of eight.

He closed his eyes and breathed in and out slowly while the corners of his mouth curled into a small, contented smile. Edie imagined she could hear him purring.

'We must make more time for each other,' he murmured, as if reading her mind. 'It's stupid we don't. I know we both work hard but we should start making a conscious effort to do things together, don't you think?'

'Uh-huh.'

With fairy fingers, she softly traced the lines of his ribs, one by one, before moving down to his hip bones and up to his collarbone, all the while feeling for any little bumps or tiny indentations.

'And I don't just mean this – what we're doing now.' He turned and smiled briefly at her before closing his eyes again. 'Although it's very nice.'

Her finger strayed to his left thigh where she drew more small circles, widening into bigger, swirling ovals and back again, then his right.

'I'd love that, I really would. But you're always in your office.'

'And you're always disappearing upstairs to do your marking.'

'True.'

She paused, with her hand resting on his leg, and thought about the parallel lives they led at home. You could be lonely even in a marriage. Fact.

He was always so reluctant to do anything with her or go anywhere different. He was stuck in a rut and neither of them had prepared for the children leaving home.

Without even realising it, they'd sunk into their own little pits of despair – so much so, she'd even considered divorce. Perhaps he had, too.

'Edie?' he said, realising she'd gone quiet. She removed her hand and pulled up the duvet, because she was suddenly cold.

'It's been such a long day,' she commented, before yawning conspicuously. 'I'm exhausted. Aren't you?'

Sensing the sudden change of atmosphere, he gave a small sigh. 'I am – absolutely knackered,' he agreed. 'Night.' He kissed her lightly on the forehead before rolling over to face the other way.

'Sleep well,' she replied in a small voice, turning her back, too, and curling into a little ball.

A painful lump appeared in her throat, but she was determined not to cry like a silly little girl.

For a few wild moments, she'd allowed herself to imagine they could get back to how they once were. But the truth was, some wounds just won't heal, no matter how many doctors you consult or different treatments you try.

7

'Here's a cup of tea, lazybones.'

Edie opened her eyes and smiled gratefully.

'Careful, it's hot.'

Gingerly, Ralph placed a yellow pottery mug on the table beside her.

Propping herself up on an elbow, Edie took hold of the mug in her free hand and blew on it, making the steam disperse in all directions.

Ralph went over to the shutters and opened them wide before walking to the other side of the bed and sitting down.

They both stared in wonder at the sky, which was such a perfect, even shade of cornflower blue, it looked like a picture postcard. Edie couldn't see the sea from where she was but Ralph could, when he straightened up and craned his neck.

'It might be quite cold at this time of year but I'll definitely go in,' he commented. 'It doesn't look rough.'

He was dressed already, in a plain navy polo shirt and tan shorts. Edie noticed his broad shoulders and upper legs, which were quite strong and muscular, thanks to all the running.

She took a sip of tea and replaced the mug on the bedside table before flopping back on the pillows.

'I was so tired yesterday.'

'Me too,' said Ralph.

Eyeing him cautiously, she imagined he might be a bit resentful about the fact she'd kind of led him on last night, only to give him the cold shoulder. To her surprise, however, he bent over and kissed her on the mouth.

'Now come on, get up! Breakfast's ready.'

'I can't,' she said with a groan. 'This bed's too comfortable.'

She rolled over, burying her face in the pillow, and he smacked her playfully on the bare bottom.

'Don't!' She laughed.

'I'll do it again unless you get a move on. The others are downstairs already. You're the last one up.'

Edie's heart sank slightly as she followed him down the stairs, through the hallway and into the kitchen. She'd managed to forget about Mac and Jessica overnight, but sensing their presence in the garden now brought everything back.

'What sort of mood is Mac in?' she whispered to Ralph, when he stopped for a moment to fetch a bottle of water from the fridge.

'Fine. Shh! He's right by the back door.'

'Morning!' Edie pinned a wide smile on her face before she stepped onto the patio.

Mac and Hannah were side by side at the table and Jessica sat opposite, nursing a mug of coffee. They all looked up when they heard Edie and smiled back.

'How did you sleep?' Hannah asked.

'Like a log. You?'

'Same. The bed's so comfy and it was amazing waking up to that view.'

The table was laid and the food looked very tempting: there was a basket of crusty bread rolls, an assortment of jams and honey, thick Greek yoghurt, fruit, orange juice, a jug of frothy hot milk and a large, almost full cafetière.

No one had eaten yet; they must have been waiting for Edie.

'Yum!' she said, sitting down beside Jessica. 'Who did all this?'

'Your husband.' Mac's eyes were wide open. 'We came down and it was all ready.'

'Do you get this sort of treatment every morning?' asked Hannah, pushing the cafetière in Edie's direction; she knew how much her friend liked coffee.

'I wish.' Edie filled her mug to about the two-thirds mark and topped it up with hot milk. 'To be fair, he does bring me a cup of tea in bed most mornings. I *am* lucky.'

Jessica remained silent while they ate, with an open novel face down on the table beside her. Edie noticed how precisely she prepared her bread roll, making sure there was a thin covering of butter and honey all over, and how neatly she ate, dabbing her mouth with a napkin after almost every bite.

'Are you enjoying this?' Edie asked, picking up the book and examining its title and cover. 'I've heard it's very good.'

'Yes, very much.' Jessica cleared her throat, as if she didn't wish to pursue the conversation, and took a sip of orange juice.

There was no mistaking the message, so Edie quickly replaced the book and asked Hannah to pass her the basket of bread rolls. Perhaps Jessica preferred complete quiet at breakfast time, she thought. Maybe she normally read while eating. She must be accustomed to being alone, after all.

When they'd finished, Ralph and Mac offered to clear away while the women headed into the village. It was almost 10.30 a.m. and, as Ralph pointed out, if they left it much later, they mightn't want to go at all as it would be too hot.

'You don't need to buy any more clothes,' he joked to Edie when she said goodbye. 'You don't wear half of them as it is.'

'I told you, I'm not looking for clothes.'

'Hm. I bet you come back with something.'

The women were a colourful-looking trio as they left the villa behind and headed down the mountain towards the village. Edie was wearing a pink shirt, blue shorts, sneakers and a baseball cap, wedged tightly over her curly hair.

Hannah was in a straw hat, sandals and the white dress she'd worn last night, while Jessica had sports gear on: black trainers, running shorts and an orange vest top. A longish plait hung over one shoulder.

The landscape looked different this morning with the sun rising higher by the minute. Wild orchids and blue pimpernel peeped through the vegetation on either side, which was so dense, it felt as if they were walking through a giant salad bowl.

Edie breathed in deeply, filling her nostrils with the scent of herbs, listening to the sound of birds chirruping in the nearby trees and goats bleating in the distance. The ground underfoot was rocky and a bit slippery in places so she couldn't totally switch off; she had to watch her step.

'Are you all right in sandals?' she asked Hannah, who needed to stop every now and again to retrieve a stone from her shoe.

'I'm OK for now, thanks. They were a bit of a silly choice, though. I'll definitely wear trainers next time.'

Katerina's neighbour, Eleni Manousaki, was outside her tumbledown cottage hanging out today's washing when they passed. Dressed all in black and bent almost double, she had numerous lines criss-crossing her face and wrinkles so deep, they seemed to mimic the Cretan landscape with its cavernous valleys and gorges.

Despite her age and evident infirmities, she heard the visitors approaching and turned to give them a friendly smile, revealing rows of stumpy black teeth.

'*Kalimera!*' Hannah said. 'Good morning!' It was one of the few words she and Edie had learned before arriving in Crete.

The old woman's black eyes, almost buried beneath folds of tanned, crepey skin, twinkled with pleasure.

'*Kalimera*,' she replied, bobbing her head in acknowledgement.

They were about to move on when she held up an arthritic hand, gesturing for them to wait. Edie and Hannah glanced at each other when she disappeared into her cottage, only to bustle out a few moments later with a basket of ripe, golden apricots.

Proffering the goods, she muttered a few words in Greek and nodded her head vigorously. Edie put a hand in the basket and looked tentatively at the old woman, unsure if this was what she was meant to do.

Eleni nodded several times again – '*Nai, nai!*' – and pushed the basket closer.

Feeling more confident, Edie chose a plump apricot with soft, slightly furry skin, and said thank you. Then the old woman proceeded to shove the basket towards the others, who did the same.

'Thank you,' they all repeated once more, this time in Greek, taking Hannah's lead: '*Efcharistó*.'

The old woman laughed and grinned, as if she'd never heard a foreigner try to speak her language before. She was so endearing and friendly, like everyone's favourite grannie, Edie wanted to give her a hug, but decided against it on the grounds it might not be the 'done thing'.

Instead, she bobbed her head and beamed and sniffed the apricot while making appreciative noises. 'Mm... yum!'

This seemed to tickle Eleni enormously, who giggled like a

teenager. They could still hear her laughing when they turned their backs and walked some little way along the track, munching on the fruit, which was sweet and delicious.

'Well, we've certainly made a hit with one of the locals,' Hannah commented, throwing her apricot stone into the bushes and wiping her mouth with the back of a hand.

Edie licked her sticky fingers, one by one.

'She was so lovely, I wanted to take her home with me,' she said when she'd finished.

Hannah laughed. 'I think her black teeth might upset you after a while. You'd have to get her some sparkling falsies.'

Before long, they came to a set of rough wooden beehive boxes, stacked one on top of another on a stony plateau.

Painted in vivid, primary colours with metal catches on the front, they looked very jolly, like jack-in-the-boxes.

Edie paused briefly to take a photo. 'I expect that's where our breakfast honey came from. They say Cretan honey's the best in the world.'

'I'm afraid I went a bit mad with it this morning and slathered it on,' said Hannah. 'Not good for the waistline.'

Jessica, who'd been very quiet up to now, paused and took a swig of water from the bottle in her small, neat backpack.

'Want some?' she asked Edie and Hannah, replacing the bottle before they had a chance to reply.

'Er, no thanks.' Edie watched Jessica buckle up her bag and swing it over her shoulders. She looked quite the professional hiker, all set for a demanding twenty-mile trek. The only item she lacked was walking poles.

'Come on,' she said, marching ahead. Hannah broke into a trot to catch up but Edie stayed behind, content to lose herself in her own thoughts.

As she walked, she found herself thinking about her children, whom she loved more than life itself, and felt truly grateful they were doing well. Also Ralph, who was being kinder and more gentle than usual. She realised she felt just a little bit lighter.

There was no way she'd let Mac and Hannah's rows or Jessica and Mac's animosity towards each other spoil things. This holiday was precious and she was determined to make the most of it.

Hannah and Jessica were deep in conversation when they approached the steep steps that led down to the village. Edie heard Hannah say, 'Wow!' and 'Amazing!' a few times and decided to hang back, keen not to get sucked in.

At one point they both stopped while Hannah took a look at Jessica's fitness watch.

'I've no idea how many steps I do, but nowhere near as many as you,' she said. 'You must be so fit. Well, of course you are, that's why you're so slim. I wish I had a figure like yours.'

Jessica seemed to have an extra bounce in her stride as she carried on down the stone stairs. No wonder. All the compliments must be terrific for her ego, Edie thought, before chiding herself for being mean-spirited.

Once they reached the bottom, Jessica announced she wanted to start at the far end of the high street and work her way back, browsing in the shops on the way.

Edie, who had her eye on a store to her right selling local herbs and honey, said she'd rather go in the opposite direction and they agreed to meet in a café somewhere near the middle in about half an hour.

She was rather hoping Hannah would stay with her, but Hannah made up some excuse about not wanting to 'go against the flow of people' and stuck with Jessica instead.

As she watched them head off, Edie felt slightly miffed and had to tell herself once again not to be petty. They weren't schoolgirls, for heaven's sake. Back then, friendships could be so intense, picking someone other than your bestie for almost anything would be considered a shocking betrayal. Thankfully, adult friendships tended to be more sensible.

Even so, after that she found she was less interested in browsing and wasn't inclined to buy anything, not even more honey.

There were so many different types, some with nuts, some a dark, amber colour, others yellow, whitish or even almost black. Overwhelmed by choice, she smiled apologetically at the young man behind the counter before moving off.

He looked a bit dejected and she hoped he'd get more customers soon. He'd have to sell an awful lot of honey and herbs to make a decent living, she reflected, deciding to make a point of coming back when she was in the right mood.

As she made her way up the street, just before reaching April's mini-market she spotted a woman in tight jeans, high heels and a leopard-print top admiring herself in a mirror, which was propped up against a wall outside one of the clothes shops. She looked so different from everyone else round here, you couldn't miss her.

Tall, slim and striking, with bright red hair tied up in a high, perky ponytail, she was shimmying from side to side, trying to see herself from different angles.

As Edie drew closer, she couldn't help noticing the woman's permanently surprised expression. Her lips were also curiously full, her cheekbones unusually high, her eyes remarkably wide and her lashes extraordinarily long, black and thick.

Not wanting to appear rude by staring, Edie would have walked past without stopping, but the woman spun round and tapped her on the shoulder.

'Are you English?' she asked uncertainly, in an unmistakable

Glasgow accent, and Edie nodded. 'I hope you don't mind. Do you think this suits me?'

She pulled on the hem of the leopard-print top, which was sleeveless and hugged her body like a second skin.

Edie frowned, thinking she might be taking the mick. But the woman seemed so shy and hesitant, crossing her ankles and looking down, she must be serious.

Unsure how to reply, Edie glanced round, hoping to pull some other unsuspecting person into the discussion, but there was no one close by.

She wouldn't have chosen the top for herself, because it was too tight and revealing and not her style at all, but didn't want to lower the woman's confidence.

'You look great,' she said at last. 'You can certainly carry it off. You've got a fantastic figure.'

Although the woman was unable to smile properly because her lips were so big, Edie could tell she was delighted by the sparkle in her eyes.

'Do you think so? Really?' she said breathlessly. 'Thank you. I can never decide on my own. I need someone else's opinion.'

The shop's grey-haired owner, in a colourful dress and chunky silver jewellery, seemed to appear from nowhere and hovered beside them, waiting to hear the verdict.

'I'll have it,' the red-haired woman said suddenly, pulling a silver purse from her bag and handing over some cash.

The shop owner nodded and unzipped the small leather bumbag round her waist before shoving in the money.

'I'm Anthea, by the way,' the red-haired woman told Edie, while she stripped off her new top and handed it over to be wrapped. She was wearing an even smaller, tighter, scarlet-coloured vest underneath.

Edie, amused, introduced herself, too. 'Are you here on holiday as well?'

Anthea shook her head. 'Oh no. I came here twenty years ago to be with my former partner, Alexandros, or Alex. Big mistake.' As she couldn't frown, she rolled her eyes instead. 'He was a waiter. He worked at one of the restaurants up the road.

'He doesn't live here now. We weren't together long, but we had a little girl, Alexa. She's eighteen now. I can hardly believe it. The time's gone so fast.

'I didn't want to move her too far from her grandparents and cousins. She adores them, and we don't have much family back in Glasgow. So I decided to stay here. I'm a freelance hairdresser. I travel to people's houses all round the area. I've got one of the newish apartments on the outskirts of the village. It's only rented,' she added, lowering her gaze again, 'but we like it.'

'Gosh! You don't look old enough to have an eighteen-year-old daughter,' Edie replied truthfully. 'You must have been a very young mum.'

Anthea tapped the side of her pert little nose and her plump lips curled slightly at the edges in a sort of conspiratorial smile.

'Och, I've had loads of work. It's amazing what you can do with a bit of Botox and fillers.'

Edie laughed. 'I'd better have the name of the person who does it for you. They're obviously very good. But I've got so many wrinkles, it's probably too late for me now.'

Anthea's eyebrows, which were already halfway up her forehead, rose a fraction higher. 'Never! You can have it at any age. I'm fifty-four, you know.'

Edie couldn't hide her surprise.

'Blimey! I thought you were about thirty!'

'I wish.'

Anthea stared at her fingernails, which were long and red,

like her hair. 'You should have seen me when I was Alexa's age. I could turn a few heads then.'

'I bet you still can.'

When Anthea shrugged, it dawned on Edie her fondness for cosmetic procedures probably had more to do with insecurity than vanity. It must have been hard raising a child single-handed in a foreign country, but she seemed to be making a success of things. Edie was impressed.

'Which way are you going?' she said at last, thinking it was time she made a move. 'I want to check out the other shops before meeting up with my friends.'

'I'll walk with you some of the way,' Anthea replied. 'I've got an hour before my next appointment. It's been ages since I had a chance to browse.'

Meaty and his little brother, Nikos, were hanging round the door of the supermarket when the women strolled by. Nikos, in a droopy nappy and pale blue T-shirt, was playing with a grubby-looking plastic yellow car, sticking it in his mouth and waving it about as if it were an aeroplane. Meaty, meanwhile, looked a bit bored.

Peering behind him, Edie spotted April in her floral apron behind the counter and waved. April grinned and waved back.

'Hello,' Anthea said to Meaty, squatting down on her high heels to his level. They obviously knew each other, but instead of smiling, he hung his head and his mouth drooped at the corners.

'What are you up to, love?' Anthea asked gently, clearly sensing something was wrong.

'I've got to mind Nikos all morning,' came the gloomy reply. 'It's my punishment.'

'Punishment for what?'

'I gave him some of Mum's English mustard. It was on the table and he was screaming and crying because he wanted it. I kept saying no but he wouldn't listen, so in the end I stuck a spoon in and gave it to him.'

'Och, no!' Anthea sounded appalled, and Edie had to suppress a giggle. 'The poor wee lamb. What happened?'

'He ate it, *obviously*.' Meaty clearly thought Anthea was a bit slow off the mark. 'Then he went bright red and screamed the house down.'

Anthea gasped. 'Jings!'

'Mum gave him some water and he was all right after that,' Meaty went on. 'But she says she can't trust me so I've got to stay where she can see me. I was supposed to go fishing with my friend.'

Tutting, Anthea rose and pulled up the front of her low-cut scarlet vest.

'Well, at least Nikos is OK and there's no harm done.' She ruffled Meaty's mop of dark hair. 'Hopefully your mam will let you go fishing later on.'

'She won't,' he said gravely.

Nikos thrust the plastic car at Edie, which was covered in dirt and dribble. She hopped back out of harm's way just in the nick of time.

'No, thank you, sweetie.'

A quick glance down established her shorts and pink shirt were still spotless. Relieved, she focused again on Anthea and Meaty.

'Your mum absolutely adores you,' Anthea was saying with conviction. 'Just tell her you're really, really sorry and you'll never do it again. And keep your word,' she added sternly, giving a cheery thumbs up to April, who was watching the proceedings out of one eye while serving a customer with the other. 'Mustard is for grown-ups, not wee bairns.'

Though very small, it turned out Porto Liakáda was a lively

place, humming with sights, sounds, smells, colours and activity. Dark-haired waiters and waitresses in smart shirts and trousers or skirts stood outside their restaurants, smiling as they passed and pointing to the displays of fresh fish on offer.

'We cook for you, beautiful ladies?' one waiter said, gesturing towards an enormous, goggle-eyed fish nestling in a bed of ice on a large metal tray. In his thirties, probably, the waiter had slicked-back hair, a big bushy moustache and a gold chain round his neck.

'We put on barbecue for you, with lemon, garlic, local herbs. Magnificent!' He opened his arms wide and grinned.

'It's a bit early in the morning for me,' Edie replied, patting her stomach to show she was still full from breakfast.

'No, no!' the waiter cried. 'You come back at lunchtime or tonight. We make proper Crete feast for you! You will love it!'

Edie laughed. 'I'm sure we will. Thank you. I need to speak to my friends first, though. I'll let you know. Maybe tomorrow or the next day.'

The waiter pulled a mock-sad face then his grin reappeared, even wider than before.

'Of course. You come back when you are ready. Rest assured, we will look after you.'

'Tsk. That's Vasileios. He's such a flirt,' Anthea muttered, rolling her eyes again. 'He tries it on with all the girls. He even had a pop at me, can you believe? I'm old enough to be his mother!'

'Do you know everyone in the village?' Edie asked, thinking she was beginning to like her new friend a lot.

'Pretty much. It's not difficult. When I lived in London for a while, I hardly knew anyone. But here, everyone talks to you and before you know it, you're telling them your life story.'

After that, Edie tried her best not to catch any other waiters' eyes, fearing she'd never get further than a few paces. But she didn't feel harassed; it was just that everyone was so friendly and full of banter.

There were quite a few stalls selling tempting summery dresses, brightly coloured cover-ups for the beach, towels, hats, sunglasses and jewellery.

The styles were right up Maisie's street – casual and a bit boho. Edie wouldn't have a problem finding a gift to take home for her daughter. She might well be tempted to buy something for herself, too, on another day.

Her attention switched to an interesting-looking leather shop on the right, with a pair of Greek-style gladiator sandals in the window. There were also bags, belts, purses, glasses cases and wallets.

When she suggested going in, however, Anthea excused herself.

'I don't need any more shoes or bags. I've got too many as it is. You take a look, though. There are some nice things. I'm sure I'll see you later, or another day. It's been lovely chatting.'

The door of the leather shop was open and when Edie poked her nose in, she was assailed by a heady scent of oil, wax, chemicals and perfume. The interior was very dark, and a quick scan revealed she was the only customer. She was in two minds about whether to enter, but then a voice called, 'Please! Come!'

Tentatively, she took a few steps inside and as her eyes adjusted to the gloom, she became aware of a very old man sitting behind a wooden counter, surrounded by untidy piles of shoe boxes in different shapes and sizes.

He had wisps of white hair, which had been neatly trimmed, a snow-white moustache, dark, deep-set eyes and tanned, wrinkled skin. He was wearing a pale blue shirt, rolled up at the sleeves, with a rather dashing red and white scarf round his neck, knotted in front like a cravat.

Although he was seated, Edie could tell he was very thin, with stick-like arms, a scrawny neck and paper-thin skin. His smile, though, was wide, generous and charming.

'Good morning, madam,' he said in a heavy accent. 'You are English, I presume?'

Edie laughed. 'Yes. Is it that obvious?'

The old man continued to smile. 'Forgive me, but I can always tell an English lady from, say, an American or European.'

'Really? How?'

'Ah,' said the man, with a twinkle in his eye. 'English ladies are more... how shall I say? *Refined*. That's the word. You are not loud and aggressive like Americans and you have better manners than Europeans. Where in England are you from?'

The old devil! He seemed harmless, but Edie could imagine him being a right one in his younger days.

When she told him where she lived, he said he'd visited London once but never Surrey. His daughter would undoubtedly know it, though.

'She's a successful artist, a painter,' he said proudly. 'Marina, she is called, Marina Makris. That's my name, Makris. She's not married,' he added, lowering his eyes. 'Though she has had many offers.'

There was a pause, then his face lit up again. 'She has been all over the world. She has her studio right here, in the village. Just a few doors down.' He pointed to the right. 'You must go and look. She's very good. She has admirers from America, Japan, Athens, everywhere!'

Edie said she'd definitely check out the studio, then asked if she could browse round the shop.

'Of course!' Mr Makris put his hands on the counter top and

started to push himself up. It obviously required a good deal of effort and Edie would have liked to help, but feared offending him.

Her heart leaped into her mouth when he gave one final push, lost his balance and flopped back into his seat with a groan.

'Are you all right?' she asked anxiously, and he waved a hand in the air.

'Old age,' he muttered, shaking his head disconsolately. 'It's so tiresome. No one wants to be weak but unfortunately it cannot be avoided, if you live as long as me.'

Time was getting on for Edie, too, and she didn't want to keep the others waiting. She took a quick look at the leather goods, which Mr Makris said he mostly used to make himself, but now imported from elsewhere.

'I'll definitely come back,' she promised as she said goodbye. He looked quite sorry to see her go.

'You are a very gracious lady,' he said, which made her secretly smile, wondering if he'd perhaps mistaken her for a minor noble in *Downton Abbey*, the famous TV series.

Then, as a seeming afterthought, he added: 'Er, where are you staying, if you don't mind me asking? Here in the village?'

When Edie told him she was renting Villa Ariadne, his response startled her.

'That place again?' He wrinkled his nose, as if there was a bad smell. 'That woman, Katerina Papadakis, makes a fortune out of people like you. You should have chosen somewhere else. I would have given you suggestions. There are plenty of beautiful villas round here.'

Edie raised her eyebrows. 'The price wasn't too bad, to be honest. I was quite surprised actually; I thought it would be more. It's a gorgeous property with amazing views.'

But Mr Makris was having none of it. He bent down and

reached for something under the counter, before passing her a white card with his name, email address and phone number on.

'Here are my details. If you come to Porto Liakáda again, call me first. I have friends who can help. They will give you a much better price than Mrs Papadakis.'

Edie left the shop puzzling over why the old man had it in for Katerina. She seemed to be kind and honest and certainly not a money-grabber. Perhaps there was bad blood between them. There must be all sorts of age-old feuds going on in a tiny place like this. Edie would love to know the truth.

She was intending to take a quick look at the studio before searching for the others but on leaving Mr Makris' shop, whom should she see but Hannah and Jessica.

They were sitting round a table in a café opposite and appeared to have company.

'Edie!' Hannah called, spotting her friend. 'Come and join us!'

The table was in the shade under a blue and white canopy overlooking the harbour. Folk were getting on and off small boats moored to the jetty and in the distance, Edie spotted the bow of one of the big passenger ferries rounding the headland.

It was after 1 p.m. now and the sun was high in the sky. She could feel how much the temperature had gone up since they left Villa Ariadne and longed for a cold drink.

'Hi!' she said, glancing at her friends as well as the newcomers.

Hannah pushed out a chair and beckoned to her to sit down.

'This is Marina,' she explained, gesturing to a very slender, olive-skinned woman with a slim face, high cheekbones, a straight nose, deep-set, dark brown eyes and long black wavy hair that ran over her shoulders and down her back like a waterfall.

She was wearing a long, flowing, beachy yellow dress with spaghetti straps and chunky silver jewellery. She was probably in her mid or even late fifties, Edie decided, but still beautiful, in an unconventional way.

'Hello, pleased to meet you,' the stranger said with a serene smile, shaking Edie's hand. 'This is my half-brother, Jean-Luc.'

Edie turned to the man beside Marina and tried not to show her surprise. For a start, he was remarkably handsome, with one of those strong-jawed, straight-nosed, angular yet sensitive faces most women find irresistible.

He looked quite a lot younger than his sister and his name didn't sound a bit Greek. Moreover, Mr Makris definitely hadn't mentioned a son, though he'd waxed lyrical about his daughter. What was going on?

'Enchantée,' Jean-Luc said, with a lazy, drop-dead gorgeous smile. He rose, took her hand and brushed the back of it with his lips.

Edie's heart fluttered and she felt quite giddy and had to tell herself to grow up.

'What brings you here to Porto Liakáda?' Jean-Luc asked, sitting down again.

Edie was more interested in asking *him* some questions but decided to be patient. Settling down beside Hannah, she explained about the holiday and the fact she and her husband hadn't been back to Crete since their long-ago honeymoon.

'How romantic!' Jean-Luc said with a grin. 'Has the island changed much since you were last here?'

'It's too early to say. We only got here yesterday. But so far, it hardly seems any different at all. It's still just as charming and unspoiled.'

The waiter came over and Edie ordered a Coke and some water. The others hadn't yet finished their coffee.

'We met Jean-Luc in a shop back there and he told us about

Marina,' Hannah explained hurriedly. 'She's an artist.' Her eyes sparkled with excitement.

Edie nodded. 'I was just speaking to her father, Mr Makris, who owns the leather shop. I was on my way to the studio when I saw you.'

Marina gave a little laugh, like tinkling wind chimes.

'He tells everyone. I wish he wouldn't; it's so embarrassing.' She glanced at Jean-Luc affectionately. 'You're almost as bad, assailing these poor women in a shop and forcing them to look at my paintings.'

Jean-Luc opened his mouth to reply but Hannah butted in.

'Oh no! We're glad he told us. We mightn't have known about your studio otherwise. I adore art.' She was leaning forwards, addressing her words to Jean-Luc, not Marina. 'Do you paint, too?' she asked, tilting her head to one side and twizzling a strand of long blonde hair round her forefinger.

'Me? No.' He crossed an ankle over one knee.

He was in a black, round-necked T-shirt and baggy, brown carpenter shorts with lots of pockets. He had a frayed string bracelet with coloured beads round his wrist and there was a tattoo on his upper arm, which was tanned and quite muscular.

'I'm a poet,' he went on. 'I live in Paris most of the time – but I was raised in Lille. My mother is French and so am I. You've probably guessed from my accent.' He smiled.

'She and Konstantin – Mr Makris – weren't together. In fact I never saw him when I was growing up. It was only when I was eighteen I found out I had a half-sister.

'Marina got in touch, you see. I thought I was an only child and I was so happy to find a sibling. Now, I come here most summers to see Marina – and my father,' he added quickly. 'This time I have rented an apartment for two months. It's very quiet, so I can write.'

The longer he spoke, the bigger and wider Hannah's eyes grew. 'A poet?' she said, leaning forward even more. 'How fascinating!'

The waiter arrived with Edie's drinks and set them on the table. Meanwhile Jessica, who'd been silent till now, watching what was going on, piped up: 'Do you write in French?'

Jean-Luc nodded. His dark brown hair was cut in a low fade and there was a hint of stubble on his chin.

'You speak French, don't you, Hannah?'

Hannah gave a modest smile. 'Only a little. I learned at school but I'm very rusty.'

'Ah!' cried Jean-Luc, taking a sip of coffee, 'you can practise on me! *Ça va?*'

At this, Hannah sat bolt upright and drew back her shoulders. *'Oui! Ça va bien, merci!'*

She grinned and Jean-Luc leaned across the table and high-fived her.

'Excellent,' said Jessica, with a small, satisfied smile. 'After French p'raps you can get on to Greek.'

'My Greek is very bad, I'm afraid,' Jean-Luc replied.

'Never mind! French is probably enough for now.'

Edie sipped her Coke and frowned. She felt rather as if she were on the set of a film, watching the action but with no role in it. Something was going on between Hannah, Jessica and Jean-Luc, but she wasn't sure what. Marina seemed clueless, too.

'Does your mother still live in Crete?' Edie asked the artist, wanting to steer the conversation in another direction. Was she being too forward? After all, she and Marina had only just met.

'No. Unfortunately, she died about ten years ago. I still miss her.'

'I'm sorry.'

Marina shrugged. 'It happens. Dad is the exception rather than the rule. He's ninety-four, you know.'

'Goodness! I'd never have guessed. He's amazing! So with it and amusing.'

'And annoying,' Marina added with a laugh. 'At times, anyway. But yes, he is amazing. His mind is razor-sharp. It's just his body that lets him down.'

'He's lived a very full life,' said Jean-Luc in a meaningful tone.

Marina glanced at her brother before focusing again on Edie.

'He was a terrible philanderer in his younger days.'

Edie started. 'Really?' She was taken aback, not so much by the information itself but by the fact the artist had chosen to reveal it to her, a virtual stranger.

Jean-Luc snorted.

'Don't say you didn't notice his roving eye! He must have lost his touch! God knows how many children he's got. They're probably all over the world. He was particularly partial to the Swedish girls who came here on holiday, so I gather.'

'I don't think there are any other kids,' Marina replied dryly. 'Just us. He would have told me.'

Edie cleared her throat. 'Did your mother know – about all the affairs, I mean?'

At this, Marina's eyes clouded over. 'I'm afraid she probably did. But she chose to look the other way. It was self-protection, I expect, and also a desire to shield me. She was a very kind, loving person.'

Emboldened by her openness, Edie now asked about Katerina.

'Why does your father dislike her so?'

'Ah!' said Marina, fiddling with the silver bangle on her slender wrist. 'He could never get over the fact she turned him down. She was perhaps the only one who ever did.'

Good on her, Edie thought, though she didn't say so. Mrs Papadakis instantly shot up in her estimation.

'There are other things, too, but I won't bore you with them now.'

Edie nodded. 'Have you any idea how Katerina came to run Villa Ariadne? Who are the owners?'

Marina examined her nails, which were short, neat, square-shaped and painted orange.

'Ah, now that's another story, too. She has looked after it for many years. The owners are no longer here, but she runs it exactly as they always wanted. She only rents it to special people who will benefit from it – like you.'

At this, Marina fixed on Edie with her dark, deep-set eyes, lined with black kohl, and made her flinch.

Edie wanted to ask what she meant, and why she and Katerina behaved as if they knew something she didn't. But for some reason, the words wouldn't leave her mouth.

'You know she has special powers, my sister,' Jean-Luc blurted, arching one eyebrow. 'At least, she thinks she does.'

Marina playfully slapped her brother's thigh and the spell was broken.

'Some people are so mundane,' she said with a laugh. 'If they can't see it, they don't believe it. I feel sorry for the poor things. There's a whole world they know absolutely nothing about.'

8

Jean-Luc turned to Hannah and asked something in French. Edie was so distracted by Marina, she didn't catch what it was. Then she noticed Jessica picking up her backpack.

'Come here,' Jessica told Jean-Luc, rising from her seat. 'Come and sit next to Hannah. Then you can gabble away in French together as much as you like.'

Obediently, Jean-Luc got up and moved to the other side of the table, where he and Hannah sort of huddled together, their shoulders almost touching, and proceeded to strike up an intimate conversation just for two.

Meanwhile, Jessica took the chair beside Edie, crossing her long legs easily, one over the other.

'Did you buy anything?' she asked.

Edie shook her head. 'Not this time.' She was gazing at Hannah's flushed face and simpering smile and wondering why Jessica seemed so keen on pushing her and Jean-Luc together. Did she find it amusing? If so, Edie didn't get the joke.

Jean-Luc might mock his father's womanising ways, but by the looks of it, he was a chip off the old block. He was certainly doing his best to bewitch Hannah, who was embarrassing herself, she was so smitten. She was like putty in his hands.

'It's good to see Hannah smiling for once,' Jessica said in a low voice, as if she could read Edie's mind. 'She seemed so tense yesterday and this morning. Like a coiled spring.'

'Oh, she's always like that at the beginning of a holiday,' Edie replied airily. 'She works like a demon most of the time and it takes her a few days to unwind. She'll get there.'

This wasn't strictly true, but Jessica needed to be reminded of Edie's long-standing friendship with Hannah. She couldn't just waltz in and make out she knew more about Hannah's state of mind than Edie did.

She didn't seem to get the message, though.

'She needs to know not all men are like Mac. There are *some* nice ones.'

A bubble of hot rage swelled and popped in Edie's stomach. She wanted to tell Jessica to mind her own bloody business. She wished she'd never mentioned she was worried about Hannah and Mac's relationship.

She was on the point of saying something when she noticed Marina fidgeting, first with her hair, then the hem of her dress. Edie and Jessica had been completely ignoring her.

'I'm so sorry,' Edie said, turning to Marina. 'How rude of us!'

Marina shook her head and leaned forward to take a sip of water from the glass in front of her.

'No, no, it's not you. I feel a bit light-headed, that's all.'

She set the glass back down with a sigh.

'That's better. It's gone now. Perhaps I was dehydrated.'

'Here you are!'

Edie glanced round and was surprised to see Mac sauntering towards them. He waved at her and gave a cheery smile but her heart sank nevertheless.

He looked quite suave in a red-and-white-striped shirt, open at the neck and rolled up at the sleeves, smart navy shorts and boat shoes. On reaching the café, he stopped right in front of Edie and ran a hand through his thick brown hair.

'I've been trying to call Hannah but she never picks up,' he said, rolling his eyes.

He glanced round the table and it was only then he noticed Hannah next to Jean-Luc. They were bent over, their knees almost touching, and so deep in conversation, they hadn't even clocked his arrival.

'Hannah?' Mac said. 'Hello!'

Hannah looked up and started. 'What are you doing here?'

Quickly pulling back her legs, she straightened up, tucked her hair behind her ears and reached for her sunglasses, which were on the table. 'I thought you were relaxing by the pool.'

'I got bored, so I thought I'd come and find you, my darling wife,' Mac replied, somewhat sarcastically. 'Aren't you pleased to see me?'

Hannah gave a small, cool smile. 'Of course. Come and join us. Would you like a drink?'

He took a chair from the empty table next door and Edie shuffled round to make room. Jessica then made the introductions, telling Mac first about Marina, then her brother.

'Hannah's been practising her French with Jean-Luc,' she said. 'It seems to be improving by the minute.'

'She speaks very well,' Jean-Luc added gallantly. 'Her accent is excellent.'

Mac looked directly at the Frenchman, examining him, it seemed, rather as you would a laboratory specimen.

'And where in France do you come from?' he asked, unblinking.

'I live in Paris now but I grew up in Lille, in the north. Do you know it?'

Mac's eyes narrowed. 'I've been through it in the car. It's not the sort of place you stop to go sightseeing, though, is it?'

Hannah squeaked like a bat. 'That's rude!'

'I've been to the Christmas market,' Edie said quickly. 'I bought all my Christmas presents there. It was great – very festive.'

Mac shifted his gaze from Jean-Luc back to his wife.

'Have you had a good look round the village?'

Hannah nodded. 'There are lots of nice shops.'

'I need some shaving cream. I forgot to pack it. Coming with me?'

He extended his hand across the table. Hannah quickly stood up and took it briefly, before letting go.

'What a shame to break up the party!' Jessica piped up. 'Hannah, you and Jean-Luc should arrange another time for French conversation. You might be fluent by the time you get home.'

It was such a provocative comment under the circumstances, Edie gave a silent gasp. Mac's eyes narrowed even more and his mouth set in a grim, hard line.

'Mais oui!' Jean-Luc replied easily. He was either unaware of Mac's hostility or he was enjoying it. Edie couldn't decide which.

Rising, the Frenchman pulled a scrap of paper from his pocket and asked his sister for a pen. After writing down his name and number, he passed it to Hannah before kissing her on both cheeks.

'Call me if you would like some more practice. I'm mostly at home writing during the day. It would be nice to have a break.'

He glanced at Mac and gave a wide, disarming smile. 'That is, if your husband will allow it.'

Mac's frown grew deeper.

'Of course he will!' Jessica cried. 'Hannah's her own woman, aren't you? She doesn't take orders from men!'

It was with a great sense of relief that Edie watched Mac and Hannah move off. If they'd stayed any longer, Mac might have punched the Frenchman in the nose.

'Right, I'd better do some work,' Jean-Luc said, fishing some cash from his pocket and putting it on the table for his share of the bill.

'I'll see you later, big sister,' he added, bending down to give her a kiss. Then he turned to Jessica and Edie and gave a small bow. 'Lovely to meet you two ladies. I'm sure we will see each other again very soon.'

Edie had finished her Coke now and gestured to the waiter for the bill.

'I'm very fond of my brother,' Marina said in a low voice, when Jean-Luc was out of sight. 'He has a good heart, but I fear he can sometimes be a little impulsive.'

'He's extraordinarily handsome,' Edie replied. 'Like a film star.'

Marina gave her tinkling little laugh. 'I'm afraid he is like our father in certain respects. Women find him hard to resist.'

Without warning, her smile vanished and she looked at Jessica full-on. 'And what do you do for a living?'

Her question seemed out of place, coming so soon after what had gone before, and Edie shifted uneasily.

Jessica uncrossed her legs and recrossed them the other way.

'I'm a teacher. I teach general and classical History at a secondary school, the same one as Edie's.'

Marina cleared her throat. 'Ah, so you know all our old myths? About the gods looking down on us humans from Mount Olympus, toying with us for their sport?'

Jessica's eyes widened slightly, but she held Marina's gaze.

'Oh yes,' she replied, deadpan. 'I love the Greek gods. Powerful yet flawed. Full of anger, jealousy and lust and *so* mischievous. They were much more interesting than today's gods, don't you agree?'

* * *

After leaving the café, Edie looked about for Anthea but didn't see her. She was probably at her next appointment by now. Before heading home, Edie decided to pop in to Marina's studio to take a quick look at her paintings. Jessica, who'd already seen them, waited by the harbour wall.

Edie liked Marina's work, which was strong, impressionistic and vibrant, focusing mainly on outdoor subjects – the sky, mountains, water, rocks, animal bones and trees.

'They're stunning,' Edie said, flinching slightly when she noticed the price tag on one of the smaller canvases. 'Sadly, I can't afford to buy one. Maybe one day. You never know.'

Marina crossed her slim arms and smiled graciously.

'There are not many people who can afford to go round buying original artwork. Unfortunately, those who can aren't always the people you'd most want to have your work hanging on their wall.' She shrugged. 'But beggars can't be choosers. And I'd rather have my paintings on display than stuck in a storeroom.'

'Of course. May I take some photos?'

Edie proceeded to take a few shots before saying goodbye and going to rejoin Jessica. There was no sign of Hannah and Mac, so they agreed to send a text and walk on home ahead of them, grabbing some supplies from April's on the way.

Meaty had gone now and April was jiggling a grizzling Nikos on one hip. She was somewhat distracted, so the women quickly chose a ready-cooked chicken, bread, salad ingredients, ripe peaches and some pastries before trudging back up the mountain with their bags.

They barely spoke en route. Edie was still cross with Jessica and afraid she'd say something rude, while Jessica seemed lost in thought.

Ralph was on a lounger by the pool when Edie went to find him. He was in the shade under a tree with a book in one hand and a glass of water by his side. He looked so comfortable and settled, she wondered if he'd moved at all since she'd been away.

'Hey!' he said, looking up from his book when he spotted her walking towards him. 'How did it go?'

While Jessica was still in the kitchen, unloading the bags, Edie quickly filled him in on what had happened.

'A busy morning, then,' he said, glancing at the page of his still-open book. It was obvious he was itching to get back to it and couldn't really be bothered with Anthea or Jean-Luc and Hannah.

In a way, Edie didn't blame him. She half wished she hadn't gone into Porto Liakáda with the others, then she'd be none the wiser about Hannah's little flirtation and the awkward moment when Mac arrived. She'd enjoyed meeting Anthea, though.

She spent most of the afternoon by Ralph's side, reading, swimming and dozing. It was just what she needed. Jessica and Hannah joined them for a bit, but they didn't see anything of Mac.

At around 6 p.m. Edie went upstairs for a shower, leaving Ralph to finish his novel. He was so engrossed, he couldn't bring himself to put it down till he'd found out what happened in the end.

On the top stair, Edie stopped dead and her heart pitter-pattered. She could hear shouting coming from Mac and Hannah's room. The door was closed but she clearly heard Mac say, 'You're a fucking cow, you hear me?'

Hannah's voice was quieter so Edie couldn't catch what she said, then Mac came back: 'You're vile, you know that?'

There was a noise, like a sob, and Hannah whisper-shouted something in reply.

Tiptoeing towards the door, Edie waited for a moment, wondering what to do. Then someone tapped her on the arm, making her start. She swung round to find Jessica right behind her. She'd obviously been listening, too.

Just then, there was another shout from Mac and the sound of something being thrown and landing with a crash.

Edie gasped. 'Oh God! What should we do? D'you think Hannah's all right?'

Jessica's features seemed to fix into a tight mask of fury. She stepped forward and put her hand on the doorknob, ready to turn it, but before she could do so, the door flew open and Mac marched out.

'She's a fucking lunatic!' he said, his face red and spit spurting from his mouth.

Edie and Jessica had no time to respond as he raced downstairs, two steps at a time. They heard a door slam and heavy footsteps on the gravel outside, disappearing into the distance.

Now he was gone, they walked tentatively into Hannah's room. She was sitting on the bed, her face in her hands and her body heaving with sobs.

Before Edie had even had time to think, Jessica hurried over and sat down beside their friend, putting an arm round her shoulders.

'What did he do? Are you all right?' she asked urgently. 'Did he hurt you?'

Hannah sniffed and rubbed her eyes. 'No, he didn't hit me or anything. He just gets so jealous. He accused me of deliberately flirting with Jean-Luc. But I wasn't.'

All of a sudden, she jerked up her head and jutted her chin. 'We were just chatting,' she insisted, staring hard at Edie, as if challenging her to disagree. Her jaw and neck were visibly tight and snot dribbled from her nose. 'I told him that. He was so angry.' Her red, puffy face crumpled again. 'He said some horrible things.'

Jessica made a tutting sound. 'It's not right, Hannah. You shouldn't put up with it. He's a bully. I heard what he said. It's emotional and verbal abuse.'

Hannah sobbed again. 'I know. He's not normally that bad, though. It's only when he sees me talking to another man, or even a woman sometimes. I don't know why he's so jealous.'

Edie was still standing by the bed, not wishing to crowd out Hannah and feeling a bit useless.

It was distressing to see her friend so upset but at the same time, a tiny worm in her ear was whispering to her that Hannah wasn't being entirely honest. She *had* been flirting. It wasn't exactly a crime, and she could at least own up to it.

Ralph would probably have been put out if he'd seen Edie behaving in that way. The difference was, he wouldn't have shouted and sworn at her.

There was silence for a moment and Jessica breathed in and out deeply.

'I'm worried about you, Hannah,' she said at last. 'Things might escalate.'

Edie was about to join them on the bed when she noticed a wood-framed dressing table mirror lying in pieces in the corner of the room.

'What happened?' She went over to take a better look; the mirror was pretty much smashed.

'Did he throw it at you?' Jessica asked shrilly.

Edie glanced at Hannah, who lowered her eyes.

'Yes.'

'Did it hit you?'

'No, it missed.' Hannah bit her lip.

'That's still assault, you know. He could be arrested for it, even if you weren't physically hurt. Imagine if he hadn't missed. We might be taking you to hospital now.'

Hannah shuddered. 'Thank God it didn't come to that.'

'No, but it could have.'

Jessica's words seemed to impregnate the air surrounding them, compressing their lungs and making it difficult to breathe.

'I think you should take my room tonight,' she insisted. 'While you decide what you want to do. I'll sleep on the sofa downstairs.'

'Thank you.'

'And remember to lock the door.'

Hannah glanced fearfully at Jessica, then Edie. 'I will.'

***

They were a sombre group at supper that evening. Ralph had said he'd have a chat with Mac and had tried calling, but Mac hadn't picked up.

Meanwhile, Jessica had stayed close to Hannah, checking on her constantly and asking if she needed anything.

Hannah seemed to need and want the attention, so Edie had taken a back seat and left them to it.

Instead, she'd prepared the meal and laid the table on the patio. Just before they ate, she'd asked Hannah if she'd like to talk in private, but Hannah had said no.

'It'll blow over, honestly. I'm sorry you and Jessica got caught up in it.'

Edie frowned. 'This is serious, Hannah. You do know that, don't you? Mac can't go on behaving like this.'

'I'll talk to him – I really will. He'll have calmed down by the time he gets back.'

They'd just finished their main course and started on the sweet pastries Jessica and Edie had bought when Mac reappeared. He stood uncomfortably in the kitchen doorway, illuminated by the light behind, with his arms crossed and his head lowered.

'Hello,' he said hoarsely.

He was met with absolute silence; no one knew what to say.

'I'm sorry about the argument,' he went on, hesitantly. 'Not what you want to hear on holiday.' He gave a humourless laugh. 'I lost my temper. I was a prat.'

Edie nervously cleared her throat.

'Look, mate—' Ralph started to say, rising, but Jessica interrupted.

'DON'T try and make light of it.' Her teeth were half clenched. 'You tried to assault Hannah with that mirror. She could have been seriously injured.'

Mac's eyes opened wide. 'I didn't—'

In a flash, Hannah abruptly stood up and pushed back her chair. 'Mac and I will sort this, won't we, Mac? The rest of you shouldn't have to get involved.'

Mac nodded.

Jessica started to protest but Hannah, who was next to her, put a hand on her arm.

'Don't,' she said. 'It's all right—'

'No, it bloody well isn't! He's a bully and a bastard. I can't stand by and watch you get hurt.'

Ignoring her, Hannah started to move away but Jessica followed.

'Leave them!' Ralph said suddenly, stopping Jessica in her tracks.

She turned to him with a deep frown and eyes that looked hot enough to scorch his pupils, but he didn't flinch.

'Let them try and sort this out themselves,' he went on. 'They don't need our interference.'

He looked at Mac and Hannah, who was now hovering nervously by her husband's side.

'Mac, mate,' he said, carrying on where he'd left off a few minutes earlier. 'Listen, stop the shouting and stuff, OK? Talk to each other sensibly. If you want a mediator or a third opinion, I'm here.'

Mac nodded. 'Thanks.'

As soon as he and Hannah turned their backs and disappeared into the villa, Jessica glared at Ralph, looking for all the world as if she wanted to kill him.

'I can't believe you just did that. Why would you? You sent her back into the lion's den.'

Ralph squared his shoulders and held Jessica's gaze, with his hands on his hips and both feet firmly planted on the ground.

Edie stared at him in wonder; she couldn't remember when she last saw him so angry yet, at the same time, completely in control.

'With respect,' he said quietly, carefully enunciating every word, 'to my knowledge, you're not a marriage counsellor. And you hardly know either of them. Do us all a favour, will you? Stop meddling and give them some space.'

9

'I'm sorry, I know she's your friend, but I can't stand her,' Ralph said, when he and Edie were finally alone.

They were lying naked on the bed in the moonlight, her head on his bare chest and his arm round her shoulders. His breathing had slowed and he was clearly drowsy, but she was too wound up to sleep.

'I wish to God I'd never asked her,' she said savagely. 'She's making things ten times worse.'

Ralph breathed in and out deeply.

'I might ask Mac to come on a walk with me tomorrow,' he said at last. 'Do you mind? We can't pretend this isn't happening. I need to ask him what's up.'

Edie raised her head and kissed her husband lightly on the neck. 'I think that's a really good idea. I'll try and get Hannah on her own for a bit, too.'

They lay for a while in silence. Edie was pretending to listen to the cicadas chirruping in the garden beyond their open window. Really, though, her ears were pricked for any sounds coming from Mac and Hannah's bedroom.

She found herself replaying scenes from the past when they'd all been together, trying to remember moments when Mac's anger had flared.

He had a temper, for sure, but she'd never imagined in a million years he could be violent. Had she missed something? If so, she could kick herself.

Her mind drifted back to the Sunday lunch when she'd first introduced Jessica to him and Hannah. Edie had thought the occasion a tremendous success, but now, in retrospect, she began to wonder.

Hannah had made quite an entrance in a new, chocolate-brown, fake fur coat.

'Wow! You look fabulous!' she'd told Edie, who'd been standing at the open front door.

'Do I?' she'd said, eyeing up Hannah's fur, which struck her as far more noteworthy. 'I'm only in jeans, and I've had this jumper for years!'

'You've got to learn to take a compliment, Edie,' Hannah had retorted. 'You *do* look great. Your skin's glowing and I don't know what you've done to your hair. It's all shiny and lustrous.'

She'd turned to Mac, right behind her, who'd agreed.

'You could be in a haircare ad.'

Edie had smiled at the unexpected gallantry and patted her head. 'Thanks. I used a new conditioner this morning. It seems to have tamed the frizz – at least for now.'

Once the visitors had come inside, Edie had taken their coats and she remembered hanging Mac's on the vintage oak rack on the wall. Hannah's was heavy so it had gone over the wooden newel post as a precaution; it might have pulled the rack down.

Ralph had been waiting for them in the sitting room, which looked out over the small front garden. He'd lit the log burner and the room had felt warm and cosy with its creamy walls and white woodwork, rusty velvet L-shaped sofa and jute carpet.

One side of the room was taken up with a floor-to-ceiling bookcase displaying books and interesting objects collected by Edie down the years. She loved vintage stores and markets and had whiled away many a happy hour at weekends and on holidays, searching for the perfect vase or picture frame. It was a bit of an obsession.

Elsewhere there was an antique mahogany desk, which had belonged to Ralph's grandmother, a richly patterned ottoman coffee table, which she'd had re-covered, and a variety of decorative lamps, including one with an unusual, elephant-shaped base.

A slow-burning candle on the windowsill was giving off a delicious scent of orange and ginger.

Edie had pale, sensitive skin and the log fire had made her face and neck flush rosy red. But the temperature hadn't seemed to affect Hannah, who was all glammed up in tight black leather trousers, big silver earrings and a long, loose, silky turquoise top that cleverly disguised the bits she didn't like and highlighted the ones she did – namely her legs, which were long and slim, and her big boobs. Meanwhile, her fair, shoulder-length hair was straight, loose and shiny.

Hannah had always liked dressing up for parties and was into designer clothes – unlike Edie, who found many of her favourite outfits in charity shops.

She enjoyed mixing and matching an old-fashioned tartan woollen coat, say, with a funny cashmere twinset from the fifties, plus jeans and new-season boots.

Or combining one of her newish dresses with an oversized granddad waistcoat. The pinkish jumper she'd had on that day was a genuine lambswool Fair Isle, which she'd picked up at a jumble sale several years ago. It had moth holes, which she'd repaired, and it looked almost like new.

Beside sparkling Hannah, Mac had looked small and a bit weaselly. His body, though thin, was quite muscular because of the physical nature of his job, but you couldn't tell underneath his pale blue shirt and nondescript navy jumper.

Because of the time of year, he'd been pale, almost grey-faced, but he still had a surprising amount of thick, wavy, brownish-grey hair, long on top and shorter at the sides.

His face lit up when he laughed – really laughed – revealing traces of the funny, talented, quirky young man he used to be. But as little seemed to amuse him much these days, this side of his personality rarely shined through.

While Ralph had fetched some drinks, Edie had warned the others about Jessica.

'She might be a bit quiet. She absolutely doted on Ernest.'

'We'll be gentle with her,' Hannah had promised. 'No dog jokes.'

'Do you know any?' Mac had asked in a sarky voice. 'I wouldn't have said jokes were your thing.'

Hannah's lips had puckered, as if she'd eaten a lemon. 'I do, actually.'

Mac had raised his eyebrows. '*Really?*'

Edie's pulse had quickened and she'd fidgeted nervously with the neck of her jumper. They were at it already! She'd have liked to change the subject, but felt duty-bound to stick up for the sisterhood.

'I've heard some of Hannah's jokes,' she'd said, a little too brightly. 'I can still remember the fish one in that famous seafood place we went to with the kids in Cornwall. The joke popped out of her mouth just as the food appeared. It was hilarious!'

'You mean: "What do you call a fish that won't shut up? A big-mouthed bass." That one?' Mac had asked.

Edie had nodded.

'That was *years* ago. The kids were only little. She hasn't told one since.' He'd grinned, trying to make out it was just a harmless tease, but no one had laughed. Hannah had made no comment but her eyes had narrowed and she'd stared down at her feet, clearly stung.

She and Mac had only been there five minutes and he'd already managed to create an atmosphere. Edie wondered why he did it.

At that moment, she'd felt like slapping him and now rather wished she'd followed it through. She could still recall feeling anxious about whether she'd be able to cope with him on holiday. Perhaps she should have given it a bit more thought before booking.

With luck, though, she'd mused, he'd relax with Ralph. The two still got on and could talk for hours about football, rugby and politics. They were both left-leaning and had been active members of the university students' union. Down the years, they'd gone on numerous protest marches together, from climate change to spending cuts to further education.

They were both die-hard atheists, too, but Edie had forbidden Ralph from raising the subject at social gatherings, after a dinner party some years ago that hadn't ended well.

Ralph had reappeared with a tray of drinks just as the doorbell rang. Dilly, who'd been snoozing in front of the fire, sprang up and yapped hysterically, making everyone's nerves jangle, and Edie had been worried the barking would upset Jessica.

She'd hurried into the hall, unable to stop the dog following close at her heels, and asked Ralph to scoop Dilly up and shut her in the kitchen.

Once the coast was clear, she'd opened the front door with a wide smile and remembered being taken aback by her visitor's appearance.

Always neat and tidy at school, Jessica was looking uncharacteristically windswept, with long, loose, messed-up hair and pink, weather-beaten cheeks.

She was wearing a khaki waterproof jacket and tan boots and thrust a bunch of mostly purple flowers into Edie's arms.

'It only took twenty minutes to get here on the bike,' she'd announced. 'It was easy.'

'Oh! You cycled?'

It was only then Edie had noticed the helmet in her friend's spare hand. 'Where did you leave your bike?'

She'd peered left and right over Jessica's shoulder. 'Do you want to bring it in?'

Jessica shook her head, pointing to the side of the house where a passage led through another door into the back garden. 'I've locked it up; it'll be fine there.'

'OK. If you're sure.' Edie had leaned forward and embraced her friend, whose cheek was slightly damp. 'Come on in! The others are here. They're looking forward to meeting you.'

Far from seeming nervous or shy, Jessica had stridden confidently inside, pulling off her jacket as she went and tossing it over the newel post, on top of Hannah's fur coat. Underneath, she had on a baggy grey sweatshirt and jeans. She'd bent down, unlaced her boots and taken them off.

'They're dreadfully muddy. I probably should have left them on the doorstep.'

Edie had glanced down the hallway, now strewn with clumps of dirt and a few leaves, and shrugged.

'No worries. How are you feeling?'

To her surprise and pleasure, her friend had seemed positively cheery, despite the recent death of her beloved pet. Unless of course, it was all show.

Jessica had straightened up. Even in just her thick red woollen socks, she was much taller than Edie.

'Good, thanks.' She'd smoothed her tousled hair, coiling it round her fingers before setting it free to tumble over her shoulders once more. 'I was gutted when I got the news. You saw what a state I was in?'

Edie had nodded.

'But I've made my peace with it now. I told you I bounce back quickly.'

She'd sounded so upbeat Edie was almost convinced, but had looked her friend in the eye to be sure. Happily, Jessica's small, clever, bright blue eyes had smiled back.

'I think you're amazing,' Edie had said, meaning it. 'You're so brave. Much braver than I would be. You must be kind to yourself, though. You've had a big shock. It might come back and hit you again when you're least expecting it.'

Jessica had touched Edie's arm and given a sympathetic sort of smile, rather as if she were doing the comforting, instead of the other way round.

'Now, I want to meet your friends,' she'd said. 'And Dilly, of course.'

Right on cue, they'd heard a volley of barks and the sound of Dilly's claws scratching ferociously at the door.

Edie had made to let her out, but Jessica had stopped her.

'I'll do it. She's in here, right?'

Without waiting for a reply, she'd marched towards the kitchen and Dilly had soon hurtled out, leaping up Jessica's legs, yipping wildly.

'She's gorgeous.'

Jessica had bent down to pick up the little dog and stroke her back and ears before picking her up and carrying her purposefully into the sitting room, while Edie followed behind.

'Hello! I'm Jessica!'

The others had paused their conversations to look at the newcomer.

'Right, that's sorted!' Jessica had gone on cheerfully. 'No more introductions needed for me! Now, what about you?'

Her bold, confident manner had seemed to put everyone at ease and soon they were all sitting down, glasses in hand, talking and laughing. Even Mac had lightened up and he forgot to have sly digs at Hannah, who'd settled beside Jessica and Ralph on the rusty-coloured sofa. Mac had chosen the armchair opposite.

While the chatter flowed, Edie had popped into the kitchen to check on the food. She'd been thinking Jessica was a revelation; she could be nerdy, scary, bossy, quiet, grief-stricken or, as it turned out, the life and soul of the party. At least Edie hadn't needed to worry her guest would find today's company boring.

The meat was cooked, so Edie had removed it from the oven and left it to rest on the side. The peas were almost done, too, and she'd used some of the boiling water to make gravy, adding the reserved meat juices, along with flour, stock, salt, pepper, herbs and a splash of her secret ingredient – sweet Madeira wine.

When everything was ready, she'd summoned in the visitors, who'd settled round the big circular table, which she'd already laid, leaving Ralph to sort out the drinks.

Jessica, who'd already removed her baggy sweatshirt, had pushed up the sleeves of her slim black polo neck and launched into a discussion about her next sporting challenge – a triathlon involving running, open-water swimming and cycling.

'I'm not a particularly strong swimmer, so I need to focus on that,' she'd said, unfolding her napkin and placing it on her lap. 'I did thirty lengths in the pool this morning and I was a limp rag by the end. Exhausted!'

She'd pulled a face and everyone had laughed.

Ralph had moved round the table, filling up the glasses with red wine.

'How far do you run each week when you're training for an ordinary marathon?' he'd asked, pausing momentarily over Jessica's shoulder to listen to her answer.

'Ooh, between thirty and forty miles, maybe, spread over three or four days. For a half-marathon, twenty-five should be enough. It all depends on your fitness to start with, of course. Obviously, you need to start slowly or you might get injured.'

Ralph had nodded. 'There's a half-marathon in June I'm quite keen on doing. It looks like a lovely route round West Sussex and the South Downs.'

Jessica had sipped some wine before responding. 'Go for it! You won't regret it, so long as you put in the work first.'

While Ralph had been carving the meat, Edie had gone backwards and forwards fetching the dishes of vegetables. Hannah had offered to help but Edie had said no.

The final item was a jug of piping-hot gravy, which she'd placed carefully on the table before sitting down herself.

'Won't Ralph have to give up booze? And live on dry chicken and lentils?' she'd asked, picking up rather late in the day on the marathon conversation. 'I don't want to be stuck with an old misery for months on end.'

She'd only been joking, but Jessica had taken her question at face value.

'Oh no, well, not for the whole lead-up, anyway. It's best to avoid drinking forty-eight hours before a race because you don't sleep as well. Alcohol's terribly dehydrating, too. Before that, though, you can drink in moderation. It depends what you want to achieve.'

'What exactly does moderation mean?' Edie had asked, passing Hannah a plate of perfectly carved roast beef and signalling to her to help herself to vegetables. 'A thimbleful of wine once a week – or half a bottle every night with supper?'

Jessica had looked shocked. 'Oh! Half a bottle's too much. I'd say a small glass or two, maximum, and definitely not the night before a long run.'

'Hm,' Ralph had said doubtfully. He'd passed a plate of meat to Hannah, who'd picked up a juicy-looking sliver in her fingers and popped it in her mouth. 'One glass hardly seems worth it.'

'Hear, hear!' Hannah had agreed, raising her own glass. Unfortunately, she'd been too quick and splashed red wine on her front, which trickled down her cleavage.

'Whoops!' She'd wiped herself with a napkin. 'Silly me!'

Edie had stared down at her lap to hide her smile. There was nothing wrong with Hannah's manners in general, but she invariably managed to spill food or drink down herself or someone else at mealtimes. It was quite endearing, so long as you weren't on the receiving end.

Half expecting Mac to make another sarky comment, Edie remembered glancing in his direction. To her surprise, though, he didn't seem to have noticed. He'd been in another world, staring into space.

'Here you go, mate,' Ralph had said, extending a plate in Mac's direction. When Mac failed to respond, Jessica, to his right, had given him a nudge and he'd quickly come to.

'Thanks,' he'd said, taking the food. 'Sorry, I was miles away for a minute.'

'He's probably dreaming about next weekend,' Hannah had

piped up, seemingly unfazed by the dark red wine now staining her bosom. 'He's going to climb Ben Nevis – on his own.'

Ralph, who was still standing over the roast meat, had looked surprised. 'Are you? That sounds adventurous. What's brought this on?'

Mac had shrugged. 'I just fancied doing something different, I guess. One of my clients climbed it recently and said he really enjoyed it. It wasn't as hard as he thought.'

Ralph had turned to put what was left of the beef on the sideboard. 'Fair enough.'

Sitting down at last, he'd helped himself to roast potatoes.

'But doesn't Jude want to come with you? Or Charlotte?'

They were Mac and Hannah's children, aged eighteen and twenty.

'I haven't asked them,' Mac had replied.

'What about Hannah?'

Ralph glanced in her direction and she'd grimaced.

'No way would he want me! He'd find me a terrible drag.'

Mac had frowned. 'Not true. Why would you say that? You know you'd hate it.'

'Not necessarily.' Hannah had cocked her head on one side. 'How would I know if I've never tried?'

'You can't stand being cold. It'll be freezing at this time of year – probably wet and windy, too. Plus, I'm sleeping in a tent. You've never liked camping.'

Hannah had shrugged, before turning her attention to Ralph. 'You see? I told you. He doesn't want me!'

Ralph had laughed. 'I don't blame him, actually. Sometimes it's easier doing things on your own.'

He'd looked at Edie. 'Fancy climbing Ben Nevis with me in the wind and rain?'

'Absolutely no way. I'd moan and groan the entire time. Camping in winter's my idea of hell.'

'Case closed,' Ralph had muttered through a mouthful of food, his eyes crinkling in amusement. 'Mac, you're quite safe. You can battle the elements solo.'

The room had gone quiet for few moments, the only sounds being the clatter of cutlery and the odd whimper from Dilly, sitting hopefully at Ralph's feet.

It was Jessica who'd broken the silence.

'You should go in the spring or summer,' she'd said suddenly, looking straight at Hannah. 'When the weather's better. I'll come with you if you like? I've done quite a few of the Munros but never Ben Nevis. It's on my list.'

Hannah had paused, her fork in mid-air. She'd seemed taken aback but soon rallied.

'Do you know, I might just take you up on that, thank you. It would certainly force me to get fit. I could do with a goal. I'd be so proud of myself if I managed it.'

Mac had remained schtum, cutting his beef into tiny, bite-size pieces with almost forensic precision, and Edie had jumped in to fill the gap.

'There are plenty of mountains to climb in Crete if you want to get some practice. Hopefully it won't be wet and windy either.'

'Where is it you're staying?' Jessica had asked next, spearing a small Brussels sprout with her fork. When Edie told her, she'd nodded knowingly.

'Ah, yes. I remember now, Porto Liakáda was the site of the ancient city of Phoenix, I believe. It was an important harbour in Hellenistic and Roman times. Crete was also the birthplace of Zeus, you know. And King Minos' daughter, Ariadne, who saved Theseus from the Minotaur.'

'Ariadne. Isn't that the name of the villa we're staying in?' Hannah had asked. 'What happened to her?'

'The myth has lots of variations,' Jessica had explained. 'According to most accounts, Theseus promised to marry her then abandoned her on Naxos. She may or may not have gone on to marry Dionysus, the Greek god of wine and pleasure.' She'd smiled. 'Let's hope she did.'

'Wow! How on earth do you know all that?' Hannah had asked, her eyes sparkling in wonder.

Jessica had glanced down, looking slightly embarrassed, so Edie had answered on her behalf. 'She's a classicist. She read Ancient Greek and Latin at Oxford. That's what she teaches.'

'Wow!' Hannah had repeated.

'There's nothing she doesn't know about ancient Greece and Rome,' Edie had gone on. 'About almost anything, actually.' She'd grinned. 'You don't need ChatGPT when she's around.'

'Rubbish!' Jessica had fiddled with a strand of hair, twisting it round and round her finger. 'You know far more about English literature than I do.'

'I doubt it.'

Edie had eyed the half potato left on her plate and downed her knife and fork in defeat. 'I can't think of a single novel I've mentioned that you haven't read. Maybe there's a few old English texts that have managed to slip through your net, but not many.'

'What about football and rugby fixtures?' Ralph had asked teasingly. 'Is she good at those, too?'

'No-I-am-not!' Jessica had said, emphatically. 'Can we please change the subject? You're making me blush.'

Edie had apologised with a laugh and risen. She'd begun collecting the empty plates and when Hannah again tried to help, she was having none of it.

'Stay where you are.' She'd signalled to the others not to get up either. 'Ralph, can you open another bottle of wine?'

The conversation had taken a different turn after that and there were no more sticky moments. Edie had mentioned that their daughter, Maisie, had recently dumped her boyfriend of two years and was now dating an undertaker called Sam.

Hannah's eyes had widened. 'Ooh! That sounds a bit gloomy. Is he always dressed in black?'

'No.' Edie had laughed. 'It's his dad's business, actually. Sam's good fun and extremely handsome. The business seems to be very successful. The parents are loaded.'

'There have been a number of unexplained deaths in the neighbourhood recently,' Ralph had joked. 'There's talk of some chap sneaking round at dead of night with a bottle of poison.'

After lunch, they'd put on their coats and boots and gone for a walk in the misty woods. Pockets of tiny white snowdrops, like little crystal bells, were poking through the hard, frosty earth along the route. It was as if they were guiding the way through the dark trees and bare branches back to open ground – and civilisation.

Edie had watched her breath swirl and spiral in the cold air but she'd been well wrapped up and didn't feel chilly. She was cheered by the fact the meal had been delicious and everyone seemed to have got on well, including Mac and Hannah – in the end.

Perhaps the wine had thawed them out. Jessica's presence had undoubtedly helped as well. Hannah, especially, had seemed very taken with her and Ralph was clearly impressed, too.

All in all, the day had seemed to go very well. It had reminded Edie of some of the big, happy gatherings they used to have before the children left.

Back at the house, they'd all had tea and cake in the cosy

sitting room. The conversation had soon returned to Crete and Jessica had suggested some places to visit.

'You must go to Knossos, the ancient Minoan capital. It's not too far from where you're staying. It's years since I went but I remember finding it fascinating. I'd love to go back.'

'I'm surprised you haven't done a school trip with your pupils,' Mac had said. 'Can't you engineer one?'

'Maybe.' Jessica had looked doubtful. 'The problem is, the school's cut back a lot on trips. Not many of our parents can afford them and the feeling is, it's unfair on the kids who can't go.'

Edie had nodded. 'It's true. It's a real shame. I'd love to take my A-level students to the theatre more. We're only allowed one or two trips a year, maximum. I remember taking one of my students, Maryam, to see *Twelfth Night* at the National. She'd never been to the theatre before and she was absolutely bowled over. She couldn't stop talking about it.'

'Isn't there a fund for pupils who can't afford things like that?' Mac had wanted to know.

'There is,' Edie had agreed. 'But you can only ask better-off parents to pay so much extra to subsidise the other pupils. Otherwise, they won't be able to afford it either.'

Jessica had sighed. 'God I'd love to see my students' faces if I could show them the ancient palace of Minos. I must go back sometime and take lots of photos.' She'd looked thoughtful. 'May would be a good time, actually. After that, it gets too hot.'

It was then that Edie had asked if she had any half-term plans and Jessica had said no. By now, it was after 6 p.m. and when Edie had got up to feed Dilly, Jessica had taken it as her cue to leave.

After thanking her hosts warmly for a lovely day, she'd said goodbye and she and Hannah had embraced.

'I've really enjoyed meeting you,' Hannah had said. 'Hope to see you again soon.'

Edie had stood on the doorstep watching as Jessica put on her helmet and started to pedal away. Just before she was out of sight, Jessica had turned and waved.

'See you tomorrow!' she'd called, and Edie had waved back. 'Thanks for coming!'

Hannah and Mac had been side by side on the sofa when Edie returned and Ralph had offered them all a drink. Edie was tired and felt quite relieved when they'd said no.

'What an interesting woman!' Hannah had commented, meaning Jessica. 'I've never met anyone quite like her.'

'You see!' Edie had cried triumphantly, turning to Ralph. 'I told you, didn't I? She knows something about everything.'

Ralph had nodded. 'And she hardly even mentioned her dog.' He'd given a wry grin. 'I was worried she was going to be in deep mourning.'

'She moves on quickly,' Mac had replied, deadpan.

Edie had glanced at him out of the corner of an eye, unsure how to take the comment. But his facial expression had given nothing away.

When Hannah had mentioned inviting Jessica, however, he'd made his feelings clearer, suggesting she'd change the atmosphere.

Hannah's shoulders had drooped. 'I knew you'd say no.'

'I didn't say no.'

Mac had glared at his wife, his dark eyes glinting dangerously, and Edie had felt herself shrink. She'd wondered if this was how he made Hannah feel if he disagreed with something she wanted. If so, he was out of order.

When she'd pretended to misunderstand his objection, she'd seen his body stiffen and he'd risen abruptly. Sensing his anger, she'd acted as if she hadn't noticed.

Looking back on it now, though, she wished she'd been braver and called him up on it.

'You OK, mate?' Ralph had asked Mac, confused.

'Yeah, fine.'

But Mac had stalked into the hall, returning with his wife's fur coat.

'Put this on,' he'd told her, and she'd taken it obediently. 'It's time to go home.'

Recalling that day in such forensic detail made Edie feel incredibly tense and also guilty, because she could see how she'd ignored a lot of signs. She was ready to spring up at any moment and go to Hannah's rescue.

'I hope they've managed to have a good talk,' she whispered to Ralph. 'Thank God you wouldn't react that way if I came on to someone. Not that I would,' she added quickly. 'It's not my style.'

She was about to start praising her husband for his magnificent display of sangfroid earlier, when Jessica had tried to push herself between Hannah and Mac. But his body twitched and he grunted and snuffled, before breathing out with a crackly whoosh. He'd dropped off.

'Night night,' she whispered, carefully extricating herself from under his arm and rolling on to the other side. Then she tiptoed over to the window to close the shutters and opened the door just a fraction, so she could hear any strange noises in the house more easily.

Finally, with a sigh, she climbed back into bed, pulled the sheet over her and closed her eyes. She tried to think happy thoughts until sleep arrived at last, wrapping her in its familiar and oh-so-comforting embrace.

10

The following morning, Edie and Ralph were in no hurry to get up and join the others and it was after 9 a.m. by the time they went downstairs.

Jessica was reading her book at the table when they poked their heads into the garden.

'Coffee?' Edie asked, managing to force a smile, though her face and cheeks felt tight and rigid.

'I've got some, thanks.' Jessica looked up and held aloft a white-and-blue-striped mug. 'I wasn't sure what time you'd be down, or I'd have made a big pot.'

'No worries.' Edie bobbed back indoors, where Ralph was filling the kettle. 'Who's there?' he asked, with a frown.

'Just Jessica. She seems quite normal today.'

His frown deepened. 'Hm.'

He and Edie sat on the opposite side of the table from Jessica while they spread butter and honey on some bread rolls from yesterday, which they'd warmed in the oven.

Jessica seemed disinclined to speak and soon put her nose back in her book, which suited Ralph and Edie fine.

They chatted quietly about this and that until they'd finished eating.

'What do you fancy doing today?' Edie asked her husband, reaching across the table for the big pot of coffee he'd made and topping herself up. 'After your walk with Mac, I mean.'

At this, Jessica glanced up momentarily before feigning disinterest and returning to the page. Edie could tell she was listening, though.

'Um, not sure.' Ralph poured himself more coffee, too. 'I haven't seen the village yet, remember. Maybe we could wander down to the beach there and have a swim.'

On hearing voices inside, they froze. Edie had a chunk of crusty bread in her mouth, which hurt her throat when she tried to swallow it down.

Soon, Hannah appeared, quickly followed by Mac.

Hannah looked quite different from last night: fresh and attractive in a pale blue sundress, which Edie hadn't seen before. Her blonde hair was still damp from the shower and she was wearing a thin gold necklace and gold studs in her ears.

'Morning!' she said with a dazzling smile, as if nothing had happened. 'How did you all sleep?'

Before anyone had time to reply, Mac, in a clean white T-shirt, jeans shorts and bare feet, stretched his arms above his head and yawned.

'I must've slept for ten or eleven hours,' he announced, still stretching.

You could see a sliver of pale tummy between the end of his T-shirt and the beginning of his waistband.

'Me too. I think we both needed it.' Hannah shot her husband a small, secretive smile before walking over to the table and helping herself to what was left of the coffee.

Then she and Mac sat down, reached for plates, knives, bread rolls, butter and honey and proceeded to eat with gusto.

Edie was so surprised she didn't know how to respond. Hannah's smile said it all: they'd obviously made up in the time-honoured way.

If the evidence wasn't staring Edie in the face, she'd have thought it was too late for that, given Mac's threatening behaviour. She presumed the others felt the same way, as they were silent, too.

'D'you fancy a walk, Mac, just you and I?' Ralph asked at last. 'I thought we could head for Sweetwater Beach along the coast. It should take about an hour and we can either walk back or get the ferry.'

Mac glanced at Hannah and the pair communicated something with their eyes.

'Actually, Hannah and I thought we'd push off on our own for a bit, if you don't mind,' Mac replied after a pause. 'We might investigate that ruined Venetian castle. We won't be gone that long. We just thought it would be nice, you know, after yesterday—'

'Of course,' Ralph said quickly. 'We can do Sweetwater another day.'

'I'm heading to Knossos.'

They all turned to Jessica, who had put down her book and was wiping the corners of her mouth with a napkin.

'I'll get the ferry to Chora Sfakion then a bus to Heraklion. Then it's just another, shortish bus ride to the ancient palace. It'll take about four and a half hours in all so I'll spend the night there tonight. I've booked a hotel. I think I'll get up very early tomorrow to look round the site. There won't be enough time today.'

'Great! You can take lots of photos for your pupils.' Mac's

comment seemed innocent enough but there was no mistaking the caustic tone.

Ralph rubbed his hands together, ostensibly to remove the breadcrumbs.

'Fine.' He looked at Edie. 'So that leaves just you and me. I guess we'll have to entertain ourselves.'

He made a mock-sad face but Edie could sense his underlying delight.

'Let's go to the village beach as you suggested,' she said, also trying not to sound too cheerful. 'We could maybe have some lunch in one of the cafés.'

She glanced at Hannah. 'We'll pick something up for supper at the mini-market. And for breakfast tomorrow, too.'

'No. That's not fair.' Mac's sudden interruption made everyone stop and stare.

'You don't want to have to carry everything home at the end of the day. You'll be too tired. I'll nip down to the village now and pick up some stuff. It won't take me long. Hannah and I can go for our walk afterwards.'

Hannah frowned. 'You'll be knackered by the time you get back. You won't want another walk.'

'She's right,' Edie agreed. 'And there'll be too much to carry for one person.'

But Mac was adamant. 'I insist.' He ran a hand through his hair. 'I'll jog both ways. I need the exercise. To be honest, it'll do me good. I've been thinking I should take up running again. I used to run a lot in my twenties and thirties. I'm not sure why I stopped. I'll probably be shocked by my speed, or rather lack of it.'

Ralph pushed his chair back and scratched his neck. 'I should offer to come with you, mate, but I can't face the uphill bit on the way back. Sorry.'

Mac shook his head. 'Nah. Don't be. I reckon I'll do it in an hour, give or take, if I don't have any stops.'

Hannah made a face. 'Well, I'm definitely not coming with you. No stops sounds like torture. I'd probably pass out. I'll save myself for the Venetian castle. I know my limits.'

Mac gave a half-smile. 'Wise move. I won't be long, promise.'

He seemed dead set on the idea, and Edie thought it *would* be a relief for her and Ralph not to have to shop later on.

'If you're sure...' she said doubtfully.

'I am.'

It was hard for her and Ralph not to cheer after they said goodbye to Jessica, who set off purposefully straight after breakfast, wearing her rucksack.

'I'll be back sometime tomorrow evening,' she said, opening the heavy oak front door and stepping out into the hot sun.

'No rush,' Ralph muttered when she was just out of earshot. 'I reckon she'll need at least two nights to soak up the atmosphere.'

Edie giggled. 'Shh.'

'With any luck she'll bump into the Minotaur in the labyrinth and that'll be that.'

Soon, Mac appeared in running shorts, a white vest top and trainers. It was noticeable that neither he nor Jessica had suggested starting the trip to the village together.

'Do you want to take some shopping bags?' Edie asked Mac, but he said he didn't want to have to carry anything except keys; he'd rather get bags at the shop.

It was only after he'd left that Edie realised he hadn't asked what food to buy. Perhaps Hannah had given him a list, or maybe he had his own ideas.

Once Edie, Ralph and Hannah had tidied up the breakfast things, Hannah went upstairs to read her book.

'I'll be amazed if Mac makes it in an hour,' she said. 'I reckon it'll be more like two.'

Ralph decided to do some lengths in the pool before he and Edie headed to the beach. She guessed he felt a bit guilty about not going running with Mac, and was trying to compensate.

Meanwhile, Edie sat at the patio table again and quickly checked her emails before phoning Maisie first, then Ollie. He hadn't been in touch since she'd been away. She wasn't surprised. Like a lot of boys, he wasn't particularly communicative and tended to ring only if he was feeling down or needed cash or a lift.

'How's it going?' he asked, sounding distracted. There was a lot of noise in the background; he said he and several friends were staying at another mate's house for a few days, while the parents were on a long weekend away.

'I hope you're looking after the place,' Edie said.

Ollie sighed. 'That's such a mum comment. Obviously, we had a rave last night and we're sniffing lines of leftover coke right now.'

Edie managed a humourless laugh. 'Very funny. Not.'

Ralph walked by in a towel, dripping water on the ground. He'd finished his lengths and was on the way upstairs to shower.

'Gotta go,' Edie told Ollie. 'We're off to the beach in a moment. Take care. Love you.'

In truth, she was quite relieved to have an excuse to wind up the conversation, which was giving her the jitters. Ollie was pretty sensible and she trusted him, mostly.

But there was always a little niggle at the back of her mind telling her everyone slipped up occasionally and could do something out of character. Especially if, like Ollie, you were just nineteen and away from home for the first time.

Rising, she picked up her phone and glass of water and

strolled into the kitchen. Her beach bag was already packed and she was ready to go as soon as Ralph came down.

As she rinsed out her glass in the sink, her ears pricked at the sound of a key in the front door lock. Someone entered the villa and she could hear footsteps on the marble hallway floor and heavy breathing.

It must be Mac. She checked the time. But he'd been gone just under an hour. Speedy.

When she went to find him, he was at the bottom of the stairs, bent over and taking off his trainers.

'Goodness! You were quick.'

She noticed the large, dark sweaty patch on the back of his top and his glistening arms and shoulders. His knees were covered in dirt and his hands, too, by the looks of it.

'Did you fall over?'

He glanced up at her, before slipping the trainers off his feet and rising. 'I tripped over a rock, annoyingly. No damage done, I'm pleased to say.'

'Are you sure?'

He showed her his palms, which were grimy but unscratched.

Edie breathed in and out slowly.

'Thank goodness. You must have run incredibly fast. I can't believe you're back already.'

Mac shifted from one foot to another and wiped his sticky forehead with the back of an arm.

'I didn't find it too difficult, actually. I was quite surprised. I expected it to be really hard as I haven't run for so long, but maybe my fitness isn't as bad as I thought.'

'Clearly not. I'm impressed!'

'Is Hannah upstairs?'

His gaze shifted up, towards the first floor. Edie guessed he must be keen to wash and prepare himself for the rest of the day.

'She's reading her book.'

It was only now she remembered the real reason for Mac's mission, but scanning round, she couldn't see any bags of food. It crossed her mind he might have left them in the porch.

'Did you get to the supermarket?' she asked, puzzled. 'I'll put the shopping away if you want to jump in the shower?'

His response wasn't what she expected.

'I-um...' he said with a stammer, before licking his lips. His eyes darted this way and that and she wondered what on earth was coming next. 'I'm tempted to lie, but I can't.'

Now, his focus settled on her and she found herself blinking more than usual under his gaze.

'The fact is,' he went on, 'I completely forgot. I'm really sorry. I was so busy concentrating on my running technique and trying to maintain my speed, it just slipped my mind. I'm such an idiot.' He slapped his forehead with the heel of his hand. 'Hannah will have my guts for garters.'

Edie couldn't help laughing. 'I haven't heard that phrase in ages. But don't worry,' she added, more seriously. 'We can get something later. It's really not a problem.'

* * *

Ralph seemed to be taking ages in the shower and Edie suspected he'd got stuck into his next book. She was about to go and fetch him when Hannah and Mac came down.

Hannah seemed to be in a remarkably cheerful mood still, despite Mac's oversight.

'Did you hear about what happened?' she asked Edie, when she found her in the garden.

Edie raised her eyebrows and nodded with a grin.

'Honestly,' Hannah went on. 'You can't trust him with

anything.' But she was smiling as she spoke. 'What's that old saying? "The rooster may crow, but the hen delivers the goods". He was so busy wanting to show off about how fast he could run, he forgot why he'd offered to go to the village in the first place.'

She and Mac soon started to head off in hats, shorts and walking boots, clutching bottles of water. Whether or not they'd had any sort of discussion last night after their row, they'd obviously completely cleared the air. They were like a different couple.

Ralph joined Edie at the front door, just as they were leaving.

'Give us a ring when you get lost,' he called as a joke when they reached the big iron gates, which slowly swung open at the press of a button.

Hannah gave him a thumbs up. 'We will!'

'Well!' Edie said to her husband as soon as he'd closed the front door again and turned to face her. 'What shall we do now?'

'I can think of a few things.'

He raised his eyebrows and the flicker of a smile crossed his features. Something deep within her stirred: memories of blissful moments, long forgotten.

Wistful, she reached out and touched his cheek, but then reality crashed in and the feeling quickly vanished.

'We should clear away the breakfast things,' she said with a sigh.

* * *

They were both hungry by the time they left the villa and made it down the mountain into Porto Liakáda. It was a bit late for lunch and too early for supper, but they found a café that served traditional Sfakian pies, thin pancakes stuffed with local, soft *mizithra* cheese, drizzled with thyme honey and topped with nuts and cinnamon.

After devouring a couple of these each, washed down with cold draught lager, they were full to bursting and ready for a siesta.

Just beyond the café lay the village's curved, shingly beach, dotted with conveniently placed sun loungers for hire.

They made their way across the crunchy pebbles to two empty chairs and sat down beneath the jaunty parasols.

Edie, who was wearing her bikini underneath her clothes, quickly stripped off and lay down. Meanwhile, Ralph grappled clumsily with his towel while he removed his shorts and underpants.

He was almost changed, just trying to shimmy into his swimming trunks, when a man came to ask for money for using the seats. While Ralph searched for some cash in his shorts pocket, the towel almost slipped off. Edie yelped before stretching over in the nick of time to pull it back up, preserving her husband's dignity – just.

'That was close,' she said with a giggle when Ralph finally lay back with a relieved sigh. 'I don't think Porto Liakáda's ready to see you in the buff.'

Ralph scratched his nose. 'Oh, I don't know. There are plenty of nudist beaches in Crete.'

'Yes, but have you seen that sign?'

She sat up and pointed to a wooden notice nailed to the wall of the hotel behind them: *'NO TOPLESS BATHING ON THIS BEACH PLEASE'*.

Ralph flopped down again. 'Fair enough. But it doesn't say anything about todgers.'

The beach was only about a quarter full and pretty quiet, save for the background murmur of people talking, the odd rumble of a boat's engine and the lapping of the waves on the shore.

It was hot but they were comfortable in the shade and it wasn't long before Edie heard the familiar sound of Ralph's snores. She didn't try to prod him awake as he only ever snuffled and wheezed when he was dropping off. He'd soon stop.

She was nodding off herself when her phone pinged in the bag beside her. It was a text message from Hannah, asking where they were.

'On the beach in the village,' Edie replied. *'Where are you?'*

'We'll come and join you. See you in a few xx,' came the answer.

Edie's heart sank slightly as she'd been enjoying having Ralph to herself, but at least Jessica wasn't around. She seemed to stir up Hannah and Mac and make everything ten times worse.

A young woman in a skimpy bikini walked gingerly across the pebbles to the water's edge, taking short, soft steps to try to minimise the pain.

It seemed to take her an age to get into the sea. She inched forward, with her arms held high, then retreated every time a wave came her way.

Edie watched with amusement, thinking the woman would do better to dive straight in; she was only prolonging the agony.

The woman finally went all the way under, only to bob up again almost immediately. But after a few more attempts, she became used to the temperature and stayed under.

She must have started to enjoy herself because she swam out quite a distance to some rocks and sat for a while, waving at her friends on the beach and looking all round.

Edie remembered herself at this age – so young and carefree – and was tempted to go in herself. But she soon heard familiar voices behind and, on turning, saw Hannah and Mac walking towards her. They smiled and waved and Edie got up to greet them.

'How was the walk?' she asked, watching Mac drag over a couple of sun loungers.

'Great.'

Hannah took a slurp of water from her bottle, which was almost empty. She looked rather hot, sweaty and uncomfortable after her exertion.

'We found the castle. We got good views from there. It was a fair old hike, though,' she added.

The pair undressed, with much less of a song and dance than the one Ralph had made, and went straight into the sea. Hannah lay on her back, staring up at the bright blue sky, while Mac dived down to the bottom, coming up with a handful of sand and seashells.

They were clearly having such a lovely time that finally, Edie couldn't resist joining them. Ralph stayed snoozing under the parasol for a while, but when he woke, he went in, too, then they all swam to the rocks and sat on top, chatting and sunbathing.

Leaning back on her hands, with her face to the sun and her eyes closed, Edie breathed in and out deeply. It wasn't the right time to quiz Hannah about Mac, she thought. In any case, at that moment everything felt reassuringly normal.

Hannah was beside her, dabbling her feet happily in the crystal-clear water, while Ralph and Mac were on the adjacent rock, talking about this and that in soothing, low voices.

'It's rather nice, not having Jessica here,' Edie said eventually, before waiting tentatively for an answer.

'Do you think so?' Hannah said.

Edie's eyes sprang open. 'Well, yes. I mean, it's nice to be just the four of us for a bit, don't you think? I hope she has a good time in Knossos,' she added quickly.

Mac started to rise. 'Shall we go back?' he asked Ralph. 'Race you to the beach.'

Ralph started to protest, knowing Mac was the stronger swimmer, but it was too late.

Mac was already launching himself off the rocks and was soon slicing through the water, using his best front crawl. Ralph would have to be quick to have any hope at all of catching him up.

While the women watched from their rock, Hannah drew up her legs and hugged her knees.

'I think Jessica's amazing. She's such a strong woman. I wish I was more like her,' she commented.

'She's certainly very independent,' Edie replied carefully. In truth, her opinion had shifted and she'd begun to think Jessica was really quite selfish. But Hannah viewed things differently.

'She told me she never wanted to get married or have children,' Hannah went on. 'She's an individualist. It's important to her not to have to rely on anyone for anything.'

'I can see that, but some of us want and need support from others. If everyone was like her, the world would be rather a lonely, disconnected place.'

'I disagree.'

Edie sat up and brushed the dirt and stones off her hands. 'Really?' She swallowed, wondering what was coming next.

'Yes. For example, I'm sick of bending over backwards for my family and getting nothing in return. It's all take and no give, as far as I'm concerned. I could do with being a bit more self-centred.'

Edie frowned. 'I know you work incredibly hard, and Mac's work is so irregular. I wish you could share the load more.'

'You don't know the half of it,' Hannah said darkly.

The comment worried Edie, but she didn't get the chance to question her friend any further.

'Come on,' Hannah said, standing up and preparing to launch herself off the rock. 'We'll get left behind.'

She and Edie adopted a more leisurely pace as they made their way towards the shore and as she swam, Edie made a mental note not to mention Jessica to Hannah again for the time being. Clearly, Hannah wouldn't have a word said against her and it would only cause friction.

They sunbathed for a while longer on the beach before gathering their things together. Edie suggested they could perhaps hang round the village for a while and have supper out. However, Hannah wanted to get changed and as no one could face the prospect of walking to and from the villa twice in one day, the idea was vetoed.

They were on their way to April's shop to buy provisions for dinner together instead when Edie spotted Jean-Luc in dark glasses, sitting on the harbour wall sipping something from a can.

She shuddered, remembering Mac's behaviour yesterday, and quickly looked in the other direction, but not fast enough.

'Bonjour, tout le monde!' Jean-Luc called, getting up and strolling towards the group. 'How are you today?'

Edie, who was behind Mac, noticed his body stiffen and his fists clench, and she could swear his pace quickened, as if he intended to push on past.

'Oh God, it's the Frenchman,' she whispered to Ralph, beside her. 'I hope Mac doesn't punch him.'

Just then, Hannah stopped, forcing her husband to do likewise.

Edie and Ralph came to a halt beside them and, without a word, Ralph stepped forward and shook Jean-Luc by the hand.

'I'm Ralph, Edie's husband,' he said. 'Edie told me she'd met you and your sister, the artist. I'd be interested to see her work sometime.'

The intervention was timely. Mac's shoulders relaxed a little and his fists unclenched.

Jean-Luc bowed his head graciously. Barefoot and wearing a khaki T-shirt over bright blue swimming shorts, he looked more handsome than ever.

'Thank you. She is very talented.'

'So I hear. Edie went to her studio yesterday. She loved her paintings.'

'It's true,' Edie agreed. 'I just wish I could afford to buy one.'

Jean-Luc held out his hands, palms up, and shrugged. 'Euh, I can't afford them either. Unfortunately there are no discounts for little brothers.'

He stuck out his bottom lip like a sulky kid, making Edie laugh.

'We must get a move on,' she said, taking Ralph's arm. 'We've got to buy supper and go home and cook it.'

She was starting to move when Hannah piped up.

'Est-ce que tu vas nager?' she asked Jean-Luc, before flashing a coquettish little smile.

Edie, who spoke some French, understood perfectly well what she'd said: 'Are you going for a swim?'

The bottom seemed to drop out of Edie's chest. Jean-Luc turned to give Hannah his full attention and Mac's face went white and pinched.

'Mais oui,' the Frenchman replied, with a playful little smile. 'And when are we going to have that French lesson? You must give me a call.'

'Um, sometime tomorrow, maybe?' Hannah suggested.

Normally, a blatant come-on like Jean-Luc's would have made Edie snort. But not when Mac was involved.

Hannah knew how jealous her husband was. After witnessing his rage last night, Edie couldn't understand why on earth she'd do anything to provoke him further, especially since the couple seemed to have made up and got back on a more even keel.

Ralph hopped from one foot to another and back again, as if the ground was burning his feet.

'Come on.' He grabbed Edie's hand and told her in a low voice to get Mac, too.

It wasn't clear if Mac heard or not, but he started walking with them, without needing to be hustled, leaving his wife behind.

Edie glanced back, hoping to catch Hannah's eye and make her hurry up, but Hannah was deep in conversation with Jean-Luc and didn't notice.

April was on her own in the shop for once, tidying a row of cans on one of the shelves.

'Where's Nikos?' Edie asked, looking round.

'With Anthea. I think you met her?'

Edie nodded.

'She offered to take him for a walk,' April went on. 'She loves little ones and they seem to adore her. When she comes here to do my hair, Nikos won't leave her alone. She has to sit him beside me in front of the mirror and pretend to cut his hair, too.'

Edie smiled. 'Did you know Alexandros, the father of her daughter?'

April raised her eyebrows, which were a slightly uneven shade of brown. She must have been in a hurry when she put on her make-up.

'That bastard?' She shook her head. 'He was before my time. He was a wrong'un, by all accounts.'

She seemed to glare at Mac and Ralph, as if they were somehow implicated, and they shuffled uncomfortably.

'He got sacked from his job for putting his hands in the till,' she went on. 'He treated Anthea really badly. Never gave her a penny or showed any interest in his child. Anthea's a toughie, though. She's a great mum; Alexa's turned out fabulous. The only thing is, I don't know why Anthea does all that stuff to her face. She's beautiful inside and out. She doesn't need to.'

'Does she have a partner?' Edie wanted to know, allowing curiosity to get the better of her. She knew she was holding the others up.

'No,' said April. 'More's the pity. I wish she could find a really decent, honourable man. We all do. She deserves it. I'm sure she's had offers, but as far as I'm aware there's been no one for years. I guess there's not many eligible types round here who aren't married. She'll have to look further afield.'

Ralph cleared his throat. 'We must get going,' he said, sounding slightly desperate.

Edie apologised. 'We need something for supper,' she told April. 'Any suggestions? It can't be too complicated.'

April thought for a moment. 'What about *keftedes* – Greek meatballs.'

She pointed to the meat section in one of the refrigerators. 'All you need is some ground beef or lamb, fresh mint, chopped onion, garlic, an egg, salt and pepper and breadcrumbs. Mix them all together, make them into little balls and fry them in olive oil. They only take about fifteen minutes. You can have them with *tzatziki* – I've got some here – and a squeeze of lemon juice. I'd serve them with pitta and a Greek salad. They're delicious and dead easy.'

Edie glanced at Ralph, who nodded and said, 'Sounds perfect.'

'Mac?' Edie prompted, because he hadn't spoken and clearly wasn't paying attention.

'Oh, yes, anything. Great.'

She looked at him properly, because he sounded far away, and his appearance shook her. He seemed lost and sort of shrunken, all his anger and bluster gone.

'You all right?' she asked, experiencing an unexpected wave of sympathy.

'Yes, fine, well...' He swallowed. 'You know, *ish*.'

She gave his arm a squeeze. 'It'll be all right, you'll see.' She wasn't sure she believed it, though.

Hannah breezed in as they were paying for the food and offered her bank card.

'It's OK, Ralph and I have got this,' Edie told her.

On the way back, Hannah made a point of staying close to Mac. She even took his hand at one point. Edie, behind them, wondered if he'd shake her off, but he didn't.

In fact, there seemed to be a new spring in his step, as if his wife's tender gesture had breathed new energy into his limbs and feet, which were landing on the ground more lightly.

Supper turned out to be a jolly affair. The wine flowed and moods were high. Ralph left the meatballs on for too long and they were rather burned, but no one cared.

Looking round the laughing faces in the candlelight, Edie felt her tension evaporating, like steam from a kettle. Perhaps Hannah and Ralph were OK and the holiday would be all right after all.

'So, what's the plan for tomorrow?' she asked, when they all rose and started to clear up the plates and glasses.

Mac and Hannah exchanged glances.

'I think we both fancy a chilled day here, right, Aitch?' It was his pet name for her. Edie hadn't heard him use it in a long while.

'Definitely,' Hannah replied, with an unmistakably cheeky grin.

11

Jessica didn't message anyone the following day and tellingly, no one tried to contact her, either.

'I wonder what time she'll be back,' Edie said to Ralph, on her left, when they were lazing by the pool in the late afternoon. Hannah and Mac were lying on her other side, both with their eyes closed.

'Late, I expect,' Ralph replied gruffly. 'Any time will be too soon, as far as I'm concerned.' He growled, like a dog guarding its supper.

Edie took a deep breath. 'At least we've had a bit of a break from her. Maybe she'll have mellowed on her trip.'

After a while, Hannah and Mac woke up in restless moods and Hannah announced she was going for a shower.

'Coming?' she asked Mac, looking all wide-eyed and fake-innocent. It was obvious what she was thinking.

Mac got up and followed her indoors.

Sometime later, Ralph said he'd had enough sun and wanted to read his book upstairs. Edie told him she'd do twenty lengths of the pool before joining him.

The task she set herself wasn't really a chore at all. She enjoyed being out there on her own as the sunlight faded and she could watch the sky slowly change colour, as if by magic.

She was thinking how easy-going Ralph seemed, despite all the tension between the others, which had nothing whatever to do with them, and how well they were getting on. She almost wished their children could see them.

Back home, Ollie, in particular, would often tell them off for 'bickering'. Once, he even asked Edie why she and Ralph were still together.

'You don't seem to make each other very happy,' he'd commented.

Edie had tried to brush the comment off, but it had really stung, and Maisie had been on their case, too. Last Christmas, she'd given them a voucher for a well-known restaurant in central London.

'You should book a nice hotel and make a weekend of it,' she'd said. 'You hardly ever do anything, just the two of you.'

Edie and Ralph had thanked her, of course, for her generous and thoughtful present. Neither had been in the mood for an overnight stay, however, and they'd deliberately timed things so they could catch the last train back.

Edie couldn't help thinking both children would be amazed to see their parents now, being so relaxed and enjoying each other's company. Not long ago, she wouldn't have believed it either.

She used the outdoor shower to wash, before wrapping herself in her towel and padding into the kitchen. She was wondering what to do about supper.

Yesterday, April had persuaded them to buy some Cretan sausages, along with the chopped lamb they'd made into meatballs. The sausages were made locally, she'd explained, from free-range, happy pigs that roamed for miles over the fields and hillsides, munching on organic acorns, roots and fruits.

They were stuffed with sage, marjoram and thyme, as well as *stamnagathi*, a wild green leaf thought to increase longevity.

Her sales pitch had worked like a charm and Edie had promptly asked for two packs. They could grill the meat on the barbecue later, she thought, unless anyone objected, of course.

Meanwhile, a quick check confirmed there was just enough in the fridge for a mixed salad, which she promptly set about making. There was also a bag of brown rice in one of the cupboards and she put two cupfuls in boiling water to cook.

She was still in her wet swimsuit and, by the time she'd finished, she was cold and keen to go upstairs and get dressed. On spotting Jessica's white flip-flops in the hall, however, she felt a stab of guilt.

Jessica was no doubt on the long journey home and would be tired. A friendly text at this point might cheer her up.

> Hope all OK and u enjoyed Knossos. What time will u be back? See u later. Edie.

She couldn't bring herself to add kisses, even though almost all her acquaintances, from the window cleaner to the doctor's receptionist, normally received at least one from her. The kisses had a habit of appearing all by themselves. Maisie used to hover over Edie when she was writing to make sure she didn't go completely mad.

'You're so *embarrassing*, Mum,' she'd say. 'It looks like you've lost the plot. You need to rein yourself in.'

By the time the two couples sat down for supper, it was nearly nine o'clock. Ralph barbecued the sausages, which were delicious, and they all had fruit for pudding, with the last of Katerina's *kalitsounia*.

'Let's eat out tomorrow night,' Hannah suggested. 'We could spend the day at Sweetwater Beach and have supper in the village on our way back.'

'Great idea,' said Ralph. 'We'll be in our beach clothes, though. Will that matter?'

Edie took a sip of white wine before putting down her glass.

'I don't think anyone cares round here. Everyone's so laid-back. What time shall we set off? Ten-ish?'

'Perfect.' Mac topped up her glass before refilling Hannah's and his own. Ralph said he'd had enough for now.

'According to my guidebook, there's a café on the beach, but we'd better bring some snacks just in case.'

All of a sudden, Hannah let out a cry. 'Oh my God! We've forgotten about Jessica. Shouldn't she be back?'

Edie explained she'd sent a message, but when she picked up her phone, which was in the bag at her feet, she could see it hadn't been read.

'That's odd,' she said, with a frown. 'It's quite late. I wouldn't have thought there'd be a ferry to Porto Liakáda at this time. Maybe she'll stay in Chora Sfakion tonight. I'll try calling her.'

The phone rang nine or ten times with no response. Edie messaged once more.

> Hi Jessica, hope all's well. Please call to let us know you're safe. Are you staying another night somewhere? Edie.

The others had lost interest already and were talking about something else, but Edie had an uneasy prickling sensation in her gut.

'I'm a bit worried about Jessica,' she said, interrupting the conversation. 'It's odd she's not answering her phone. What shall we do?'

'Nothing,' Ralph replied firmly. 'She's an adult; she's perfectly capable of looking after herself. You know what she's like; she does what she wants when she wants, with little thought for anyone else. She'll have booked herself in somewhere and she's probably stuck in a book right now, with her phone on silent. She'll be back tomorrow, you'll see.'

Mac nodded in agreement. 'I always thought it was odd going to Knossos for just one night. There's so much there, from what I hear. My guess is she's staying another night. She'll be OK.' He chuckled. 'To be honest, I wouldn't fancy anyone's chances if they tried to attack her. She'd make mincemeat of them.'

Ralph laughed politely at his friend's joke, but Edie could tell he wasn't greatly amused. Hannah, meanwhile, looked furious.

'That's the most stupid, sexist thing I've ever heard.'

Edie shuddered and Mac's mouth twisted in a strange way.

'Violence against women is as high as ever and it's all around us,' Hannah went on, glaring at her husband. 'You should know that. It doesn't matter how strong a woman is, if a man wants to hurt her, he will. You should never, ever make jokes about it.'

Mac seemed to shrivel into his chair; he wasn't a big man and Edie could swear he lost several more inches in height and girth.

'I-I'm sorry,' he said with a stutter. 'I wasn't thinking. It was foolish of me – insensitive and wrong.'

Hannah's eyes narrowed and she pursed her lips, as if she'd bitten into a lemon. Her husband's abject apology might have come at the right time and knocked the wind out of her sails, but there was no way she'd forgive him yet.

'Look,' said Ralph firmly, sounding like a referee at a football match. 'It's late and there's nothing we can do now. If we haven't heard from her by about lunchtime tomorrow we'll make a plan, OK?'

He looked round the group to garner support, and everyone

concurred. The party was definitely over, however, and when Edie rose, the others copied, helping to clear the table in virtual silence.

'Let me know if you hear from her,' Hannah told Edie as they went upstairs. Ralph waited at the bottom to turn off the hall light. 'I'll keep my phone on. It doesn't matter what time it is, I want you to wake me, all right?'

Edie said she would.

'Promise?'

'I promise.'

* * *

Edie had a bad night, tossing and turning, while Ralph somehow managed to sleep soundly beside her. Every now and again she'd check her phone, hoping for a message from Jessica, but none came.

At daybreak, when light started to peep through the shutters, she decided there was no point trying to doze off any longer so she rose and hurriedly put on some shorts and a T-shirt.

After splashing her face with cold water in the bathroom, she glanced in the mirror and was dismayed to see a pair of puffy, bloodshot eyes staring back at her, with ugly dark circles underneath.

Her hair was all over the place, too. She tried patting it down, but the curls sprang up again immediately, even tighter than before, as if to mock her.

'Bloody hell!' she muttered to herself, turning away in disgust. 'What a fright!'

She tiptoed downstairs, so as not to wake the others, and put on the kettle, hoping several cups of strong coffee might sort her out. She was reaching for the coffee pot when someone spoke, making her nearly jump out of her skin.

'Mac!' she exclaimed, spinning round. He was standing just outside the kitchen door. 'I didn't think anyone was awake.'

Mac looked pale and tired and, like her, he'd obviously flung on the first clothes he could find – a crumpled navy T-shirt and shorts.

'I hardly slept,' he said, running a hand through his thick, messy hair. 'Hannah kept looking at her phone, hoping you'd have heard something.'

Edie leaned back, her hands gripping the work surface behind, and crossed one bare foot over another.

'Me too. I kept imagining the most horrible things. You know how the brain works on overdrive at three in the morning?'

He nodded.

'To be honest, though,' Edie went on, 'I'm properly anxious now. I know Jessica's very independent but as far as I can tell, she hasn't opened any of my messages. We're going to have to call the police.'

Mac's eye twitched. 'That's a bit over the top, don't you think? I mean, she's only been officially missing one night.'

He wrapped his arms round his chest, as if he was giving himself a hug. 'Have you tried her again this morning?'

Edie nodded. 'No answer.'

'But the phone was working OK? It rang normally?'

'Yes.'

'Well then, she's probably just decided to have a break from it. Some people do that, you know. A friend of mine turns his off completely every Sunday. He says it helps him relax and it's good for the family as well as his mental health.'

He sounded so utterly convinced by his own argument, Edie

didn't bother to dispute it. He'd failed to calm her nerves, however.

When Hannah joined them in the garden half an hour or so later, she and Edie agreed they couldn't possibly go to Sweetwater Beach or anywhere, in fact, until they knew Jessica was safe.

It was hard just trying to sit still. Both women kept getting up and pacing round the patio, until Mac told them to stop, as they were putting him more on edge, too.

Edie was relieved when Ralph finally made it downstairs at around 10 a.m. His calm, steady manner helped to settle her mind a little, but he could tell she and Hannah were in a mess.

'Pass the coffee, will you?' he asked Edie, before pouring himself a large cup.

He took a swig then sat back with his legs apart, one ankle resting on the other knee.

'Right,' he said purposefully, reaching in his pocket for his mobile. 'I've had enough of this.'

Edie swallowed. 'What are you going to do?' Her voice sounded oddly high-pitched.

'Ring her,' Ralph replied. 'What's her number?'

Edie read it out to him and he pressed the digits. When there was no reply yet again, his eyes darkened and his sandy brows moved so close together, they almost met in the middle.

Swiftly, he tapped out a WhatsApp message, which Edie asked to see.

> We're all very worried about you. Please get in touch immediately. Ralph.

Edie looked over her husband's shoulder while he checked if the message had been delivered, which it had. But the two ticks, which went blue if it had been read, failed to light up. 'I think she's playing games with us,' Mac said suddenly, and they all turned to look at him. He was fiddling with the teaspoon he'd used to stir his coffee.

'What do you mean?' Edie wanted to know.

'I mean, I believe she's extremely manipulative. She's used to getting her own way and she can't stand it when she doesn't. She's really put out and this is her way of getting revenge.'

Edie placed her elbows on the table and rested her chin in her hands. She was staring at Mac, struggling to read him, as if he was a book written in a foreign language.

'So, are you saying you think she's gone into hiding and this is all deliberate? She wants us to be worried sick. She's trying to get even? But why would she be put out? We haven't done anything wrong. Also, that's very dark. You make her sound like a pantomime villain. She might be selfish, but she's not *that* bad.'

'It's ridiculous,' Hannah added, fixing on her husband, too. 'Just because you've taken against her doesn't mean she's evil. I think you're jealous because she's cleverer than you – and she and I get on really well.' She jabbed a finger at him, making him recoil. 'You hate that, don't you?'

Edie shivered, wishing Hannah would stop now, but she was only just getting into her stride.

'You're threatened by it,' Hannah went on. 'You tried to stop me being friends with her from the word go. In fact, you'd love it if I had no friends at all, maybe just Edie because she's your friend, too. You want me all on my own, isolated and miserable.'

Edie swallowed and she noticed Ralph was shaking slightly. She scarcely breathed, waiting on tenterhooks for Mac to retaliate. Instead, though, he rose abruptly and stalked towards the villa without uttering a word.

There was silence for a moment while they all digested what had happened.

'Does he really try and stop you having friends?' Edie asked at last in a small voice.

Hannah, who was trembling, bit her lip and stared at her lap.

'You can tell us,' Edie persisted, meaning her and Ralph. 'We've known each other forever. You know you can trust us, don't you?'

'Of course.' Hannah looked up again with tears in her eyes. 'He's OK with you and Ralph. He's really fond of you both. Plus, we go back such a long way. But if I ever mention meeting someone new – male or female – and say how much I like them, he gives me the silent treatment. Either that or he goes off on one. He says I bend over backwards for everyone else and hardly give any attention to him. Apparently, there's no room in my life for new friends; I've got too many as it is.' She gave a humourless laugh. 'He certainly doesn't want to meet anyone new either. He's not interested. That's why we hardly socialise together these days. If we ever get invited anywhere, he refuses to come.'

Edie exchanged glances with Ralph, who was chewing his thumbnail. She rolled her shoulders, which were stiff and achy all of a sudden.

'This isn't good,' she said gently, leaning forward to touch Hannah lightly on the knee. 'It's classic controlling behaviour – you know that, don't you?'

Hannah's bottom lip quivered. 'Yes,' she whispered.

Edie sat up straight and took a deep breath. 'This can't go on, Hannah. It's not right. Would he agree to marriage counselling, do you think?'

'I asked a while ago. He refused point-blank.'

'I can have a word with him?' Ralph suggested. 'Edie and I found counselling helpful ten years ago when we... when I... you know...'

His voice trailed off, but Hannah knew what he was referring to. She'd been Edie's main source of comfort and support after she'd found out about the other woman.

Hannah was silent for a moment while she considered his proposal.

'Thanks for the suggestion, but now's not the right time,' she said finally. 'He's too angry and I think it would make him feel cornered. He'd know we'd all been talking about him.

'It'd be better to wait for the right moment. Maybe you and he could go for a drink sometime when we're back in England? You could broach the subject then.'

She shivered, despite the heat, and reached for her cardigan on the back of her chair. 'Check with me first, though, so I can be prepared.'

Ralph nodded gravely. 'Of course.'

Edie gave a big sigh. 'But I'm worried about you *now*, Hannah. Seriously, should you even be in the same room as him after he threw that mirror at you?'

Hannah gave a brave smile. 'I appreciate your concern, but it'll be fine, truly. He'll have simmered down by the time I go up and if he hasn't, I'll sleep on the sofa.'

Edie knitted her brows. 'It's your call, of course. But remember, Ralph and I are always here for you. You can ask us for anything.'

12

Edie, Ralph and Hannah sat in the shade by the pool for a while and tried to read, but none of them could concentrate.

When Hannah's phone rang, they all jumped, but it wasn't Jessica. It was Hannah's eighteen-year-old daughter Charlotte.

Hannah got up and took the call at the other end of the pool, so as not to disturb the others, but they could hear her anyway.

A few moments into the conversation, Edie couldn't help noticing a frown appear on her friend's forehead, and her face, normally round and smooth, turned pale and pinched.

'For God's sake, Charlotte! What the hell were you thinking?'

Edie glanced at Ralph, who rolled his eyes. He was no doubt reflecting, as she was, that things surely couldn't get much worse, yet it seemed they just had.

Charlotte had always been a bit of a wild child and Hannah and Mac had briefly sent her to boarding school, hoping it would sort her out. But they couldn't really afford the fees and she'd hated it anyway, so they'd pulled her out after just one term.

Maisie always said Charlotte was attention-seeking, and

Maisie was usually right. She also said Charlotte couldn't wait to get away from home as her parents hated each other and the atmosphere was toxic.

At the time, Edie had dismissed this as youthful exaggeration, but she now feared it wasn't far from the truth.

'It's your problem. You sort it out…' she heard Hannah say in a whisper-shout. And: 'I'm not giving you a penny… borrow it from somewhere… I don't know… I don't care…'

When she'd finished speaking, Hannah stomped back to Edie and Ralph with a big scowl on her face.

'Trouble?' Edie asked anxiously.

Ralph, beside her, pretended to bury his nose in his book, but she knew he was all ears.

'She bought a second-hand laptop from some acquaintance she'd only just met,' Hannah said angrily. 'Her old one broke. She paid a ridiculous amount for it and of course it crashed immediately. Now the person who sold it to her has disappeared. He's not replying to any of her calls or texts. Apparently the laptop's not worth fixing.

'She took it to a computer repair place and they said there's too much wrong with it. She spent all her savings on it, can you believe? Now she doesn't have a laptop for her exams. I told her, tough. It's her fault for being so gullible. She'll have to sort it out.'

Hannah's mouth clamped shut and her pupils shrank to small, black, glittering dots. For the second time today, Edie was taken aback by her friend's rage. Before this trip, she'd have described Hannah as pretty even-tempered, and she'd never realised how strict she was with her kids.

Though Charlotte could be demanding and difficult, she was still young, and Edie felt sorry for her. She'd made a foolish mistake and was no doubt beating herself up about it.

A laptop was essential for her end-of-year exams. If Maisie had done the same thing at that age, Edie knew without a shadow of doubt she'd have been upset, angry and exasperated, for sure, but one way or another, she'd have helped her daughter out.

In fact, she and Ralph wouldn't have expected Maisie to spend all her savings on a laptop in the first place; they'd have bought it for her or, if they couldn't afford it, contributed as much as they possibly could.

'What a nightmare,' she said. 'I bet that bastard who flogged it to her has done it before, too. If I were you, I'd be tempted to lend Charlotte the cash for a new one. She could set up a direct debit and pay you back an agreed amount each month?'

'No way.' Hannah's jaw jutted and the veins in her neck protruded. 'She's always been useless with money. She's got to learn.'

Edie decided to leave it there. Charlotte was Hannah's daughter and there was no point arguing. Besides, Jessica was the more pressing worry.

It seemed almost pointless to try calling yet again, but Edie did so anyway, to no avail. After putting her phone back down, she turned to Ralph.

'It's one o'clock. We said if we hadn't heard anything by now, we'd make a plan.'

Ralph removed his sunglasses and rubbed his eyes. His face looked lined and drawn, and Edie felt a rush of guilt, because it was her fault Jessica was here.

'You're right,' he said, replacing his shades and sitting up straight. 'I googled emergency contacts this morning. I've got a number for the Greek Tourist Police in this area. They're available twenty-four-seven. I'll give them a call.'

The sun was high in the sky now and even in the shade, Edie

felt hot and slightly nauseous. Listening to her husband on the phone to the police, describing Jessica and the situation they were in, seemed unreal.

Edie imagined she was looking down on herself from some distance away, as if she were a character in a play.

'Yes, we've tried contacting her numerous times...' she heard Ralph say, in a far-off voice, and, 'No, not to my knowledge. She didn't mention anyone she knew...'

The police wanted to know what she was wearing, what she'd taken with her and what her behaviour was like before she left.

'We didn't know she was going to Knossos till that morning... out of the blue, yes... History teacher... very fit... single... independent...'

He held the phone away from his ear and looked at Edie.

'Do we know anything about her family? Or close friends?'

Edie shook her head. 'She never mentioned parents or any brothers or sisters. She didn't seem to have friends either, not even other teachers. I was the only one, really – to my knowledge, anyway. And Hannah, of course, but she's much more recent.'

As she spoke, it dawned on Edie how little she actually knew about Jessica. Their conversations had mainly centred round Jessica's numerous interests: books, ancient Rome and Greece, films, running and so on.

Edie had certainly spoken to her about Maisie and Ollie and she'd been to the family home. In fact, she was probably far more knowledgeable about Edie's private life than the other way round.

Ralph interrupted Edie's train of thought with another question.

'Can you send me some photos of Jessica? Close-ups if you've got them, and full-length ones. As soon as you can.'

He glanced at Hannah. 'You too.'

Both women scrolled through their collections, shared what

they had and Ralph forwarded them straight away to an address he'd been given. When he finally came off the phone, he said the person he'd spoken to had very good English and seemed sympathetic, helpful and professional.

'The police are going to make some enquiries in the village and around Knossos. It's a shame we didn't ask which hotel she was staying in the first night. There are so many in that area. It could have been any of them.'

Edie curled into a little ball on her lounger and hugged her knees. She wished none of this was happening and it was just a bad dream. It felt like one.

'What about us? What can we do?' she asked, pressing her palms together and squeezing.

Ralph stood up and stretched his back; he'd been sitting for too long.

'We wait here for a bit, then the police want to meet us in the village at 5 p.m. They're obviously going to be asking round to see if anyone's seen or knows anything. They're based in Chania, so we've arranged to meet in a café. They might take this whole thing more seriously once they've put faces to our names and they'll be able to see how worried we are. To be honest, though, they sound pretty competent, like they know what they're doing. I suspect people, visitors I mean, probably go missing on the island all the time.'

Edie and Hannah nodded.

'I can't help thinking about Michael Mosley,' Edie said with a shiver, remembering the UK doctor who'd recently gone for a walk on a different Greek island and who'd tragically died, most probably of heatstroke.

'He was much older than Jessica,' Ralph pointed out. 'And the circumstances were completely different. We haven't had lunch,' he added, deliberately changing the subject. 'What is there? I don't mind making something.'

Neither of the women was hungry but he insisted they should eat to keep up their strength.

'I think we've got bread and there should be some leftover cheese,' said Edie, rising too. 'And a few tomatoes. Let's have that. We can buy some other stuff in the village for later.'

As they all walked towards the villa, Edie suddenly stopped in her tracks and let out a small cry.

'What about Mac? I completely forgot about him. Do we even know where he is?'

Ralph and Hannah looked blank.

'Oughtn't we to find him and tell him what's happening?' Edie went on. 'Shouldn't we ask him to come with us later, too?'

Hannah's body stiffened and her face twisted into a grimace. 'Absolutely not. I expect he's upstairs in our room, sulking, waiting for me to go and apologise. If he was at all concerned about Jessica, he'd be down here with us now. I really don't think he cares about her at all,' she added, narrowing her eyes. 'To be honest, he'd probably rather she was dead.'

* * *

Hannah's comment left Ralph and Edie speechless and the three of them barely spoke over lunch or opened their mouths on the walk to the village.

The Libyan Sea in the distance was deep turquoise and it glittered and gleamed like the surface of a brand-new car, but Edie barely noticed.

She was reflecting on the fact that though she couldn't take Hannah's words seriously, they'd still managed to shock her.

Edie wouldn't have believed her friend could even think such a terrible thing about her husband, let alone say it out loud – and with such conviction.

Hannah must hate Mac yet, at the same time, she seemed to want to stay with him and he with her. Edie couldn't understand it.

Compared with those two, her own marriage seemed pretty good. Yes, Ralph had strayed, but he'd owned up, apologised and said he bitterly regretted it. And Edie was as certain as she could be it hadn't happened again.

They both missed the kids terribly since they'd left home, and they'd stopped doing things together and having fun. But despite all the dramas on this holiday, it had proved she did still like and fancy Ralph. And his calm strength had reminded her just how wonderful he was in a crisis. Perhaps there was hope for them yet.

On reaching Porto Liakáda, the three of them soon spotted two police officers, a man and woman, in dark blue peaked caps, pale blue shirts and navy trousers.

They had official-looking badges and guns on their hips, but they didn't seem threatening.

The man, who was tall and broad, with a pot belly and a big black moustache, seemed to be sharing a joke with a waiter in the café where they'd all arranged to meet.

Meanwhile, the woman, in dark sunglasses, had long, loose blonde hair, an attractive face and a large, shelf-like bust, straining at the buttons of her shirt. It was quite difficult to ignore.

After a moment or two, she left her male colleague chatting to the waiter and made her way towards April's shop. Edie, Ralph and Hannah were a few minutes early and watched her go in.

When the male officer looked round and saw them at the

bottom of the stone steps leading to and from the village, he ended his conversation and headed in their direction.

Soon, he was shaking hands and introducing himself as Police Officer Ioannis Karanasios, from the local Tourist Police department. He seemed very friendly and approachable.

Edie noticed he was holding a clipboard, attached to which were some of the photos of Jessica that she and Hannah had forwarded.

Goosebumps ran up and down her spine. Suddenly, Jessica had turned from a normal, flesh-and-blood woman to a 'missing person', in a strange, hazy category all of its own.

The policeman cleared his throat and Edie, Ralph and Hannah edged closer so as not to miss anything.

'First things first, my colleague and I are trying to establish if anyone saw your friend in the village,' he said, sounding official. 'We have also alerted our colleagues in Heraklion and Knossos.'

A moment later, the woman police officer left April's shop. Ioannis waited for her to join the group before introducing her as Police Officer Aikaterini Skouras.

She glanced at her colleague, who gave an almost imperceptible nod.

'Before we go any further, I need to ask a few more questions,' she said.

Ralph, Edie and Hannah responded in unison. 'Of course.'

Gesturing to the café, Aikaterini led the way to an empty table where they all sat down.

'I've just obtained the CCTV footage from the supermarket,' she began. 'The owner was in the shop at around the time your friend would have passed, but didn't notice her. Let's see if the footage is able to help. We've spoken to the ferry operators, but they do not appear to remember a woman of your friend's description boarding the boat.'

At this, Edie's insides squirmed uneasily.

'You think she hasn't left the village?' she asked in a shrill voice.

Ioannis made an impatient clicking noise with his tongue. 'I'm not saying that. It's not unusual for the ferry crew not to remember someone; they see so many people in one day. It's important not to jump to conclusions. I'm merely saying it's *possible* she didn't leave. At this stage we are in the dark,' he admitted, before flashing a reassuringly cheery, lopsided smile. 'But we are very good at our job. We will soon find out what has happened to your friend and, we trust, return her to you none the worse for wear.'

Edie took a deep breath and sat back, before glancing at Ralph. He looked a bit less tense, too. Hannah, though, was a bundle of nerves, hunched over and picking at the corner of a fingernail, making it sore.

One of the waiters approached to ask if they wanted anything, but Aikaterini waved him away.

Her walkie-talkie crackled, as it did every so often, and she spoke in a low voice into the microphone.

The small group was attracting quite a lot of attention now. Edie noticed shopkeepers and restaurant staff busying themselves nearby, pretending not to pry.

Meanwhile, other folk were slowing right down as they passed, clearly hoping to catch bits of what was being said.

When Aikaterini had finished speaking into her device, she leaned forward.

'We'd like to ask a little more about Jessica's frame of mind before she left for Knossos. Was there anything at all unusual about her demeanour? Anything you have forgotten? Any reason why she might have been upset or agitated?'

There was a brief pause while Edie, Ralph and Hannah

considered the matter. For the umpteenth time, Edie thought back to the night before Jessica's departure, and Hannah and Mac's terrible row.

Jessica had been furious with Ralph for telling her not to interfere. By the following morning, however, when Ralph and Edie joined her for coffee in the garden, she seemed to have simmered right down.

It wasn't until Mac and Hannah appeared, surprising them all by having made up and being so affectionate with each other, that Jessica had announced her Knossos trip.

Edie had wondered earlier this morning if the argument and its aftermath might be worth mentioning, but it was a delicate matter. She hadn't wanted to raise it herself, she'd rather leave it to Hannah and Mac, and she assumed Ralph felt the same.

Now, though, Edie felt duty-bound to speak up and braced herself to begin. Luckily, however, Hannah jumped in first.

'There is something...' she began to say, and both police officers straightened up. 'My husband and I had a bad fight the night before,' she said, staring down at her lap. 'He was angry with me for speaking to a man in the village. He... he threw a mirror at me and it smashed.'

Aikaterini's eyebrows rose and Ioannis scribbled something on a notepad. They were both on full alert, listening attentively.

'Jessica and Edie overheard the shouting. They came to help me. I was very upset. Mac had already taken against Jessica for some reason and vice versa. There was quite a tense atmosphere between them. Mac stormed off after the argument but later, when he came back, Jessica accused him of trying to assault me.' Hannah glanced up and gave the policewoman a meaningful look. 'Obviously that didn't go down very well.'

'Did he say anything to Jessica?' Aikaterini asked. 'Did he argue with her?'

Hannah shook her head. 'He and I went upstairs. We wanted to talk things through and try and sort out our differences.'

'And did you – sort them out?'

Aikaterini was watching Hannah intently.

Edie's mind flashed back to her friend's secret smile to Mac, and their healthy appetites the morning after the row. But Hannah pulled a face.

'Not exactly. Well, on the surface, yes. We agreed to try and get on for the rest of the week. We didn't want to spoil everyone else's holiday. But it was all a bit of a sham. Underneath, I was still really upset and he was seething.'

'About what? About that man you were speaking to?'

'No, well, partly that. He was more annoyed about Jessica, to be honest. He thought she shouldn't intervene; she should keep her nose out. As far as he was concerned, our relationship was none of her business.'

Aikaterini dragged her chair in a bit further and rested her hands and elbows on the table. Edie noticed her neatly trimmed nails, coated in clear polish, and her thin gold wedding band.

'Did Jessica believe in you and your husband's – how shall I say it – reconciliation?' Aikaterini asked now. 'How did she take it?'

'Badly, I think,' Hannah admitted. 'I think it's maybe why she decided to go to Knossos. She may have wanted to get away.'

Edie rubbed her eyes, which were sore and stingy.

'She wanted to go before then, though, remember? She talked about Knossos back in England, that time when you all came for lunch at our house.'

'Yes. But she never told us when she might go until the morning she left. It was so abrupt.'

Edie frowned. 'True. Maybe it *was* related.'

Aikaterini took a deep breath and sat back, crossing her arms.

'That's helpful, thank you.'

The interview was over and when she rose, Ioannis followed suit.

'Your husband is at the house now?' the policeman asked Hannah, who confirmed that he was.

'We will finish our enquiries here, then go to the villa to talk to him. Please warn him of our visit and ask him not to leave the building until we've seen him.'

13

Edie stood and watched the two police officers heading up the high street in the direction of the jetty. Before they got there, however, Ioannis disappeared into a store, possibly Mr Makris' shoe shop. Meanwhile, Aikaterini ventured a little further before entering Marina's art studio.

'We forgot to ask if we can do anything to help,' Edie commented, turning to the others when she could no longer see the officers, and sitting back down.

'We should probably leave them to it while they make their initial enquiries,' Ralph replied, scratching his head. 'Hopefully someone will have seen something. I'm sure the police will get us involved further down the line, if we need to search the area, say.'

He swallowed, wincing slightly as if it hurt. 'Let's just pray it doesn't come to that.'

Hannah, who'd been staring into space, came to all of a sudden. 'God, what a nightmare! I wish we could rewind the clock and tell Jessica to stay with us.'

'What do you think's happened?' Edie asked, wrinkling her

forehead. 'Do you get the feeling she's OK?' She hesitated for a moment while her eyes darted this way and that. 'Or not?'

Hannah gave a helpless shrug.

'There's no point trying to guess,' Ralph said, slightly tetchily.

He beckoned to one of the waiters, who'd been lurking close by when the police officers were there, but was now standing in his usual place near the café entrance, with his back to the wall.

'I need a drink,' Ralph told the women as the waiter approached. 'I'm thirsty. Anyone else?'

Both Edie and Hannah ordered Cokes, while Ralph wanted an espresso and sparkling water.

His leg had started bouncing under the table again, doing its nervous jig.

Edie reached out and put a hand lightly on top of the back of his.

'You all right?' she asked in a low voice, giving his hand a gentle squeeze.

'Sort of. You?'

'Same,' she replied, with a tense smile.

It felt wrong to be sipping drinks in a seemingly leisurely fashion, watching the small boats coming in and out of the harbour and listening to the happy chatter of fellow customers and passers-by.

Edie was impatient at the best of times and hated having to play the waiting game, but there was nothing useful she could do to further the investigation right now.

Her spirits lifted somewhat when she spotted Marina coming towards the café. She must have finished speaking to the policewoman, who was now chatting to a group of folk outside the artist's studio.

Marina was wearing a loose, multicoloured dress and sandals, and her long, wavy black hair fanned out freely round her shoulders.

Her stance was anything but relaxed, however. She was walking very fast, with short, determined steps, her arms tight against her sides and her gaze fixed firmly ahead.

She failed to acknowledge Edie's wave but on reaching the café, she stopped abruptly before making her way to the table and sitting down without being asked.

Ralph, being gentlemanly, started to rise but Marina shook her head.

'Please, don't get up,' she said firmly. It was more of a command than a request and he did as he was told.

Everyone was so alarmed by her grave expression, no one spoke a word.

Edie's heart started pounding and her stomach keeled like a ship in a storm. 'What's happened?' she finally managed to mutter in a raspy voice. Her mouth had gone dry. 'Have you heard anything about Jessica?'

Marina crossed her slim, bare arms and the bangles round her wrists jingled merrily, as if determined to try to lighten up the sombre atmosphere. 'No,' she said, fixing her deep-set, dark brown eyes on Edie. 'I don't know where she is, but I need to tell you something.'

Her gaze was so intense, it made Edie shiver and Hannah gasped.

'What?' Edie asked, before swallowing.

'You need to know, things are not always as they seem and what you think is real may be a lie,' Marina said quietly, still staring into Edie's eyes. 'Keep an open mind and try to trust the process. Nothing happens in this world by mistake. So long as you keep the faith, all will be well.'

'Wh-what do you mean?' Edie said with a stammer. 'I don't understand—'

'Leave it, Edie.'

She stopped mid-speech and stared at her husband, whose eyes flashed in warning.

'Why can't—?' she began, but he raised his hand like a halt symbol.

'Look,' he said, turning his attention to Marina, 'I'm sure you mean well, but I don't believe in visions or special powers, or whatever you like to call them. Edie and I aren't remotely religious either.

'Our friend's gone missing and we're all under a lot of pressure right now. We're worried sick. No offence, but it really doesn't help if you give me or my wife strange warnings that don't make any sense. Please keep them to yourself.'

Ralph's bluntness embarrassed Edie and she felt her cheeks and the tips of ears turn red. At the same time, though, she was grateful to him for shutting Marina down, so to speak.

As he said, they were under quite enough stress already without the artist getting involved and giving them the heebie-jeebies. And he was probably right when he'd said Marina, like Katerina, was just a bit fey and Edie should ignore her.

Even so, she couldn't help feeling strangely drawn to the artist and somehow knew she wouldn't be able to forget her chilling remarks, however hard she tried. She'd keep going over them in her mind, trying to work out what they meant. She wouldn't be able to stop herself.

If Marina was offended by Ralph's put-down, she didn't show it.

'I'm sorry for disturbing you like this,' she said calmly, before rising. 'I know you're very anxious. I hope Jessica turns up soon.'

Ralph thanked her and she was about to leave when Jean-Luc

approached from behind and tapped her on the shoulder, making her start.

'Greetings, my fair sister!' he said in a silly, over-the-top English accent. He grinned at Hannah, inviting her to share in his joke, and, still silent, she smiled back.

Marina, though, wasn't amused. 'Have you heard about Jessica?' she asked with a frown.

The Frenchman took a step back and raised his dark eyebrows. 'Jessica? No. What's happened?'

Glancing round the table, he noticed Edie's and Ralph's serious expressions for the first time and his face fell. As soon as Marina had finished filling him in, he pulled out an empty chair and plonked down, as if his legs were in danger of buckling.

Marina needed to get back to her studio, but he wanted to stay behind to recover. Unsurprisingly, he also had a lot of questions. Hannah was the one who seemed keenest to answer them, so he moved to the chair next to her. They were soon hunched over, their heads almost touching, deep in conversation.

The waiter returned to ask if there were any more orders and Jean-Luc wanted an espresso. Ralph decided he was hungry, having eaten very little all day, and persuaded Edie and Hannah to have something more, too.

'We may as well wait till the police have spoken to Mac,' he said.

Hannah explained she'd sent a text to warn him of their visit and all he'd said in reply was, *'OK'*.

Jean-Luc looked amused and sat back, smoothing his hair. 'He is a man of few words, your husband? He is not, as we say in France, a *raconteur*.'

'Not remotely.'

Hannah, who was in a shortish skirt, uncrossed her long bare legs and crossed them again. 'All he really likes talking about is sport.'

'Ah.' The Frenchman leaned in again. 'Some men are obsessed with sport. I have friends who talk about it all the time. Personally, I'm more interested in art, films, books, culture and—' there was a pregnant pause '—and women.'

Hannah's eyes widened and she gave a simpering little smile.

Edie, who was watching, felt her muscles tighten and the blood rush to her head. She turned away quickly and tried to focus on the plates of food the waiter had just put on the table instead.

Ralph had ordered a selection of *mezze* to share, including *dakos* – twice-baked barley bread brushed with olive oil – topped with chopped tomatoes and local *mizithra* cheese and sprinkled with oregano. There were also *dolmades* – vine leaves stuffed with rice, pine nuts and minced meat – plus *tahini* – a dip made from sesame seeds, olive oil and lemon juice.

Some other small bowls contained pale pinkish *taramasalata*, made from fish roe, *tzatziki*, and *fava*, made from split yellow peas and onion.

Everything looked delicious, including the basket of warm pitta bread, but Edie still had little appetite.

She couldn't quite believe Hannah was flirting with Marina's brother again, while the police were searching for Jessica. As every hour passed, the need to find her became more urgent, yet to look at Hannah now, you'd think she hadn't a care in the world.

It was Jean-Luc who polished off most of the *mezze*. Ralph and Hannah had just a small amount, while Edie could only nibble on some pitta. She'd been keeping an eye on the police officers, going in and out of the stores, and realised she hadn't seen them in a while. Perhaps they'd gone to speak to Mac now.

The bad news was, they couldn't have obtained any vital

information yet that would lead to Jessica's discovery, or they'd have surely told Edie, Ralph and Hannah. Edie could only hope their colleagues in Knossos were having better luck and there'd be a breakthrough soon.

Bored with sitting round twiddling her thumbs while Jean-Luc and Hannah chatted each other up, she rose and wiped the crumbs off her lap.

'I'm going back to the villa. Anyone coming?'

'Me,' Ralph replied, tossing his napkin on the table and rising, too.

Edie glanced at Hannah, who looked up, all wide-eyed and innocent.

'Oh! I wouldn't mind some coffee first. I'll catch you up. I won't be long.'

'See you,' Jean-Luc added, clocking Ralph's and Edie's anxious faces again and remembering not to smile.

Deep worry lines appeared between his eyebrows, but as soon as Edie's back was turned, he and Hannah resumed their heart-to-heart.

Edie saw them huddled together in the corner like two lovesick teenagers, laughing animatedly at some private joke or other and blind to what was going on around them.

Once she and Ralph were out of earshot, her frustration seeped out, like air escaping from a punctured bicycle tyre.

'I think it's weird the way Hannah's behaving, don't you?' she said, sticking her hands in the pockets of her shorts.

Ralph glanced sideways at his wife.

'What do you mean?'

'You must have noticed! She's all over that man like a rash.'

'Yes,' Ralph agreed. 'Very odd. And inappropriate.'

'Inappropriate?' Edie repeated, with a hiss. 'Outrageous more like! I wouldn't have believed it if I hadn't been there. I don't know what's come over her. Maybe she's having a nervous breakdown or a midlife crisis or something. I've never seen her like this before.'

'I have.'

Edie stopped in her tracks and stared at her husband, open-mouthed. 'What do you mean?'

'I've seen her flirting at parties sometimes.'

Edie made a scoffing sound. 'What? When she was a student? That doesn't count.'

Ralph rubbed his nose as if he had an itch. 'No, much more recently.'

'Really?' Edie's eyebrows shot up. 'When?'

'I can't remember exactly, but I know I've seen her coming on to people – quite subtly, but it was obvious what she was up to. Mac mentioned it to me once. He said it happened quite a lot and it made him feel humiliated. He said he thought it was something to do with her wanting validation, but he didn't know why she felt the need. She got plenty of praise and reassurance from him.'

He resumed walking and Edie had to hurry to keep up. She was silent for a few moments, processing what she'd just heard, before coming to the conclusion Mac's word couldn't be trusted.

'Well, I never noticed Hannah doing anything to embarrass him,' she replied dismissively. 'I do know the slightest thing made him jealous. She only had to look at a man and he'd freak out. She probably feels like letting her hair down now after years of being under his thumb, and I don't blame her. The way he acted the other night was appalling.

'I just think, with Jessica missing, she should stay away from Jean-Luc for the time being. He's a bit of a creep anyway, in my view. But if she's planning on taking it any further, it's because Mac's driven her to it. The blame is all on him.'

A young, dark-haired girl walked by in a pink and white

spotted dress, holding two enormous, fat, fluffy black dogs on leashes. She could only have been about eight years old and was such a skinny little thing, the dogs could easily pull her over. They looked quite docile, however, ambling obediently on either side of their mistress, only stopping every now and again to sniff something.

Edie remembered April saying she had two big Bernese dogs and guessed these must be them. The girl was probably Meaty's sister.

Sure enough, the animals paused outside the supermarket entrance and waited for her to lead the way inside.

When Ralph stopped again, Edie watched the dogs plod one by one through the open door. The very last things to disappear were the tips of their furry tails.

The idea of living in a small flat with two such enormous creatures made her shudder. But reflecting on the dreadful prospect didn't distract her enough to make her lose her previous train of thought entirely.

'How come you never told me about Hannah's flirting before?' she asked, picking up the threads of their conversation.

Ralph pretended not to hear. 'We should probably get some food for tomorrow,' he said, gazing in the supermarket window, with his fists perched nonchalantly on his hips. Edie wasn't so easily fooled. Pushing forwards, she wedged herself between him and the shop window, jutting her chin.

'Don't try and avoid the question. Why didn't you tell me?'

Ralph rubbed his stubbly cheek and shifted slowly from one foot to another, as if playing for time.

'She's your friend,' he replied at last. 'I didn't want to badmouth her. Anyway, flirting's not a crime. I just felt a bit sorry for Mac, that's all.'

If Edie had a shred of doubt about whether any part of Mac's story was true, she wasn't going to admit it. Hannah – and the sisterhood – would always come first.

'Well, I don't feel sorry for him,' she said with a snort. 'Not one little bit. I hope Hannah dumps him the minute we get home.'

* * *

Naturally, April was thrilled to see the couple as it gave her the chance to do some digging.

She was standing behind the shop counter, flicking through a magazine, but looked up the moment they entered.

'I'm so sorry about your friend,' she said, closing the magazine quickly and shaking her head. 'Bad business. I'm surprised no one saw her get the ferry, mind.'

She eyed them slyly while they put some cheese and a packet of cold meat into their basket.

'That's if no one did see her,' she continued, before raising her eyebrows, which were rather badly pencilled in, as usual. 'Did they?'

She looked a bit different today because her blonde hair, usually scraped back, was loose. It was rather dry and brittle, owing, perhaps, to too much straightening, but she was wearing an attractive, short-sleeved, white lace top that showed off her tan, plus eye-catching blue earrings and a matching necklace.

Edie knew she was fishing for juicy information, but didn't mind. Naturally, April was curious, anyone would be.

'The police haven't told us anything yet,' Edie answered honestly. 'I think they're up at the villa now, having a word with our other friend, Mac.'

April pretended to straighten a pile of greaseproof paper on the counter, which she used for wrapping meat.

'Fancy a few sausages?' she asked. 'Those Cretan ones you had the other day? You said you liked them. You can have them on me.'

Edie started to protest but April wouldn't hear of it.

'It's the least I can do. Treat yourself, why don't you? You deserve it, what with everything you're going through.'

Without further ado, she scooped up a string of six or seven sausages from the chilled display cabinet and wrapped them in paper.

'Was she meeting anyone in Knossos – your missing friend, I mean?' she asked, resuming her not-so-subtle line of enquiry as she popped the parcel of sausages on the surface beside her.

Meanwhile, Edie took a tub of Greek yoghurt from one of the fridges, along with a pot of hummus.

'No, not that we were aware of. Unfortunately, she didn't say where she was staying and we didn't think to ask, which doesn't help.'

Walking over to one of the shelves, she selected a couple of packets of sweet biscuits, deciding she needed some comfort food. Meanwhile, Ralph found a big bar of chocolate to add to their growing grocery pile.

April was just getting into her investigative stride when one of the huge dogs reappeared from upstairs and lumbered over to her side, wagging its tail and looking up at her with moist, expectant eyes.

It was soon followed by Meaty, who was blowing a huge bubble. When it popped, he was left with a mess of sticky gum all over his nose, cheeks and mouth.

April stared at the dog, then Meaty, and back again.

'What's she doing here?' she snapped, pointing at the animal, which promptly plonked itself down on its haunches and continued to gaze at her adoringly.

She glared at Meaty once more. 'Take her upstairs – now! And for Christ's sake, wash your face. You're an embarrassment.'

There was a pause while Meaty tried, unsuccessfully, to pick off the gum with his grubby fingers. Meanwhile the dog, sensing a brief window of opportunity, heaved itself up and took a surprisingly agile flying leap at the counter.

Before anyone realised what was happening, it had grabbed the packet of sausages and waddled upstairs as fast as its legs could carry it, clearly thinking its birthday and Christmas had come all at once.

April threw her arms in the air and screamed. 'After her – this minute!'

Meaty turned tail and raced after the dog, his feet thumping on the wooden steps as he went. Bang-a-bang-bang.

April, Edie and Ralph stared at the ceiling, listening in silence as a torrent of thuds and crashes erupted overhead.

'I hope nothing's broken,' Edie said rather lamely after a while.

'I don't think the sausages will have survived,' Ralph muttered darkly.

At last, they heard a shout and Meaty hurtled back downstairs.

'Got them!' he yelled triumphantly, holding aloft a torn package with a few bits of chewed pink meat still clinging to the wrapping.

He was about to proudly present the parcel to Edie and Ralph, as if it were a gift, but April whipped it off him just in time.

'Don't be ridiculous. You can't give it to them now. There's nothing left!'

The look of horror on her face, along with Meaty's surprise, made Edie giggle; she couldn't help it.

'Oh well.' She glanced at Ralph, who was biting his cheeks,

trying not to laugh, too. 'At least the dog's had a slap-up meal. I guess she's partial to a Cretan sausage as well – and who can blame her!'

* * *

April insisted on giving them some more, unchewed sausages and after saying goodbye to her and Meaty, they trudged back to the villa with the shopping bags, cursing themselves for buying too much.

'I can't think why I got all that stupid cheese,' Edie grumbled. 'No one feels like eating anything anyway.'

By the time they arrived, the police had left and they found Mac sitting on his own by the pool, hunched over, with his hands clasped between his knees, staring into space.

He looked up when he heard them and gave a small smile, but his eyes were dull and lifeless.

'Hi,' Ralph said, trying to sound a bit cheery. 'How are you doing?'

Mac shrugged. 'Same as you, I guess. This whole thing is a shitshow.'

Edie and Ralph pulled up another lounger and sat side by side.

'Did you speak to the police?' Ralph asked, and Mac nodded. 'How were they?'

Mac sat up straight and crossed his arms. 'Pretty aggressive, to be honest.'

'Oh!' Ralph couldn't hide his surprise; they'd seemed so pleasant and helpful earlier.

'They were asking loads of questions about my marriage,' Mac went on. 'They wanted to know if Hannah and I were happy or not, and what we argued about the other evening.'

He looked Ralph straight in the eye, before shifting his gaze to Edie.

'Did you tell them about the fight?' he said. 'What did you say?'

Edie's pulse started racing and she fidgeted with the hem of her shorts.

'We didn't... I mean *I* didn't, actually. I was going to, because I didn't want to keep anything back in case it was relevant. But then Hannah started talking about it, so I left her to it.'

'And?' Mac's blank expression made Edie shiver; she couldn't work out what was going on in his head.

'Basically, she told it as it was,' she said.

Mac gave a hollow laugh. 'You mean she gave her version of events?'

Edie was confused. 'Well, yes. Why not? Surely that's normal? She didn't lie, if that's what you mean.'

Mac swallowed. 'She also told them I didn't like Jessica, correct?'

Edie glanced at Ralph, who was sitting completely still, listening carefully.

'She said you'd taken against her for some reason, and vice versa.'

'Too right.' Mac exhaled with a long, loud puff.

'Where is Hannah anyway?' He glanced round, looking for her, as if she might suddenly appear, like an apparition. 'Didn't she come back with you?'

Ralph jumped in to answer before Edie got the chance.

'She's on her way. She won't be long. Did the police say anything else about Jessica? Do they have any leads?'

'None at all,' Mac replied. 'Not that they mentioned to me, anyhow. I got the impression they didn't exactly take to me. God knows what they said about me after they left.'

14

Ioannis, the police officer, rang Ralph at around 7 p.m. that evening to give an update. He confirmed investigations were continuing and would do so throughout the night.

Police were checking CCTV in all the likely places where Jessica could have been, and appeals were going out on local radio and TV stations, as well as on social media.

So far, checks with her bank revealed she hadn't withdrawn any cash, hadn't made or picked up any phone calls and hadn't been admitted to any local hospitals.

'The police chief said he's surprised no one remembers seeing her in the village or on the ferry or any of the buses she was supposed to use, but it doesn't mean something bad has happened to her,' Ralph explained to the others, once he'd put down the phone. 'Apparently, most missing people are found or return in the first few days, which is encouraging. We must hold on to that.

'He thinks she's low risk, because she's so used to travelling on her own. They do seem to be doing everything they can to locate her, though. They'll be in touch again tomorrow – unless they've got news, obviously.'

Ralph took a deep breath. He and Edie had been in the pool when the phone rang, doing lengths in a bid to distract themselves.

He'd leaped out of the water the moment he heard the call, and had stood talking by the stone balustrade, looking out at the sparkling sea stretching far into the horizon.

Soon, Edie had got out too, and fetched a towel to wrap round her husband's shoulders. Mac, who'd been on a lounger, attempting to read his book, had put it down straight away and listened in on the conversation.

The three of them were now gathered on the top pool step, sitting side by side, while Ralph related what he'd heard.

'I don't understand why she's low risk,' Edie commented, bending forward to rest her elbows on her knees and staring into the distance. 'She's been missing for two days and nights. When does she become high risk?'

Mac, who was between her and Ralph, lowered his legs so his feet dipped in the cooling water.

'I'm not sure,' Ralph replied hollowly. 'I guess in a day or two, if they still haven't found her.'

'Shouldn't they be searching the area?' Mac asked. 'If no one saw her in the village, isn't it possible she changed her plans at the last minute? She might have decided to go for a walk before catching the ferry. What if she fell? Have they considered that?'

Ralph nodded. 'Our chap said they've done a preliminary search and found nothing, but I'm sure things will ramp up if they have to. That's when they'll get us involved. Probably the locals, too.'

They all looked up when Hannah appeared and joined them

by the pool. She'd returned from the village about an hour and a half after Ralph and Edie and had gone straight to her room.

She'd obviously had a shower and had changed into a long white T-shirt and black leggings. Her hair was still wet and her face was bare of make-up and shiny with moisturiser.

Ralph repeated almost word for word what he'd told the others.

'I just feel so helpless,' Hannah said with a sigh, when he'd finished speaking. 'If only there was something we could do now.'

'You could make supper.' Mac gave a sardonic smile. 'Some hope.'

Hannah pulled a face, as if she'd caught a whiff of sewage. 'If you're hungry, why don't you make it? We had some *mezze* in the village. I don't want anything else.'

Mac rose and looked calmly at Ralph and Edie, ignoring his wife completely. 'Do you fancy something? I'm happy to walk down to the village if we need anything.'

Edie explained what there was, and she and Ralph agreed they might be hungry in a while.

Mac nodded. 'OK, great. I'll light the barbecue and put some things together. If anything's left, we can have it tomorrow.'

He was about to leave when Hannah piped up. 'It just occurred to me – did you see Jessica when you went for your run on the morning she vanished? You were very quick. You must have overtaken her?'

Edie inhaled sharply and she heard Ralph do the same. All eyes were suddenly beaming in on Mac. He paused for a moment, like an actor preparing to deliver a monologue, and looked down at his wife, who was still seated.

'No, I didn't see her,' he said, slowly and deliberately. 'I didn't stay on the path. I decided to go off-piste.'

'Ah.'

The silence that descended was so loud, it made Edie's head hurt and her vision blur. There was a sour taste in her mouth and her tongue felt as if it had been coated in sawdust.

Mac walked away but his words seemed to hang in the air, circling round her brain in a bizarre sort of dance, which made her sick and giddy.

She shuffled right up close to Ralph, who put an arm round her shoulders and squeezed tight. Meanwhile, her head was suddenly so unbearably heavy she could hardly support it, and it fell against his chest.

* * *

It was completely dark by the time they sat down for supper, so black, Edie felt as if she were floating in a cauldron of dense, sticky coal tar.

Only the flames of the candles could pierce through the lightless void; human eyes were useless.

She'd grown so accustomed to the loud, rhythmic clicking of the cicadas that she scarcely noticed them, but they all heard an owl, hooting eerily in the distance. Once or twice, a bat fluttered by, quite close to Edie's face, and made her squeal.

'They're harmless; they won't hurt you,' Ralph reassured her, but chills ran up and down her spine all the same.

The scent of the sausages cooking on the barbecue had made her stomach rumble. They smelled of smoke, meat and wholesome, aromatic herbs and tasted even more delicious than she remembered.

Hannah, who wasn't eating, had opened two bottles of wine – one red and one white – and Edie found herself greedily gulping the alcohol. Soon, her head was pleasantly buzzing, she felt her muscles relaxing and, at long last, her mind began to quieten down.

The others were clearly craving a release just as much as she was and they, too, kept reaching for the wine to top themselves up. Soon, both bottles were gone and Ralph went inside to fetch some more.

'Wouldn't it be amazing if Jessica rang now, out of the blue?' Edie commented, with a forkful of food suspended in the air in front of her.

'Yes,' Ralph agreed, plonking two more wine bottles on the table. 'If only.'

Edie's phone was beside her plate and she'd checked it several times since sitting down. They were all doing the same and now it was Hannah's turn to have another try.

'I've got this awful feeling we're not going to see Jessica again,' she said, glancing at her screen before shaking her head and setting her mobile aside.

'Don't!' Edie replied, with a shudder, noticing for the first time that Hannah's face was deeply flushed. Her eyes looked glossy and adrift, too, floating aimlessly round her surroundings.

Edie hadn't been watching how much her friend was drinking, but it must have been more than the rest of them. No one else was wasted.

She was quite relieved in a way, because it was harder to take Hannah's gloomy prediction seriously.

Ralph made no comment and took another swig of red wine, but Mac banged his fist on the table, making everyone jump. 'Why would you say that?' he said, through half-clenched teeth. 'You don't know anything more than the rest of us.'

Hannah's mouth was slack and drooping slightly on one side. Her eyes, though, stopped drifting and descended on him. 'No, but I know *you*,' she said, jabbing a finger clumsily in his direction.

Her gaze floated off again briefly before refocusing. 'You and your filthy temper...' She paused to hiccup. 'You killed her, didn't you? Hic... You did the dastardly deed.'

The last two words were accompanied by emphatic nods. She didn't need to underline them, though. No one could mistake the meaning.

Edie's mouth dropped open and Ralph froze like a statue. Meanwhile, Mac's expression switched from anger to shock. 'I can't believe what I just heard. You're insane!'

His upper body swayed slightly from side to side and, even in the gloom, Edie could see his face had turned pale, almost grey.

Hannah, oblivious, ploughed on. 'It's obvious, isn't it?' She was slurring her words. 'As soon as Jessica said she was going to Nosh-er-Knossos... suddenly, you... you were dead keen on running... hic... not that you normally run... in fact you're pretty bloody lazy most of the time, no *all* the time...' She laughed and her arms flailed clownishly.

'I reckon you whacked her on the head... hic... didn't you? See? I'm Miss Marple...' Another laugh. 'You whacked her on the bonce and chucked her in a... in a gully, or whatever you call them... Job done.' She dusted her hands off, as if wiping them clean of something. 'Nice one, Mac.'

She tried to high-five him across the table, but he backed away sharpish and seemed to shrivel into his seat like a snail retreating into its shell.

Edie was speechless and felt dazed and panicky. She couldn't forget the fact she, too, had thought it slightly strange when Mac had suddenly decided to go for a run. Also, that he'd failed to buy the shopping, which had been the main purpose of the trip.

Although he'd come back surprisingly soon, he'd probably

still have had enough time to harm Jessica and even hide her body somewhere, too. What's more, he'd arrived home covered in dirt. When Edie had asked him about it, he'd dismissed her concerns, claiming he'd fallen over but wasn't hurt.

Perhaps it was all untrue and at this very moment, Jessica's poor body was lying in a shallow grave somewhere on the mountain. Edie had a painful lump in her throat when she tried to swallow and her eyes felt hot and stingy.

Marina's strange words from earlier came flooding back.

'Things are not always as they seem... what you think is real may be a lie...'

Was she referring to Mac? Did he have more than just a bad temper? Was he a *murderer*?

Edie stooped down and picked up her sweatshirt, which had fallen off her chair onto the ground. All of a sudden, she was freezing cold, with chattering teeth.

Even once she'd put the sweatshirt on, however, she still couldn't stop shaking. She pulled her feet up onto the seat and hunched into a small, self-protective ball.

Ralph's voice sliced through the silence.

'We've all had too much to drink,' he said, trying to take control of the situation. 'We should get some sleep.'

He pushed back his chair, ready to rise, but Hannah hadn't finished yet.

'So, Mac,' she said scornfully, 'how shall... I mean, what do you suggest... hic... how exactly do I tell the kids their daddy's killed someone?'

Despite feeling weak and exhausted, Edie managed to uncurl her legs, sit up straight and stare hard at Hannah. She was willing her friend to look her in the eye and calm down.

'Hannah, I—'

She wanted to say – stop now and go indoors before it's too

late – but Hannah was like a steam train hurtling towards its final destination.

'You do realise this means our marriage is over?' Hannah told her husband, lurching to one side as she spoke and only just managing to save herself.

Smiling grimly, she drew her right index finger slowly across her neck, from one side to the other, in a macabre cutting motion.

'That's it, we're finished. Kaput!'

A loud crash made everyone turn and stare. Ralph had risen and accidentally knocked over his wooden chair.

'I'm going to bed,' he announced, bending down to pick the chair up. He fixed on Hannah, who stared at him blankly as if she had no idea who he was. 'I think you should too.'

Edie was about to get up and join her husband when she was distracted by another sound, like someone tearing through thick fabric, followed by a series of rapid inhalations.

On glancing at Mac, her stomach twisted and her hands instinctively fluttered to her chest.

His head was bowed and he was sobbing. Proper, big, hot, salty tears were running down his cheeks and his thin body was shaking uncontrollably. He also seemed to be gasping for breath.

Her instinct was to run over and give him a hug and try to comfort him. But she felt as if someone or something had strapped her down, binding her arms and legs so tightly she could barely move.

She'd only seen Ralph cry once, after he'd admitted to cheating on her, and she'd been profoundly shocked, so rare was it for him to show any vulnerability.

Mac's tears appeared to have melted away all his anger and sarcasm, and he looked as small and weak as a newborn baby.

'Hey, Mac—' Ralph said softly, but Hannah interrupted before he could finish the sentence.

'Stop it! Stop crying!'

She was gripping the edge of the table so hard, her knuckles had gone white. By contrast, the skin on her face and neck was stained blood red.

Edie held her breath, uncertain now whether to stay or go and dreading what was coming next.

Mac looked up at his wife through wet, swollen eyes. 'I haven't hurt anyone, I swear,' he said in a trembling voice. 'Please don't leave me. You're everything to me. I'd be lost without you.'

He looked so abject and pitiful, Edie thought at any moment he might fall to his knees and beg. She wouldn't be able to bear it.

Part of her wanted to shake him and tell him to get a grip; the other part wanted to take away his suffering. Whatever he might or might not have done, it was profoundly upsetting to see him in so much pain.

Ralph plonked down on his chair again, looking worn out and defeated. However this was going to play out, it seemed he and Edie were destined to stay till the bitter end.

Hannah, unmoved by her husband's despair, gave him a look of such cold, hard contempt, it would have made a monster recoil.

'I always knew this would happen,' Mac said quietly. 'I knew you'd leave me in the end. I've tried so fucking hard. I thought if I loved you enough, you'd eventually fall in love with *me*. But it didn't work, did it?'

He gazed at her, pleading, but she turned her face away.

'I was never good enough for you,' he added, with a crack in his voice. 'Not like all your other men...'

A howl, like a wild animal's, filled the air, chilling Edie to her bones. It was a frightening, primeval sound that seemed to come not from him, but from someone or something else, way back when, at the very dawn of time.

Hannah's glare set Edie's nerves jangling.

'I could never love you,' she said, through gritted teeth. 'Look at you! You're so weak. Even the slightest sound makes you jump.'

Picking up her fork, she took a step towards her husband and he cringed, like a beaten dog, staring up at her with frightened eyes.

'Don't hit me.'

Hannah laughed. 'See! You're scared of your own shadow.'

Watching in silent horror, Edie felt as if cloudy films, like cataracts, were being removed from both her eyes. All of a sudden, she had twenty-twenty vision, and the light was almost blinding.

In a flash, she was certain she could see the truth. It was as if she'd been struck by lightning and nothing would ever be the same again.

'Mac?' she said, scarcely recognising her own voice, which had become surprisingly strong and steady. 'Did you throw that mirror in your bedroom the other night – or was it Hannah?'

He swallowed and his eyes darted this way and that. He was in a quandary; she could imagine the cogs in his brain working overtime to figure out the right response.

'It was her, wasn't it?' Edie gently pressed.

She was aware of Hannah, who'd sat down again, shifting noisily, scraping her chair on the paving stones beneath.

'You're wrong!' she hissed, but Edie remained fixed on Mac; she was willing him to open up, to allow light to enter the darkness, possibly for the first time.

'Mac?' she repeated.

He licked his lips. He'd stopped crying but his hands were trembling and his body shook, like a building in an earthquake.

At last, he opened his mouth and the word that came out was so quiet, she could barely hear it. But she knew, without a shadow of doubt, from the shape his lips had made, what that word was.

'Yes.'

'Enough!'

They all turned to look at Hannah, who was standing again, clutching onto the back of her chair for support.

'I'm not listening to this. It's a lie. He's a liar.'

She stooped down to pick up her bag from the ground and began to stagger towards the villa. Once or twice, she stumbled, but no one ran to help. They couldn't seem to move.

Once she'd gone, Edie, feeling sick as hell yet emboldened, too, straightened up and spoke again.

'It's not the first time she's hurt, or tried to hurt you, is it?'

Slowly and reluctantly, Mac shook his head.

Edie glanced at Ralph, whose jaw was clenched and his face had turned white with anger.

'Those cuts and bruises I've seen on you – were they her, too?' he asked urgently, and Mac nodded.

Edie didn't know anything about them; Ralph hadn't told her.

Her husband's face crumpled and he let out a small cry of anguish, which made her heart hurt.

'I'm so sorry, mate,' he said, putting his head in his hands. 'I should have realised something wasn't right. I should have asked more questions. It just never occurred to me.'

'You don't have to put up with this any more,' Edie added gently, shuffling closer to Mac. 'Why didn't you say anything? You should have spoken to us, or rung the police. Or preferably, both.'

Mac sniffed and wiped his red, puffy eyes with the corner of his napkin.

'I don't know. Fear, I suppose.' He laughed bitterly. 'Hannah's right, I *am* weak and pathetic. She tells me that all the time. And she says if I leave, I'll never see the kids again. Plus, I'll have nowhere to live and nothing to live on. She's threatened to ring my clients and tell them I'm a wife beater. She says no one will believe it's the other way round and I'll lose my business and she'll make sure I don't get a penny from her. I know she's right; she always wins. I wouldn't stand a chance against her in court.'

Edie took a deep breath. She'd read about women who abused their husbands, but had never been able to imagine how the situation could arise in reality, given that men are physically so much stronger.

Now, here was the evidence, sitting right beside her, and suddenly she understood completely. Mac was no different, really, from women who suffered domestic abuse; he'd been broken down, bit by bit, until he had no self-esteem and couldn't see a way out. He felt trapped.

A sudden thought crossed her mind.

'Don't you ever fight back? I mean, don't you want to hurt her after she's hurt you?'

'No.' Mac was emphatic. 'I've never laid a finger on her. I couldn't. I wouldn't hit any woman; it's been ingrained in me virtually since birth.'

He seemed truthful and Edie wanted to believe him. But she had one more question.

'Do you know anything about Jessica? You can tell us, you know. We're friends and we'll do everything we can to help.'

She watched him carefully and to her immense relief, his expression didn't change.

'The last time I saw her was just before she left the house to go to Knossos,' he replied. 'While I was running I was all alone. I didn't see her at all – I really did go off-piste. There was a lot on my mind and I completely forgot about the shopping. Jessica thinks I'm the devil and I dislike her intensely, but I wouldn't want anything bad to have happened to her. Like you, I'm desperately afraid.'

15

They didn't see Hannah again that night and Mac slept in Jessica's room. Edie and Ralph sat up in bed and talked into the small hours, trying to piece together everything they could remember about the times they'd spent with the other couple, both individually and together.

Edie found it hard to set aside her previous assumptions, especially about Hannah, whom she'd considered to be one of her best friends.

She'd seemed so plausible when she'd talked about Mac's filthy temper, and Edie had never doubted her.

Now, Hannah's ability to manipulate, and the lengths to which she'd gone to deceive everyone, took Edie's breath away.

Given her behaviour with other men, and her fondness for rubbing Mac's nose in it, his jealousy made complete sense. He must have felt so miserable, frightened and insecure, never knowing when she'd next lash out – or tell him the marriage was over. Edie doubted he'd ever fully recover.

She was angry with herself for being so blind, but as Ralph said, Hannah was an excellent actress. And though Ralph blamed himself for failing to question Mac more about his injuries, the truth was, they'd seen very little of each other lately and their conversations had been pretty superficial.

When Edie and her husband finally dropped off, they slept fitfully, and Edie woke with Marina's strange words filling her ears:

'You need to know, things are not always as they seem and what you think is real may be a lie. Keep an open mind and try to trust the process. Nothing happens in this world by mistake. So long as you keep the faith, all will be well.'

Edie had always been sceptical of psychics, clairvoyants and the like, but the artist's pronouncement seemed strangely accurate now.

She couldn't help thinking if Marina hadn't told her to *'Keep an open mind'* about what was real and what wasn't, she mightn't have been willing to challenge her perceptions about Mac and Hannah's relationship.

With her mind closed to the possibility there could be another version of events, she might have remained loyal to Hannah, perhaps helping to condemn Mac to yet more years of misery with his wife.

But what did Marina mean by saying, *'Nothing happens in this world by mistake'* and *'Keep the faith'*?

Was she suggesting all this was *meant* to happen, even Jessica's disappearance? It sounded like mumbo-jumbo to Edie.

Furthermore, why had Katerina warned Edie and Ralph: *'Look after what you have. It's very precious'*, as if she knew their relationship was about to be put under a lot of strain?

Edie couldn't wait for the nightmare to be over and to get back to Surrey, to her and Ralph's lovely home, to their dog and their two, precious children. She quite decided from now on, she'd never complain about Ralph, or anything else in her life for that matter, ever again.

'Penny for your thoughts,' Ralph mumbled in a sleepy voice, rolling over to face her with his eyes still half closed.

Edie had assumed he was still snoozing.

'Oh, nothing really,' she replied, reaching for his hand, which felt warm and comforting. 'Just hoping we get some news today.'

She didn't want to discuss Marina and Katerina with him; he'd only tell her they were nice, but nuts.

She'd rather keep to herself her newfound notion that there might, possibly, be something bigger out there, and that maybe everything happening to them was, in some strange way, supposed to be.

When Ralph's phone rang, they both jumped like wide-eyed deer and Edie let out a squeal. 'Quick! Answer it!'

As soon as she heard the now-familiar voice of Ioannis Karanasios, from the Tourist Police department, she sat bolt upright, all her senses on alert.

After just a few seconds, Ralph held the phone away from his ear to speak to his wife. 'They've found her. She's OK.'

Edie's heart thumped wildly and she burst into involuntary tears, all the pent-up fear and anxiety of the past few days exploding in a torrent of sobs.

Ralph raised an index finger to his mouth – 'Shh' – before placing his hand reassuringly on her thigh, and squeezing.

Clamping the phone to his ear again, he continued the conversation. Meanwhile, Edie buried her face in her pillow to stifle her blubbing and tried to catch what was being said.

Of course, she was desperate to know everything, every last detail, but she had to wait on tenterhooks for the phone call to end before Ralph could properly fill her in.

When he turned to her at last, she threw off the sheet and knelt beside him, her hands resting in her lap.

It seemed Jessica had been located in a small guest house in the city of Kissamos, in north-western Crete, some two and a half hours by road from Knossos.

She'd been visiting the city's archaeological museum, beaches and other local sites, having changed her plans at the last minute and decided to head to Knossos later.

Her intention had been to return to Porto Liakáda sometime tomorrow or the next day; she wasn't sure exactly when. Her phone was on silent, because she didn't want to be disturbed. She hadn't checked her messages and had absolutely no idea a frantic search for her was underway.

In fact, when police arrived at the guest house and told her they'd been looking for her, she thought they'd got the wrong person. She said it had never crossed her mind her friends would be worried about her. They knew she often travelled solo and was perfectly capable of looking after herself.

It took Edie a few moments to absorb the information, then she heaved a big sigh.

'I can't believe anyone can be so selfish and self-centred,' she said at last, rubbing her eyes and wiping her nose with the back of a hand. 'Not to even drop us a text to say where she is. It's mind-boggling.'

'I know.'

Ralph clasped both Edie's hands in his and gently shook them up and down.

'Look,' he said earnestly, 'I know we both think the same – she's vile, a total egoist. When we get back home, I never, ever want to see her again. You'll bump into her at school, unfortunately. But hopefully, you won't have to speak to her that much.

The thing is, though, the police are bringing her back now. They'll be here in two or three hours. I think we should try to keep our feelings to ourselves for the time being and focus on the fact she's safe. We need to thank the police. They've been great. We couldn't have asked for more. And there's Mac to consider, too.'

Edie nodded. 'What do you reckon he'll do?'

Ralph paused for a moment and scratched his head. 'I think he needs our help. Lots of it. The last thing we want is for him to reconcile with Hannah.

'I bet once she's sobered up and hears about Jessica, she'll take back everything she said last night, including about the divorce. It suits her to have him at her beck and call. I reckon she likes the power and control. But it will be a disaster for him if he listens to her and gets bullied into staying. He needs to get out now, but he won't be able to do it on his own.'

Edie tilted her head to one side. 'So, what do you suggest?'

'I think he should stay with us, just while he sorts himself out and gets the divorce proceedings going. He could have Maisie's room, or we could turn the downstairs family room into a temporary bedroom.

'I know it's not ideal, but I've known him forever and I really want to support him. That's what mates are for. How would you feel about it? Could you cope?'

Edie didn't hesitate for a second. 'Of course.'

It occurred to her Hannah would regard this as a massive betrayal, but she didn't care. Perhaps the falling-out would bring Hannah and Jessica closer together. They were welcome to each other.

After that, Ralph popped out to tell Mac the news. Edie couldn't face knocking on Hannah's door, so she texted her instead.

Jessica's been found safe and well.

She deliberately waited a while before going downstairs and by the time she joined the men, Ralph had had a serious talk with Mac, and he'd accepted the offer of moving in with Ralph and Edie.

Sitting round the patio table drinking coffee, the three of them came to the conclusion that as there were only two more days after this one before they were due to leave Crete, they wouldn't try to change their flights.

'We'll just keep out of Hannah's and Jessica's way,' Edie said with a shudder. 'If we stick together, I don't think either of them will dare come near.'

To her relief, Hannah slept in late, probably nursing a terrible hangover, and at around 10 a.m. Edie braced herself and went upstairs.

She hadn't told Ralph or Mac her intentions; she just knew that for her own peace of mind, she had to talk to Hannah and try to understand. They'd been friends for such a long time, after all.

Her pulse was racing when she knocked on the door and heard Hannah's reply, in a quiet but steady voice: 'Come in.'

Not knowing what to expect, Edie entered with trepidation. To her surprise, Hannah looked remarkably composed, sitting on the edge of the bed combing her hair. Neatly dressed in a clean white T-shirt and shorts, her face was clean and make-up-free, her hair shiny, the skin on her arms and legs tanned, smooth and moisturised.

Beside her were all the things she'd need for a day on the beach or by the pool: swimsuit, book, sun cream, sunglasses, beach bag, flip-flops and hat.

Smiling coolly at Edie, she beckoned to her to sit down beside her while she continued to comb her hair.

'About last night—' Edie began nervously.

'I don't want to talk about it,' came the rapid reply.

Edie swallowed, unsure how to proceed. She'd imagined Hannah might be a total mess, puffy and red-eyed from weeping and lack of sleep. The fact she appeared so serene and unruffled was dumbfounding.

'I, I had to ask him, you know,' Edie went on. 'Mac, I mean. I don't understand why—'

'I told you,' Hannah responded, with a sniff. 'I don't want to talk about it. He's a liar; he lies about everything. But if you choose to believe him not me, that's your call. There's nothing I can do about it.'

'But why would he lie?' Edie asked, genuinely baffled and wanting answers. 'I understand why he wouldn't want us to think he's been violent towards you, but what about the cuts and bruises? Did he inflict them on himself? Really?'

Hannah's eyes narrowed and turned cold and Edie felt herself shrink. She hardly recognised this woman she'd thought she knew so well.

'Get-out-of-my-room,' Hannah said, slowly and deliberately, with an ugly snarl on her face. 'I don't want to speak to you ever again.'

Edie's mouth dropped open. She wouldn't have believed Hannah was capable of speaking to anyone like this, let alone one of her oldest and dearest friends, and yet she just had.

Tears pricked the corners of Edie's eyes but she didn't cry; she couldn't. For a few minutes she was stunned into silence and just sat there, staring at Hannah as if for the first time.

The spell was only broken when Hannah got up and stalked into her adjacent bathroom, banging the door closed and locking it behind her.

Too astounded to feel hurt, Edie realised there was nothing

more she could do. Hannah had shut her up and booted her out of her life just like that. There was no going back for either of them.

She rose slowly and went downstairs to join the others by the pool. Ralph, who was reading, looked up briefly and gave a small smile. Edie decided to wait till they were alone to tell him what had happened. She didn't want to involve Mac and besides, she needed time to process.

It was soon after midday when they heard voices on the front drive and the sound of feet crunching on gravel.

Edie jumped up, as if she'd been stung, before reminding herself Ralph wanted them both to act composed.

She must welcome Jessica back with a smile, but wouldn't go over the top. There was no need to fawn. The police deserved much more of a fuss, and she'd make sure they knew just how grateful she and her husband really were.

Ralph went to the door and he was soon being followed into the garden by the two police officers they'd first met – Ioannis and Aikaterini – and, of course, Jessica.

Edie wasn't sure what frame of mind Jessica would be in, but imagined she might be tearful and apologetic. So she was taken aback yet again when she saw annoyance and frustration written on Jessica's face instead.

'What a nuisance!' Jessica said with a frown, plonking her rucksack on the patio table and sitting down. 'I was just about leave the guest house where I was staying when suddenly police descended and said I was a missing person.

'I didn't know what they were talking about. I told them I was very much *not* missing, and I was on my way to the beach, but they wouldn't listen. They insisted on bringing me back here and I haven't even been to Knossos yet. It's infuriating.'

Taking a green apple from the pocket of her bag, she

proceeded to crunch into it, seemingly completely unaware of, or indifferent to, the hell she'd put her friends through.

Edie felt the blood rise to her neck and cheeks and when she glanced at Ralph, she could tell from his narrowed eyes and clenched jaw, he was incandescent, too.

However, reminding herself again of what he'd said in bed this morning about keeping their feelings to themselves, she fixed on Jessica, sitting opposite, and managed to summon a smile.

'Thank goodness you're OK,' she said coolly, leaning back and crossing her arms. 'We were concerned because we hadn't heard from you.'

Jessica shrugged. 'I hate phones. At home they're a necessary evil. The last thing I want is to be glued to my mobile when I'm on holiday.'

Bile rose up from Edie's stomach and burned her throat. Unable to guarantee she wouldn't blow if Jessica tried to justify herself any more, she offered to make tea, coffee or a cold drink for the police officers, then disappeared indoors.

Hannah must have crept past her in the kitchen because by the time Edie returned to the garden, she was beside Jessica at the patio table, laughing at something Aikaterini was saying. She didn't glance at Edie once.

Jessica was silent while Ralph praised the police and thanked them warmly for their kindness, speed and professionalism.

'I'm sorry for bothering you unnecessarily,' he said. 'But we didn't know things would turn out so well. As soon as I spoke to you, I knew we were in good hands. I never doubted you'd get to the bottom of this – and I was right.'

Ioannis dipped his head modestly.

'You really were amazing; we're so grateful,' Edie added. 'You kept us informed and reassured us when we really needed it. I'll never forget what you've done.'

Slapping both his thighs, Ioannis grinned widely. 'It's all ended happily – that's just what I like. If only all our investigations were the same.'

Aikaterini nodded. 'When someone goes missing on the island, we mostly find them in one piece. But unfortunately, every now and then there's an exception and we find out something tragic has happened. I'm so glad that wasn't the case here.'

At this point Jessica, who must have been biting her tongue, could stand it no longer.

'The whole sorry episode's been a huge waste of police time,' she said, glancing round at the assembled group with pursed lips, her body rigid with anger.

'Edie, Mac and Hannah, if you'd thought about things rationally, instead of panicking, you'd have realised I'd decided to extend my trip. It's hardly surprising I didn't want to stick round here,' she added, rolling her eyes. 'Forgive me for wanting to get away from the horrible atmosphere. I've never known anything like it.'

Her small, bright blue eyes fixed accusingly on Mac, and Edie noticed his body slump and his bottom lip start to tremble.

Something gave way inside her, and the feelings of outrage and fury she'd been bottling up came gushing out before she could stop them.

'Do you realise what you've done?' she said, rolling back her shoulders and glaring at Jessica.

'Edie, don't—' Ralph started to say, but she wasn't listening.

'You've ruined our holiday and on top of that, you deliberately stirred things up between Hannah and Mac and made things much worse. Now they're getting divorced.'

Jessica snorted then gave a smug half-smile.

'Good! I'm glad. But you can hardly accuse me of ruining the marriage. Mac managed to do that all by himself.'

Edie's eyes narrowed to thin slits. Her face was burning and she clenched her fists under the table. She was tempted to get up right there and then and punch Jessica in the mouth.

'You have no idea what's been going on between those two. You just waded in like you knew everything – but you got it all wrong.'

Drawing back a little, Jessica arched her eyebrows and smiled sarcastically.

'Excuse me. I've never claimed to be a relationship expert. I'm not even married, remember. Thank God.' She gave an exaggerated shudder. 'And after witnessing you lot, I'm even more convinced it's a bad idea. I value my freedom and independence,' she continued, looking pointedly again at Mac. 'No one tells *me* what to do.'

While she was speaking, both police officers were quiet, watching the proceedings, it seemed, with a mixture of shock and astonishment.

Ralph had kept schtum, too, but now launched into a slow hand clap.

'Bravo!' he said, staring coldly at Jessica. 'You crack on and enjoy your splendid isolation. But if you don't mind, Edie and I will still look out for each other and try to support the people we love and care about. If everyone did the same, the world would be a better place.'

Jessica shrugged. 'Do what you like. I don't care.'

'Cheers,' Ralph replied, deadpan. 'We will.'

When the police officers got up to leave, the others rose, too, and Edie noticed Hannah sidle up to Mac. She tried to hook her hand under his arm but he shook her off and stepped away, out of reach.

He glanced back at Edie, who was standing just behind, and

she gave him a subtle nod of approval. It was a good start, she thought.

* * *

Now that Ralph and Edie were no longer sick with worry about Jessica, the last few days of their holiday took a wholly different turn. They were both tired, and spent most of their time with Mac on the local beach, reading their books, chatting quietly and soaking up the sun.

They had no idea what Hannah or Jessica were up to, and they chose to eat out each night in one of the little restaurants in Porto Liakáda. They were afraid of bumping into either of the women at the villa and perhaps getting dragged into an argument.

On their final morning, they popped into the supermarket to say farewell to April.

'It's not been very relaxing for you,' April said, shaking her head. 'You'll have to come back next year.'

Edie promised they'd try, and gave April a hug. 'It's not been easy,' she admitted, 'But we've had some really good moments, haven't we, Ralph?'

She turned to her husband with shining eyes and felt a shudder of pleasure, remembering the night before. They'd finally made love, and she could swear it had been the best ever.

He put an arm round her shoulders, bringing her back to the present, and pulled her into his side.

'Porto Liakáda's a wonderful place,' he said warmly. 'And the people are wonderful, too.'

April's cheeks and the tips of her ears went pink with pleasure and embarrassment, and she stared down at her bright-blue-painted nails.

Edie, Ralph and Mac were in a café drinking coffee when they saw Marina and Katerina walking, arm in arm, towards them.

The women looked very relaxed and comfortable in each other's company, like mother and daughter. Marina was considerably taller and she was stooping slightly, listening intently to something Katerina was saying.

Once or twice, the older woman waved an arm around, in an expressive gesture, and Edie heard Marina's tinkling laugh, like wind chimes blowing in the breeze. She wondered what they were talking about and wished she could ask.

It was very hot, and she and the men were sitting at a table overlooking the harbour. They'd been watching the sun's reflection on the surface of the water, making it twinkle like diamonds.

Mac had been quiet and looked fragile and a bit lost, but he hadn't listened to Hannah's pleas and seemed determined to break from her at last.

As soon as Marina and Katerina were close enough, Edie got up to say hello and invited them to join her and the others for a coffee, but Katerina shook her head.

'Thank you, but it is too late in the morning for coffee for us locals,' she said with a smile. 'And too early for an aperitif. We are creatures of habit, you see.'

'Indeed,' Marina agreed. 'I've become terribly stuck in my ways. I can't cope with any changes to my routine.'

Edie laughed. 'Well, at least come and say hello and goodbye to everyone.'

She pointed towards their table.

Slightly reluctantly, it seemed, both women followed her across the terrace to the water's edge, and Ralph drew up a couple more chairs.

'I guess you two have known each other forever,' Edie commented, noticing how synchronised their movements were.

When Katerina crossed her legs, Marina did the same. And when Marina frowned or wrinkled her nose, the older woman copied.

They didn't seem aware of what they were doing; it was quite subconscious. And they even looked a little alike, though Edie understood they weren't related by blood.

On hearing Edie's question, Katerina glanced at Marina, who tucked a coil of her long, dark hair behind an ear before giving an almost imperceptible nod.

This seemed to be the prompt the older woman needed.

'I've known Marina since birth,' she said, quickly adding, 'since before she was born, in fact. I read to her and taught her English – I'd been taught the language by my lady, the owner of Villa Ariadne. I always knew Marina was special, from the moment I set eyes on her. She has the gift, you know. She sees things others don't.'

Edie was aware of Ralph, beside her, wriggling uneasily, but she ignored him.

She was about to probe further, but Katerina changed the subject. In a new, business-like tone, she gave Edie instructions on how to lock up the villa when they left and leave the key under a flowerpot by the front entrance.

'I hope you've enjoyed at least some of your stay?' she asked politely, but Edie wouldn't be put off quite so easily.

'If Marina can see things, and maybe you can, too, why did you let us rent the villa? You must have known there was going to be trouble, with Jessica going missing and so on. Surely it would have been easier to rent the place to someone else?'

Katerina thought about this for a few moments before taking a deep breath.

'Ah!' she said at last. 'We have no say in who stays and who doesn't. Guests write to me and ask, for sure, but Villa Ariadne chooses whether to say yes to them or no. It's never the other way round.'

Ralph couldn't disguise his irritation and began tapping his fingers on the table, as if he were playing the piano. He stopped for a few moments, when Edie put her hand on his knee, but started up again soon after.

Edie found herself staring into space while she reflected on how easily she'd found Villa Ariadne online, how it had looked and sounded tailor-made for her and Ralph, and how it had, indeed, brought them closer together. Also, on how intrigued she'd been by Katerina's responses to her emails and how much less the villa had cost to rent than she'd imagined.

Whispering a silent prayer, she thanked the villa for exposing Hannah's abuse, for bringing Jessica back safely and, most of all, for rescuing her and Ralph's marriage.

Whether or not her prayer would be heard, she had no idea, but it couldn't do any harm, anyway.

She opened her mouth to enquire if any of the old woman's other guests had also had strange experiences and if they, too, had come to believe in Villa Ariadne's mystical energy.

The idea seemed so ridiculous, however, she couldn't bring herself to say the words out loud and closed her mouth again.

Some things, she concluded, simply couldn't be explained.

16

As they left the café, Ralph broke the news to Edie that he'd booked a restaurant for tonight for just the two of them.

'Let's head back to the villa. I'll tell you more later.'

'What about Mac?' Edie asked.

'It's OK,' Mac reassured her as he walked alongside them. 'I'm going to laze by the sea. I'll probably hang out there till suppertime and eat in a taverna. I'll be fine.'

They were about to part ways when Edie spotted Anthea strolling up the beach towards them. She looked pretty amazing in a bright pink bikini, with her long red hair hanging loose over her shoulders.

On recognising Edie, she waved enthusiastically, as if they were long-lost friends.

'It's so nice to see you! How are you?' she asked, once she was close enough. 'I was just going to the supermarket to get a cold drink. I've got the day off, so I'm topping up my tan. Bliss!'

Edie introduced Anthea to Ralph and Mac before explaining they were leaving for the UK tomorrow.

'Och, that's a shame. I was just getting to know you,' said

Anthea. 'I heard about your other friend going missing. That must have been horrible for you. I'm so glad she turned up.'

'Thanks,' said Edie, before suggesting they exchange email addresses and phone numbers.

'Come and see us in Surrey, if you're ever in the area. I'd love to show you some of the local sights.'

'And you have to book a holiday here again next year,' Anthea replied.

Mac glanced at the beach behind her, which was fairly full, and said he hoped he'd be able to find a spot for his towel.

'You can sit next to me,' Anthea offered. 'I can make room.'

If he was at all put off by her big lips and permanently surprised expression, he didn't show it. In fact, he seemed very pleased with the suggestion.

'That'd be great. Thanks. Yes.'

Anthea's eyes lit up and she nodded in the direction of the mini-mart. 'Let's grab a cold drink first.'

Edie and Ralph watched with interest while the pair headed off, side by side.

'Maybe this could be the start of a grand new romance,' Edie said with a grin.

Ralph frowned. 'Steady on. Mac's not even properly left Hannah yet. And I'm not sure he goes for big lips and eyelashes and all that stuff.'

'Well, he seemed very happy when she asked him to join her. You never know.'

As they ambled back up the hill, the subject returned to tonight's plans.

'Where's the restaurant?' Edie asked, but Ralph went all mysterious and wouldn't tell her.

'It's a surprise.'

Fortunately, there was no sign of Jessica or Hannah at the villa and after a quick, scrappy lunch, he told Edie to get ready. 'And bring a cardigan or something warm. We'll be on a boat for some of the journey.'

'How long will it take?' Edie pressed.

'Ooh, a couple of hours.'

This only made her more curious. Wherever he was taking her was quite far away. What on earth was he up to?

It seemed he'd got everything arranged and she was wearing her favourite, strappy red frock when they strolled down to the harbour, where a private boat was already waiting for them, complete with cold drinks.

Edie sipped on some white wine while they made the fifteen-minute trip to Chora Sfakion, then they hopped straight in a taxi and headed up into the mountains.

By now, it was about 4.30 p.m. and Edie still had no idea what was up. After about an hour, however, she began to see road signs for a place she recognised and the penny started to drop.

'Rethymno,' she said, pointing to one of the signs. 'We went there on our honeymoon, didn't we?'

Ralph gave an enigmatic little smile. 'We might have.'

'Is that where the restaurant is?' she asked, but he pressed a finger to his lips and shrugged.

'Grr! You're such a tease.' She gave him a playful slap and he laughed. He was clearly enjoying every moment.

When they finally entered the old Venetian town, with its medieval buildings, narrow streets, mellow stone walls and honeycomb of cobbled alleyways, Edie's memories of the place came flooding back.

'I remember that,' she said, pointing to an impressive old fortress on a hill overlooking the town. 'We walked there. It took ages.'

'And you kept complaining so I carried you up the last bit on my back.'

She could just about picture them as the two young, attractive people they'd once been, both madly in love. He was slightly bent over while she clung to his shoulders, with her legs wrapped round his waist.

'It was very gallant of you,' she commented. 'I don't suppose you'd do it again now.'

'I would – if the reward was right,' Ralph added, with a grin.

The taxi stopped near the ancient harbour, presided over by a honey-coloured lighthouse, and the couple got out.

Looking round, Edie could see the place was filled with boats and lined with tempting-looking bars, shops and tavernas. Old men fished off the harbour walls while numerous tourists meandered along the street, stopping to look in shop windows or at restaurant menus.

She was so busy soaking up the atmosphere, she quite forgot what they were here for.

'Come on. This way,' Ralph said, taking her firmly by the hand. 'We don't want to miss the cocktails.'

He led her a short distance up the road before stopping outside a gorgeous-looking restaurant. Tables and chairs under white parasols spilled out onto the pavement, and the open doors and windows were surrounded with pink bougainvillea.

'Oh my!' Edie said excitedly. 'We ate here, didn't we? I said it was the nicest restaurant I'd ever been to.'

Ralph nodded. 'And I had sea urchins, which made me feel slightly peculiar. I think I was showing off, pretending to be macho. I won't make the same mistake again.'

He gave his name to a waiter in a white shirt and black trousers, who ushered them upstairs. Edie had expected to be seated at one of the ground-floor tables, but Ralph had specifically asked for the terrace, overlooking the harbour, which was where they'd sat all those years before.

Beneath palm trees and a slowly darkening sky, they drank champagne and ate tuna carpaccio with lime, chives and sesame oil and grilled squid with tomato, onion, lemon, peppery rocket and olive oil. This was followed by seafood linguine for Edie and a juicy steak for Ralph.

For pudding they shared a deliciously light, fresh panna cotta with hazelnuts, pomegranate and a sweet wine sauce, and a slice of sponge cake, made with tangy oranges.

When they'd finished, Edie sat back with a satisfied sigh.

'Thank you so much for planning this. It's been such a treat,' she said. 'And this is *still* the best restaurant I've ever been to.'

Ralph agreed. 'It really can't be beaten.'

They watched in silent awe as the golden sun dipped below the horizon, casting a warm glow over everything and painting the water orange, pink and purple.

Edie realised she felt serene and contented in a way she hadn't been for ages, perhaps not since before Ralph's devastating fling. She wished she could capture the feeling in a bottle and wear it like scent whenever she chose.

When it was finally time to leave, they walked hand in hand to their waiting taxi.

'What a perfect evening!' Edie said, climbing into the car while Ralph held the door open for her. 'We must make sure we come back one day.'

'We will,' he promised.

They both dozed off on the drive home, but were wide awake when it was time to board the boat and trudge back up the hill to their villa. It was pitch-black, but luckily Ralph had brought a torch.

When they climbed, exhausted, into bed at last at around

2 a.m. Edie assumed lovemaking would be off the agenda, but Ralph rolled onto his side to face her. They were so close, she could feel his warm breath on her cheek.

He kissed her lightly on her forehead, the tip of her nose, her lips. Meanwhile, his fingers crept down the length of her spine and back again, making her shiver.

'I do love you, you know,' he murmured.

'Me too.'

'Did you lock the door?'

She nodded.

'Good.'

'Lights on or off?'

'Ooh, off, I think.'

He reached round and flicked off the switch.

At that moment, they might have been plunged into complete darkness, but a small gap in the shutters allowed a sliver of moonlight to creep, unnoticed, into the room.

Slowly, silently, it spread its silvery limbs across the wooden floor, before tiptoeing up the bed towards them.

Right up until morning, the poor moon tried its best to find a chink of dark space between them into which its light could slip, but they were nestled so tightly together, like spoons in a drawer, there was none.

* * *

The following afternoon, Ralph checked his watch.

'Not long now, we should land in about twenty minutes. Did you book a taxi?'

Edie nodded. 'Hopefully they'll be there, waiting for us.'

She gazed out of the aeroplane window at London's densely

packed streets far below, hoping to recognise some key landmarks.

Her heart skipped when she spotted the winding River Thames, and it leaped again, on the final approach, when the Houses of Parliament and Buckingham Palace came into view.

'I can't wait to get home,' she said with feeling.

'Me too.'

'Do you think Maisie will come and see us tomorrow?'

Ralph stretched his back and shoulders and groaned.

'She said she would. We've got a lot to tell her. We won't know where to begin.'

'I'll pick up Dilly in the morning.'

The dog had been staying with the pet-sitter she always went to when they were away.

'Good idea. I bet she'll be pleased to see us.'

The flight attendant passed by with a black bin bag, and Edie popped in her sandwich wrapper and an empty can of Coke.

Glancing over to her left, she spotted Hannah, staring out of the window, while Mac's head was turned the other way and his eyes were closed.

Jessica was two rows in front of them, with her nose stuck in a book. Edie had wondered before the flight if she'd offer to switch seats with either Mac or Hannah, as the two weren't speaking, but of course she'd done no such thing.

The truth was, she was so wrapped up in herself it probably wouldn't have even occurred to her. And if one of them had asked, she'd have said no, she wanted her own space.

Thoughtful acts and selfless gestures weren't her thing at all. With Jessica, it was all about Number One. The rest of the world could go hang.

The sounds of the engine changed from rattles and whirrs to

a loud rumbling as the flight spoilers on top of the wings were employed to slow the plane down.

Edie's ears popped just as the cabin crew were told to prepare for landing and she regretted not having asked for a sweet to suck on. It was too late now.

Landing was her least favourite part of flying and she closed her eyes and reached for Ralph's reassuring hand. Her stomach lurched when the wheels touched down and she was forced forward in her seat by the plane's rapid deceleration.

When they finally stopped moving and the lights came back on, she turned to her husband and smiled.

'Thank goodness that's over. I can breathe again now.'

It felt strange, stepping off the plane, and walking down the long passageway towards the terminal, without saying anything to Jessica or Hannah.

Jessica was way ahead, marching purposefully towards the baggage reclaim area, while Hannah lagged a few metres behind her.

As far as Edie could tell, there was no love lost between them. Hannah's hero worship had clearly come to an abrupt end.

Perhaps she now blamed Jessica, to some degree at least, for destroying her marriage. Edie doubted she'd ever admit to herself or anyone else the part she'd played. Bullies like her rarely did.

Edie and Ralph stayed close to Mac while they went through passport control and waited for their bags to arrive. Edie felt protective of their friend and hoped Hannah wouldn't lose her rag and cause an upsetting scene.

As they passed through the arrivals gate, she noticed Hannah gaze at Mac with moist, puppy-dog eyes, trying to attract his attention. Edie grabbed his arm, hustling him along as fast as possible, and luckily, he didn't notice.

After that, they didn't see Hannah or Jessica again. In the taxi home, Edie chatted to Mac about the temporary living arrangements, where he wanted to work, what he liked to eat and so on. He seemed low and tearful and she was keen to distract him.

The house was in darkness when the taxi pulled up and she was concerned it might feel cold and unwelcoming, but she needn't have worried. As soon as she'd walked in, dumped her bags in the hall and turned on some lights, the place seemed to spring to life again.

The shiny new kitchen gladdened her heart and even the simple act of turning on the kettle filled her with joy because it was *their* kettle, and they were *their* mugs she was using. She wouldn't take anything for granted any more.

When she pressed her nose to the back window and looked out at the garden, bathed in moonlight, she could see the row of white azaleas she'd planted last year had come into bloom.

She'd bet she'd be greeted by a beautiful blue cloud of ceanothus, too, when she ventured out of doors tomorrow morning. She'd always liked the months of May and June in the UK best.

'Home sweet home,' she said, spinning round with a wide smile and looking first at Mac, then her husband, whose soft, lingering gaze warmed her heart right through.

'Everything's going to be all right.'

* * *

MORE FROM EMMA BURSTALL

ACKNOWLEDGEMENTS

Heartfelt thanks to my brilliant agent, Elly James, and my super-talented editor, Rachel Faulkner-Willcocks. Also to the fab team at Boldwood Books who have worked so hard to bring this book to fruition. Finally, a big thank you to my readers whose support spurs me on, warms my heart and makes it all worthwhile.

ABOUT THE AUTHOR

Emma Burstall is the bestselling author of women's fiction, including the Tremarnock series. Emma studied English at Cambridge University before becoming a journalist for local and national newspapers and women's magazines. She lives in London and has three children.

Sign up to Emma Burstall's mailing list here for news, competitions and updates on future books.

Visit Emma's website: www.emmaburstall.com

Follow Emma on social media:

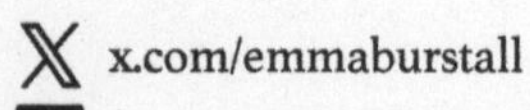

x.com/emmaburstall

facebook.com/emmaburstallauthor

instagram.com/emmaburstall

ALSO BY EMMA BURSTALL

Beneath the Lemon Trees

Beside the Turquoise Sea

www.ingramcontent.com/pod-product-compliance
Ingram Content Group UK Ltd.
Pitfield, Milton Keynes, MK11 3LW, UK
UKHW041258250625
6581UKWH00036B/695

9 781835 615478